Invisible Invader

Schaefer turned; the room was empty.

He looked through the hole in the wall, and the room on the other side was empty as well.

He stepped away from the wall and slowly turned a full 360 degrees, ending up facing the hole again.

He didn't see anything—but the light was poor.

And a good hunter used camouflage. The prey wasn't *supposed* to see him.

And these hunters might have *perfect* camouflage.

He started to turn again—and all of a sudden it was *there*, just at arm's length.

It wasn't human. It stood on two legs and was shaped more or less like a man, but it was too big, and too fast. He saw its feet in their heavy silver sandals, saw the four toes with their curving black talons. He started to turn, and saw the grayish-yellow legs, the gleaming metal greaves, the black netting that covered its body.

It was the hunter Dutch had talked about, it had to be. . . .

Don't miss any of these exciting *Aliens* and *Aliens vs. Predator* adventures from Bantam Books!

Be sure to look for all of Bantam's classic Star Trek *novels:*

Complete your Bantam Star Wars *library:*

PREDATOR™

CONCRETE JUNGLE

Nathan Archer

Based on the Dark Horse Comics graphic novel by
Mark Verheiden

BANTAM BOOKS
NEW YORK TORONTO LONDON SYDNEY AUCKLAND

PREDATOR: CONCRETE JUNGLE
A Bantam Spectra Book/May 1995

ISBN 0–553–56557–5

Published simultaneously in the United States and Canada

Bantam Books are published by Bantam Books, a division of Bantam Doubleday Dell Publishing Group, Inc. Its trademark, consisting of the words "Bantam Books" and the portrayal of a rooster, is Registered in U.S. Patent and Trademark Office and in other countries. Marca Registrada. Bantam Books, 1540 Broadway, New York, New York 10036.

PRINTED IN THE UNITED STATES OF AMERICA

RAD   10   9   8   7   6   5   4   3   2   1

Dedicated to
the memory of
Kevin Peter Hall

Acknowledgment:

The author wishes to thank Lt. Adam Kasanoff, NYPD, and Mr. Mark Verheiden, who provided essential background information.

(Any remaining inaccuracies are the author's doing, not theirs.)

PREDATOR™

CONCRETE JUNGLE

1

New York was sweltering through the worst heat wave in years. The descending sun reflected off a million windows in orange fire, turning the asphalt and concrete oven hot. Heat shimmered over the streets like an enormous translucent ocean—but felt more like a swamp.

As any cop will tell you, tempers fray when the temperature rises. The normal aggravations of life in the Big Apple are all a little more aggravating when it's 90 degrees Fahrenheit and ninety percent humidity—especially when the air-conditioning quits, or was never there in the first place.

A disagreement that would end in a quick apology or a grumbled curse in February isn't so easy to stop in August, when the thick hot air is holding the traffic fumes and the stench of uncollected garbage close around your face. Little things that wouldn't mean much on a calm spring day get in there with the sweat that's sticking your shirt to your back, and itch and itch and itch and they just won't go away until you find a way to scratch.

It was all just the little things that finally got to Al Napolitano, that drove him over the edge. They were nothing, really—the last beer gone from the fridge, the unwashed dinner dishes, the noise and stink of the city spilling in through the wide-open windows, Rose sitting there in front of the TV with the remote in one hand and that last can of beer in the other, and Christ, she wasn't even finishing it, she was letting it get warm, what a goddamn *waste* that was ... they were nothing, really, just little meaningless annoyances, Al could have handled it, he was pretty sure he could have handled it, they were adding up all right, they were getting on his nerves, but they weren't too much for him, even with the heat. He could have handled it—if it weren't for what she was watching as she sat there letting the beer get warm.

If she'd been watching the Home Shopping Network, he could have taken it, no problem. Her bowling shows, hell, those would've been just fine, he'd have maybe even pulled up a chair himself.

But she was watching *Green Acres*, some goddamn idiot cable channel had programmed reruns of *Green Acres* back to back, and she wouldn't switch channels or even turn down the sound, she wanted to hear it over the traffic, and it was when the second one came on, with that idiot theme song, that Al Napolitano couldn't take it anymore, and scratched that awful itch with a twelve-gauge shotgun at point-blank range.

Both barrels. One for Rose, one for the TV.

Detective Rasche, there to collect Al and otherwise do his bit toward keeping the peace, looked over the blood-spattered wreckage of the TV, and of Rose, after Al had explained it all to him.

"Dumb son of a bitch," Rasche muttered to himself. "I *like Green Acres.*"

Then the uniforms cuffed Al and led him down to the street, Rose's blood still red on his sweat-soaked undershirt, and the ambulance crew collected what was left of Rose on a stretcher and followed.

Rasche had given Al his Miranda rights, not that it made a whole hell of a lot of difference in a case like this, so he walked alongside and listened to whatever Al had to say, just in case the poor bastard said something that could be used to screw the inevitable insanity plea—anything Al said now was admissible.

"First time we'd had decent reception all *week,*" Al shouted as they left the old brownstone, "and she had to watch *that,* for God's sake! I mean, Jesus, when I heard the part about 'fresh air, Times Square,' something just went!"

Rasche mopped sweat from the back of his neck with a thoroughly saturated handkerchief. No question, there wasn't any goddamn fresh air within twenty miles of Times Square, but so what?

"Everybody's a goddamn critic," he said.

He hated homicide work. So much of it was like this—no mystery, no suspense, just some poor son of a bitch who lost it for a moment. There was nothing for a detective to do but try to clean up the mess—and who needed a detective for that?

He hated Homicide.

Narcotics, now—he'd *liked* narcotics work. There you were doing something positive, stopping the stuff from reaching the street, not just mopping up when it was too damn late to help anyone. You were saving kids, maybe kids like his own two boys, you were saving lives, not just watching the victims get carried out in a bag or under a blanket.

And you were up against people who fought back, not some poor schmuck with a glazed look in his eye who'd barely had the wits to drop the shotgun when the cops burst in. It took some real detecting to move up the chain following the drugs back to the source, to know what was going down, to know who was important and who was nothing, to know where to be when; it took guts, too.

Of course, you could get carried away in narcotics work. Rasche knew that, no question. He'd seen it. He'd been there when his partner had pitched the district chief of the Cali cartel off the roof of that fancy brownstone apartment house, and he had to admit that Schaefer had been just a bit over the line, doing that.

Schaef hadn't been out of control or anything; Rasche didn't think he'd even been angry. Heaving the guy over the parapet had seemed like a good idea at the time, under the circumstances, and the switchblade that was still in the smarmy bastard's hand when he landed, despite all the bones in that hand being broken, had convinced the powers that be in the NYPD that it wasn't *that* much of an overreaction.

But it had gotten Schaefer and Rasche transferred to Homicide, because that little incident had struck a nerve in the coke-dealing community, and things had gotten just a little too hot—even before the stinking heat wave began. The two detectives were on the hit list of every ambitious dealer or desperate doper in the city; anyone who wanted an in with the Colombians and could point a gun would be only too happy to blow them both away.

The captain had figured that if they stayed on the street working narco, it was just a matter of time before someone got lucky, and though losing Schaefer might simplify Captain McComb's life in some ways, it wouldn't be good PR, and it wouldn't help morale.

So Rasche and Schaefer were working homicide and hating every minute of it.

At least Rasche was; Schaefer had no comment.

Generally speaking, Schaefer wasn't much for unnecessary comments on anything. Rasche respected that.

Rasche got Al Napolitano properly on his way, safely tucked into the back of a prowl car, then found his own unmarked vehicle and climbed into the passenger side. Shadows had stretched across the streets and were climbing the buildings; the streetlights were coming on.

Schaefer and Rasche were on the evening shift at the moment; they wouldn't be getting off for another five hours, and that was assuming they didn't pull any overtime.

Schaefer was behind the wheel, staring straight ahead. He hadn't bothered to come up to the Napolitano apartment.

Rasche didn't mind. Schaefer was always there for the important stuff, and he did his share on the paper pushing, so Rasche didn't care if he blew off some of the little things on occasion.

"Yo, Schaef," Rasche said. "You want to take care of the paperwork now, or let it wait and get some coffee?"

"Coffee," Schaefer said, putting the car in gear.

Rasche nodded. He sat back in the seat, wishing he'd never seen Al Napolitano, and wondering what was happening on their old beat a little farther south on the Lower East Side. What were the druggies, the gangs, the dealers, the importers up to since Schaefer and Rasche's transfer? Had the Colombians managed to take any turf from the local outfits, the way the word on the street had said they wanted to? Had that slimy little cipher Lamb patched things up with his chief rival, Carr, to keep the Colombians out? The two had been fighting over market share for two years now, Lamb running his organization with calm, cool precision, Carr keeping up his side through sheer psychotic violence.

Carr had always been a lunatic.

Rasche wondered where Lamb and Carr and the rest were, at that very moment.

And as he wondered, Carr and four of his lieutenants were marching down a fifth-floor corridor six blocks farther downtown, in a boarded-up tenement. A holstered .357 hung on Carr's hip; three of the others carried sawed-off pump-action shotguns, while the last cradled an M-16.

The two men who met them at the door to the meeting room were armed as well—one with a

.38-caliber semiauto, the other with an Uzi. The weapons were all conspicuously visible, but not aimed at anyone.

Yet.

Carr stopped, his garishly painted face inches from the guard with the .38.

"Tell that pussy Lamb I'm here for the peace talks," he said.

The two figures were a striking contrast—the guard stood almost as tall as Carr's six foot three, but weighed perhaps half as much; where Carr wore a sweat-soaked sleeveless T-shirt, jeans, and black biker boots, the guard was nattily dressed in a blue pinstripe suit and red power tie, his only concession to the heat being the lack of a vest. Lines of red war paint that might have just been lipstick were slashed across Carr's face, and gold rings gleamed in his nose and left ear; his red hair was receding, but what was left was pulled back into a foot-long braid. The guard's face was clean and redolent of expensive aftershave, his hair in a hundred-dollar razor cut. Carr's eyes gleamed with madness; the guard's were cool and dark.

The guard was a man who'd seen dealing drugs as a way to earn money and respect; Carr, so far as anyone could figure out, had gotten into the drug business, with its guns, money, and violence, purely for the guns and violence.

For fun, in other words.

The guard nodded to his partner without turning away from Carr for an instant.

The man with the Uzi knocked twice on the door.

"Carr's here," he called.

A muffled voice answered, and a moment later the door swung open.

The room beyond was large, but as ruinous as the rest of the building; shards of glass were scattered on the floor, mixed with fallen ceiling plaster. Three empty windows were sloppily boarded over, with light from the lingering twilight and the remaining streetlights spilling in through three-inch gaps between planks. Enough air seeped in to layer the city's distinctive petroleum-based stench on top of the building's own dusty, mildewed reek.

An overturned stove sat in the center of the room, and a dapper young man leaned casually on the stove. Four others stood ranged behind him, all of them armed.

"Carr," the young man said coolly, "I'm glad you could make it."

"Cut the shit, Lamb," Carr said, striding into the room. "We got nothin' to talk about. I'm just here because I figured you might want to surrender."

"Wrong, Carr," Lamb replied. "We've got *everything* to talk about. We've got the whole damn city to talk about—not to mention our own survival."

Carr stopped a yard or so away from Lamb, planted his feet, and folded his arms across his chest. His four men straggled in behind him and took up positions around the room, dividing it into two armed camps. Edgie and Bonamo took a corner near the door, Hatcheck stood at Carr's right hand, and Crazy Charlie settled himself onto an ancient radiator, his back to a glassless window.

"Carr, just look at the situation," Lamb continued. "The cops are taking us down piece by piece, and what they miss, we finish for them with this stupid turf war. We're both pulling down serious money with our street operations, and throwing most of it away on this crap—there'd be enough for both of us if we stopped shooting at each other. There's enough that the Colombians would just *love* to step in and grab it all."

Even with the boards there was a faint whiff of a breeze there in the window, and Crazy Charlie was enjoying the feel of it on his back under his vest as he listened to Lamb's speech. He wasn't wearing a shirt, not in this heat, and even the vest was hot, and that air felt good. He was paying more attention to that, and to the taste of the Camel he was smoking, than to the little wimp's spiel. He could see sweat on Lamb's forehead, but he had to give the runt credit—it was probably the heat that did that, not fear. Lamb might not be much of a man, but Charlie knew he didn't get control of half the local drug traffic by being scared.

And Charlie knew that if *he* were in Lamb's position, he'd be scared—anyone who wasn't scared of Carr had to be crazy. Crazy Charlie *was* crazy, but not in that particular way.

"So?" Carr said. He looked bored.

"So we can do *better*, Carr," Lamb replied. "We can have it all."

"Yeah?" Carr grinned briefly. "You got any suggestions as to just how that might work, Lamb?"

Charlie took a drag on his cigarette and tapped ash on the floor.

"Yeah, Carr, as it happens, I do," Lamb said. "I know we're never going to agree on boundaries, not and make it stick—you know that, too, and I'm impressed that you're here. It shows that maybe you're as sick of this fighting as I am, and you're looking for another way. And there *is* another way, Carr!"

Carr just stared at his rival. Charlie allowed himself a grin. He knew that stare.

"I'm talking about a merger," Lamb continued. "We put it all together, combine our organizations, you and I split the net even. Together we can set prices, consolidate the police payoffs—the savings on that alone will be enormous! And the Colombians—the only way the Colombians can get a toehold in New York is by pitting the gangs against each other. If we merge, we can keep them out until hell freezes over!"

Carr shifted his weight from one foot to the other. "Only one small problem," he said.

Lamb stopped, hands spread questioningly.

Carr smiled. "One problem, Lambikins," he said. "I don't give a shit about the Colombian muchachos, and I couldn't care less about maximizing profits or cutting overhead or any of that crap. Screw your merger. I'm in this for the kicks, and you and your suits are *boring*—if I had to work with you, I'd go batfuck in a week."

Lamb's hands dropped.

"So," Carr said, "why don't we just cut this 'peace' shit and get on with it? What say we have us a dainty little game of winner-take-all . . ."

As Carr spoke, Lamb's hands were behind his back, and Crazy Charlie didn't think it was just so he could twiddle his thumbs, he'd have bet his eyeteeth that the sneaky son of a bitch had a piece back there, and besides, it sounded like Carr wanted to make this one big shooting gallery in here, which Charlie didn't think was that great an idea, if the truth be known, but Carr was the Man, and Charlie was just muscle.

If there was going to be any shooting, Charlie intended to be on the sending end, not receiving; he started to bring his shotgun around, but as he did, he sensed something, he wasn't sure what. He turned and glimpsed three little spots of some kind of red light, like those laser beams in the checkout at the 7-Eleven, crawling across the window frame and onto his back.

"What the . . . ," he began, interrupting Carr.

And then white fire flashed and Crazy Charlie's chest exploded, spraying gore across the room as the blue-white blast tore through him.

2

Everyone whirled at the sound of the blast; everyone saw Crazy Charlie's body twitch convulsively and fall to the floor, chest blown apart, bits of rib and heart and lung scattered like confetti in the plaster dust.

"It's a setup!" Carr bellowed as he drew his Magnum; a streamer of Crazy Charlie's blood had drawn a dark red line across his boot.

"It's *not*, Carr, I swear . . . !" Lamb began.

"Someone's outside," Lamb's second in command shouted. "Cover me!" He kicked a half rotted board off the nearest window and leaned out, assault rifle ready in his hands. "I'll take care of it, Lamb," he said. "Whoever the shooter is . . ."

That was as far as he got; the sentence ended in a gurgle and a grunt as the man was yanked out,

tearing more boards away as he was dragged upward, legs kicking wildly, spine arching unnaturally.

Half a dozen weapons were cocked and ready
now, searching for targets as Carr grabbed Lamb's
tie and shoved the .357 up under his rival's chin.

"*You son of a bitch!*" Carr roared. "We're five
floors up! Who the hell is out there?"

"*I don't know!*" Lamb shrieked. "Not *my* men!"
Then realization dawned in Lamb's eyes. "Colombians!" he said.

"*Fuck* the Colombians!" Carr replied. He shoved
Lamb away and looked over his men, Hatcheck
and Edgie and Bonamo, standing with their weapons ready, aimed at the windows, just waiting the
word.

Lamb's men were looking at him expectantly, and their weapons were aimed at the windows,
too.

"You and me'll finish up later, Lamb," Carr said.
"Right now I'm for blowing the balls off whoever's
out there, and I don't give a shit if it's the Colombians or the cops or fuckin' Santa Claus." He
waved to his men. "*Do* it!"

The room exploded in gunfire, in an unbearable
chaos of sound and flash, as Carr's and Lamb's
men all opened fire on the room's outer wall.
Splinters flew; planking shredded under the hail of
gunfire, and plaster showered from the ancient
walls. Window frames cracked, sagged, collapsed,
lath and studding shattered, and the brick veneer
beyond crumbled as the barrage continued, round
after round of high-caliber ammo blasting at the
aging structure. Carr's delighted yelling as he

pumped rounds from his Magnum was almost inaudible over the noise.

At last, as ammunition was exhausted, fire ceased; the echoes died away, booming down through the streets below, and the last fragments of wood, plaster, and masonry rattled to rest.

When his ears stopped ringing and he could hear again, Carr exclaimed happily, "That was *fun!*" He blinked drifting dust and gun smoke from his eyes and looked at the gaping hole where two of the three windows had been; they were gone completely, leaving a hole seven feet high and ten feet wide through which New York's famous skyline glowed in outline, black against the fading sunset.

"Nice view," he remarked.

"Jesus," Lamb said, surveying the destruction.

There was no sign of the man who had been yanked out the window, he noticed; the body must have fallen to the street, along with the remains of whoever had done the yanking. Nothing could have lived through that firestorm.

Edgie, Bonamo, and Hatcheck looked at the wreckage, at their leaders, and began reloading; Lamb's men did the same. Crazy Charlie's corpse lay ignored under a coating of debris, in a surprisingly small pool of blood.

Each side had lost a man, but the leaders were still talking; nobody aimed anything.

Lamb stepped forward, toward the hole, with the intention of looking down at the sidewalk to count the bodies; Carr's heavy hand on his shoulder held him back.

"Now, about that treaty . . . ," Carr began, grinning.

Lamb didn't turn; he still stared at the hole, at the broken line of bricks where a window had been. "Oh, my God," he whispered.

Carr glanced at the hole. Just like that sorry excuse for a man to be impressed by a blown-out wall. He and his men carried guns; hadn't they ever seen what they could do before?

Then Carr saw where Lamb was staring.

There was a hand holding on to the bricks—or was there? It seemed to flicker as Carr looked; at first he saw a big yellowish hand with long black nails, then a ghostly blue flicker like faint sparks jumping, and then the hand was gone, and there were just the bricks and a shimmering in the hot air.

"What *is* that?" Lamb asked.

The hand was back, and this time it stayed—a big, strong hand, bigger than Carr's own, with nails like claws, and Carr realized it wasn't human, it had to be a fake, one of those costume gloves you could buy in the discount stores.

It was moving; someone was trying to climb up into the room. Somehow, someone had lived through the barrage.

Whoever it was must have been on the floor below, out of the line of fire. Carr let go of Lamb's shoulder and stepped back, .357 at ready.

Whoever it was in the monster gloves must've thought he was being cute with those things.

"Son of a bitch thinks it's Halloween," Carr said as the fingers flexed and a shadowy shape rose into view. "Hey, bozo!" He pointed the heavy pistol. "Trick or treat!"

He pulled the trigger.

Then the world fell in on him.

Six blocks away Rasche handed Schaefer a plastic cup that was not steaming. Ordinarily, that might have pissed Rasche off, but in this heat he didn't think he cared if the coffee was cold. At least *something* was.

He took a gulp from his own cup and almost spat it out again. The stuff tasted like raw liver.

"Jesus," he said, "why would anyone pay gang prices for drugs? A cup of this'll make 'em feel just as awful for half a buck." When Schaefer didn't respond, Rasche glanced at him and saw that Schaefer was sitting motionless, staring up out the car window, the coffee untasted in his hand.

"What is it?" Rasche asked uneasily. Schaefer had been acting weirder than usual lately, and while Rasche didn't believe in any of that psychic shit, he knew Schaef could pick up on stuff other people missed; his weird moods usually meant trouble. Worried, Rasche leaned over and looked out past Schaefer's shoulder.

All he saw was empty sky, darkening to indigo. The first few stars were appearing.

"Something's wrong," Schaefer said. "The city doesn't feel right."

Rasche snorted and straightened up. "That's like saying battery acid doesn't taste right, Schaef. This is New York, remember? The city where we busted a satanic cow cult last month? Where good ol' Al Napolitano blew away his wife a couple of hours ago because she wouldn't change the channel?"

"I know that," Schaefer said, "but this is something else. Was that thunder a few minutes ago?"

"I didn't hear anything," Rasche said. "I was in there." He jerked a thumb at Bud's Deli and Diner.

"I thought you might've heard it anyway. Loud. Didn't sound right."

Rasche stared at his partner in disgust.

They'd been together for six years, but every so often Rasche still forgot just how weird Schaefer could be when he started getting mystical. "How the hell could thunder not sound right? It was probably heat lightning or something."

"Sounded like guns," Schaefer said. "Like a fucking army. But it must've been thunder, right? Who'd be firing that much at once?"

Before Rasche could reply, the car radio crackled. "All units in vicinity respond—shots fired, corner of Beekman and Water."

"That was it," Schaefer said, and Rasche almost thought he could see Schaefer's face relax in relief. "Like a fucking army. Roll."

That would figure, Schaef being relieved that the sound really *was* guns. Anyone else would be scared, but Schaef was more concerned that he might be losing his feel for the city than that they were about to drive into a war zone.

Rasche climbed into the driver's seat and slammed the door. "At least it'll be that much longer before we have to write up Al the TV critic," he muttered as he turned the key.

The streets were running the wrong way, and traffic and the junk along the curbs were thicker than usual but not bad enough to make Rasche use the lights or siren, so by the time they arrived on the scene, four other cars were already there, uniforms cordoning off the area around an abandoned five-story walk-up tenement. One of them jumped in front of Schaefer as he climbed out of the car.

"Sorry, Detective Schaefer," the officer said, "I've got orders to keep the building clear of all personnel until Captain McComb arrives. He wants to handle this one himself."

Schaefer nodded once, slowly, but Rasche didn't like the set of his partner's shoulders. He knew that Schaef wanted to get in there, get after whoever it was had put out that roar like thunder.

Well, he'd have to wait.

Rasche looked up at the building, just a casual glance, but he found himself staring.

A chunk of brick wall on the fifth floor had been blown out, littering the sidewalk with debris; it looked as if a bomb had gone off, not like anything done with firearms. And he could hear distant thumping somewhere in that direction—not guns, something else. "What the hell," he said. "*Shots* fired? Not an explosion?"

One of the uniforms heard him. "Yessir," he said. "A *lot* of shots."

"That wasn't a bomb did that?" Rasche asked, pointing at the hole.

The patrolman glanced up. "We don't know," he admitted, "but we heard shots. Lots of 'em. Like a gang war or something." He shrugged. "So far we've got 'em tagged for reckless endangerment, illegal discharge of a firearm within city limits, God only knows how many violations of the Sullivan Act, disorderly conduct . . . Hell, we can thrown in exceeding noise restrictions. . . ."

Just then a sharp crack sounded as boards burst out from one of the fifth-floor windows, followed by a gurgling scream as the man whose body had burst them out sailed across the street and plummeted to a hard landing atop a police cruiser, shattering light bar and windshield spectacularly.

Shocked into silence, the cops all stared for a moment as shards of glass and plastic tinkled to the pavement and across the cruiser's hood, and as broken boards thumped and clattered to the neighboring sidewalk.

Then the silence broke as men hurried to check on the condition of the fallen figure, and someone called in for an ambulance—no, several ambulances.

The patrolman who had been talking to Rasche swallowed and said, "Guess we can add destruction of police property to the list."

Somewhere above, gunfire rattled, and a shrill scream was suddenly cut off short.

Calmly, Schaefer drew his 9mm service pistol and chambered a round.

"Screw McComb," he said.

The officer who had met him at the car door stepped back. "I guess we can make an exception on that no-admittance thing, Detective Schaefer, if you feel it's warranted—I mean, you're here, the captain isn't."

He was still babbling when Schaefer pushed past and trotted into the building, pistol ready.

Rasche followed, grumbling and tugging his own piece from its holster.

The door was open, the ground-floor hallway empty and dim; Rasche followed Schaefer to the stairwell, pistol gripped firmly in both hands. Up above he could hear hoarse shouts and loud thumps.

"Sounds like a ninja movie up there," he said quietly. "Who the hell do you think's up there, Schaef? Isn't this Lamb's turf?"

Schaefer grunted affirmatively. "Gang-bang central," he said. "Lamb uses it when he takes his goddamn meetings." He took a look up into the darkness, then headed up the stairs, weapon ready.

The middle floors were dark and silent; Rasche took a quick glance down each hallway, pistol aimed at nothing, and saw only garbage and emptiness.

Schaefer didn't bother even to look; he was headed where the action was.

On the fifth floor dim light spilled into the hallway from an open door; the thumping had stopped, but someone was screaming steadily, a scream of pain and terror like nothing Rasche had ever heard before. Gun smoke was drifting in the air, and the whole place reeked of it.

"Jesus, you *hear* that?" Rasche asked, crouching on the top step.

"Yeah," Schaefer said, standing in the hallway. "They're really starting to piss me off in there."

The scream ended in a choking gurgle.

"Cover me," Schaefer said as he approached the door, his back to the wall. "I'm going in."

Rasche didn't bother to reply; Schaefer didn't give him time, anyway. Almost as soon as he'd finished speaking, Schaefer was around the door frame, charging into the room with his gun ready.

Rasche moved cautiously up the corridor, back to the wall, trying to ignore the fact that there were a dozen goddamn bullet holes in that wall, and his back was sliding right across them, begging for another few high-velocity rounds to come punching out.

He heard Schaefer's footsteps go in, then stop somewhere in the middle of the room.

And then he didn't hear anything but a thick dripping sound, like steak sauce going on.

"Oh, Christ," Rasche muttered to himself, very quietly.

He imagined that he could feel that wrongness now, the same thing Schaefer had mentioned back at Bud's Deli. Something wasn't *right*. The all-out firefight, the blown-out wall, now that heavy silence, and something intangible and indefinably *wrong*, in a way the city had never been wrong before, in all the years Rasche had lived there.

Just as Schaefer had said.

"Schaef?" Rasche called quietly.

Schaefer didn't answer; Rasche heard his boot scuff on grit, but Schaefer didn't say anything at all.

Rasche stepped forward, pistol ready, and swung around the door frame.

Then he stopped, frozen, staring into the room beyond.

It's odd, what goes through a person's head at certain times—or at least Rasche thought so, as he took in what lay beyond the doorway. Because what he immediately thought of, upon seeing it, was his mother.

He remembered her holding him, crooning soothingly to him, when he was maybe four, five years old. He remembered the soft touch of her hands, and how long and thin her fingers seemed, and how one curl of her hair brushed against his forehead as she held him close.

The rest of the memory came back, and he decided that maybe it wasn't so very odd after all.

Because the reason she'd been holding him and comforting him is that he had woken up screaming in the darkness, shaking uncontrollably with nameless terror, after some nightmare he couldn't remember, something about monsters in the night, about suffocating in his own blood, about the *things* that wanted to hurt him.

And she had rocked him gently in her arms and had told him softly, "Those bad things are just dreams, they're not real. They can't hurt you. There are no monsters in the night, not really."

As he looked at the big room on the fifth floor, the room where one wall had been party shot away, the room littered with broken glass and spattered blood and plaster dust, the room where his unflappable partner Schaefer was standing dumbstruck, Rasche knew that his mother had lied.

Because the monsters had to be real. Nothing else could have done this.

The two cops stared silently for a long moment.

Finally Schaefer spoke.

"Gang war, my ass," he said.

3

The bodies were swaying gently in the breeze from the blown-out wall, and the blood that dripped from their dangling red fingertips drew loops and whorls on the floor.

There were eight of them in all, hanging by their feet; something had smashed away most of the ceiling and tied the corpses to a joist. Even in the dim light of the city outside they were all bright red, from heel to head.

It was obvious what had been done to them, what the monsters in the night had done, but Rasche had to say it anyway.

"They've been skinned," he said.

Schaefer nodded.

"Some of them are Lamb's men," he said, "and some are Carr's. An equal-opportunity massacre, that's what we have here."

Rasche stared at him—which was better than staring at the bodies, anyway. "Jesus Christ, Schaef," he said, "how can you *tell*? They don't have their goddamn *faces* anymore!"

"They don't have the skin, the faces are still there," Schaefer said. "That's Edgie, and Hatcheck—Carr's boys. That's Fiorello, one of Lamb's—and here's the real kicker, Lamb himself. Look at the eyes, they're still there."

Rasche looked before he could stop himself, before he could remind himself that maybe he didn't want to, and he felt a sudden surge of nausea. Sweat dripped down his face, cold sweat despite the heat, and he couldn't make himself move to wipe it away. He couldn't take his eyes off the bloody bodies. He couldn't move his feet, either; if he stepped forward, he'd be walking in blood, and he couldn't step back, he wasn't sure why but he couldn't, it felt as if the monsters in the night would get him if he stepped back.

And there were cartridge casings everywhere, and guns were lying in the blood, covered with blood, blood coating the grips and barrels, and the room stank of gun smoke and meat. These men hadn't died without a fight.

"Jesus," he said again. "Schaef, who . . . It would've taken an army to . . ."

He didn't finish the sentence, because there was a sound, and in Rasche's condition just at that moment any sound he couldn't account for had to be monsters, and you didn't talk to monsters. He crouched and whirled, gun ready.

A fallen section of ceiling was moving, a broad chunk of lath and plaster that had been torn away and flung aside to uncover the beam that held the hanging bodies.

And when a bloody figure rose slowly out of the fallen plaster, it was all Rasche could do not to fire, his finger was squeezing down on the trigger but he stopped it, it was like stopping a runaway truck, it was the hardest struggle of his life to keep from squeezing that last fraction of an inch, but the figure was a human being, it wasn't the monsters, and he was a good cop, a good cop didn't shoot the last survivor of a massacre, not without knowing who it was and what was happening, not unless it was the only way.

This was a man, a man with long red hair tied back in a thick braid, but he was so covered with blood and bits of debris stuck to the blood that Rasche couldn't make out his face at first.

He rose to his knees, dazed, staring wildly about, and then his eyes focused on Schaefer.

Schaefer's 9mm was hanging at his side unthreateningly, and Rasche thought to himself that maybe he should lower his own weapon, but he couldn't bring himself to do it.

White teeth gleamed through the bloody ruin of the man's face; he coughed, then said, in a voice thick with dust and emotion, "Well, if it isn't my old pal, Detective Schaefer." He groped for something in the wreckage. "You missed one, Schaefer. The *wrong* one."

"Carr?" Rasche asked, wonderingly.

Carr was looking around at the dangling bodies and the debris, but all the time one hand was still searching for something.

"Hey, Schaefer," he said conversationally, "I've

seen you cops pull a lot of crude shit, but nothing like this. Man, I'm *impressed*."

"You're *crazy*, Carr, you're fuckin' insane," Rasche said, unspeakably relieved to have a human opponent to shout at. "*Cops* didn't do this, cops couldn't *begin* to do this. . . ."

"You didn't see them?" Schaefer asked, his flat, calm voice cutting Rasche off short. "You didn't see who it was that did this?"

"All I saw was some geek in a trick-or-treat mask climbing in through the window, then someone brought the ceiling down on me," Carr said. "Maybe it was cops and you're covering, maybe it wasn't, I don't know—and you know, Schaefer, I don't give a shit. It doesn't really matter. 'Cause I may be crazy, I may be fuckin' crazy as a bedbug, but while I'm crazy, you're just plain *dead*!"

And his hand finally came up with what he'd been looking for, and the sawed-off pump-action shotgun came up fast, Carr pushed himself to his feet and brought the gun to his hip and fired all in one motion.

Rasche had been on a hair-trigger since he'd first set foot in the building, he didn't need to have the ceiling fall in on *him*; he dived the instant he saw Carr's hand come up full, he was rolling for cover in the shattered plaster before Carr's finger could tighten on the trigger.

The roar of the shotgun seemed to shake the weakened building right down to its foundation, and Rasche's ears rang even before the second blast put buckshot through a space where Schaefer had been standing a fraction of a second before. He couldn't hear Carr's footsteps as the gang leader started running, couldn't hear if Carr had said anything else, couldn't hear him curse when he ratcheted the pump and got an empty click and realized the goddamn shotgun had only had two shells left in it.

Then Rasche's hearing began to come back, and he did hear Schaefer bellow, "Freeze, you son of a—"

Schaefer's 9mm barked three times, and by that time Rasche had finally gotten himself turned over and headed back to being upright, and how the hell had Carr gotten so far down the corridor already, and how'd Schaefer get into that solid shooting stance?

But Schaefer wasn't as calm and in control as he looked, because he missed with all three shots, and while Schaefer wasn't exactly Annie Oakley, he didn't generally miss *three* times at that range, and it sure as hell wasn't due to any worries about *wanting* to hit his target, not when Carr had just tried to blow him away.

Carr was yelling when he went through the window at the far end of the corridor, but he wasn't hit, it was pure adrenaline, a scream of challenge, not pain, and Schaefer was already running after him, and Rasche wondered as he often did, how the hell did Schaef *do* that? How could anyone be that strong, that fast, when he spent his time at a desk or in a car, instead of working out at the gym?

Rasche got to his own feet and trotted heavily down the passage, to find Schaefer standing in a shattered window frame, his hands on either side of the sash and one foot on the fire escape beyond, staring up the street.

Rasche stepped up beside him and watched as Carr dodged the four cops assigned to watch that particular alley, watched as they hesitated, conferred among themselves, and didn't leave their post to pursue.

". . . son of a *bitch*!" Schaefer said, stepping out onto the fire escape.

"Damn! We lost him!" Rasche said as Carr vanished around a corner.

"Not lost," Schaefer corrected him, "just misplaced. There's nowhere he can hide that we can't get him eventually." He leaned over the rail of the fire escape and called after Carr, "To be continued, punk!"

He stood like that for a moment, then started to turn back to the building . . .

. . . and froze.

"What?" Rasche said, looking down, expecting to see Carr coming back.

"Shut up," Schaefer said. "Listen."

Rasche shut up and listened.

"I don't hear anything," he said—which wasn't literally true, because of course he heard the wind and the distant traffic and the voices of the cops surrounding the building and all the other noises of New York by night, but he didn't hear anything that could account for Schaefer's behavior.

"Something's out there," Schaefer said.

"Like what?" Rasche asked.

"I don't know," Schaefer said.

Rasche looked around at the empty alleyways, the waiting cops, the broken glass and rotten wood of the shattered window, the dim corridor that led back to that bloody scene straight out of hell.

He didn't see anything wrong—except the obvious, of course, the broken window and the room where the monsters had done whatever it was they did.

But he didn't see anything that might begin to explain it, and he didn't hear anything that could mean anything, while at the same time he could almost feel whatever Schaefer was talking about.

Something was out there. Something wrong.

"This is starting to *scare* me, man," he said.

"I've got a feeling that's the whole idea," Schaefer answered, stepping back into the building.

And then there were footsteps pounding up the stairs, but neither Schaefer nor Rasche bothered to raise a weapon, because that was the familiar sound of police boots; no one else stomped quite like a squad of cops.

"Seal it up!" a voice shouted, a voice that Schaefer and Rasche both recognized. They looked at each other with expressions of resignation.

"All of it!" the voice continued. "Seal everything! Nobody gets in here!"

"McComb," Rasche said. He grimaced. "I mean, *Captain* McComb."

Then a stream of blue-clad men burst out of the stairwell, rifles at ready, fanning out through the building.

One tugged at another's sleeve and pointed, and Captain McComb turned to see Schaefer and Rasche standing in the end of the corridor, in front of the demolished window.

For a moment McComb just glared; then he stepped forward and growled, "You stepped in it this time, Schaefer—orders were to secure the building from outside, not cowboy around like some damn TV supercop! I heard shots—if you fired that piece of yours, you better be able to write up a convincing report of why. I want it on my desk by midnight, and I want it in triplicate."

Schaefer pointed down the corridor. "Have you seen those bodies, McComb?"

"So there's some dead punks? You think that justifies disobeying my orders?"

"It's not just some dead punks, McComb. This was a slaughter. It's like a butcher shop in there."

"So the gangs play rough—"

Schaefer cut McComb off. "Don't give me any crap about a gang war," he said. "You go take a look in there and tell me what kind of weapon these gangs have that'll do that kind of damage. You look at those holes and tell me that was just a riot gun or an Uzi did that."

McComb stared at Schaefer for a moment, then shook his head and said through gritted teeth, "You don't have a clue, do you? I don't give a shit *what's* in there—that's not the point. The point is, I told you to keep the fuck out, and you didn't. This isn't your case, and don't you worry your pretty blond head about it, Schaefer. You just stay the hell out of this one, you got it?"

Schaefer didn't answer; Rasche patted him on the back and said, "Come on, Schaef."

Together, the two detectives pushed past McComb and started down the stairs.

When they were out of earshot, Rasche muttered, "If they sold stupidity on the stock exchange, we could bust McComb for illegally cornering the market."

Schaefer grunted.

Rasche looked at him; the grunt seemed to mean something.

"You think he's hiding something, maybe?" Rasche asked. "You think he got paid off by someone to let this happen?"

Schaefer shook his head. "Not his style," he said. "Someone might be hiding something, but not that."

As they stepped out of the building, Schaefer added, "And whatever it is, I don't think it's gonna *stay* hid."

4

It was two o'clock in the god-
damn morning, but the streets outside were still
sweltering hot.

McComb wasn't on the streets, but he was still
sweating. The air-conditioning in his office was
working just fine, but he was sweating all the same
as he dialed the number he'd been given.

"Yes?" said the voice on the other end. No name,
no greeting—just "Yes?"

"This is Captain McComb," McComb said. "Let
me talk to General Philips."

"Just a moment," the voice said.

After a pause a new voice, one McComb recognized, barked, "Philips."

"McComb here, General," the police captain
said.

"Go on."

"You were right, General," McComb said. "There was an attack." He swallowed.

Philips heard the swallow, noted the pause. "Bad?" he asked.

"Yessir," McComb replied. "Real bad. Eleven men dead. Eight of them were skinned alive and hung upside down inside the building, one was thrown out a window, and the other two were on the roof. The two on the roof had been decapitated and badly mangled—we haven't found the heads."

"You won't," Philips said.

McComb was silent for a moment, taking that in.

"Who are they?" Philips asked. "Your men?"

"No," McComb said. "A bunch of hoodlums. Gang members, worked in drugs."

"No great loss, then," Philips said. "They were heavily armed?"

"We found enough weapons lying around . . . Yes, heavily armed."

"That fits."

For a moment McComb sat silently in his office, staring at the closed door, trying unsuccessfully to think; then he asked, "General, what the hell is going on? What happened to those men?"

"I told you before, Captain," Philips replied, "I can't tell you that. It's a federal matter, and out of your hands—all you do is keep us posted and keep everyone else out, and we'll take care of it."

"So . . ." McComb hesitated. "So there are going to be more attacks?"

"Maybe," Philips said. "We don't know, not for sure—but there could be, yes."

"You don't know?"

"No, Captain, we don't. This isn't something

we're responsible for, it's just something that we saw might be coming."

"But if you saw it coming, couldn't you . . . can't you see whether it's going to happen again?"

Philips sighed. "Look, Captain, I can't explain why, but it's damn near a miracle we know as much as we do about this, and it's just dumb luck that we spotted . . . that we got a hint something like this might happen in New York. We have no idea whether it'll happen again, or how often, or for how long—and it's not your job to worry about it. It's your job to keep everyone away from the scene, and to keep everything quiet, and that's all. We don't want any of your men involved, and we sure as hell don't want the press to get even the slightest whiff of this."

"Just keep it quiet," McComb said.

"That's right," Philips agreed. "Other than that, we'll handle it ourselves. I'll be coming up there to-night with my people, and we'll be conducting the investigation. You just keep your men clear."

"Yessir," McComb said.

He hung up and sat back, the sweat starting to dry.

He didn't like being ordered out, he didn't like being told what to do by the feds—but this was a special case. It wasn't the FBI or some of the other Treasury boys this time—Philips was army, some kind of special unit, and McComb's instructions to listen to him had come from the mayor, who'd said that *his* instructions came from the White House.

And this wasn't just some drug bust. At first McComb had thought that was it, that the feds had decided to turn the whole goddamn army loose on the drug traffic; but then he'd seen what was in that tenement on Beekman.

The army hadn't done that. Not the *U.S.* Army, anyway. Some third-world terrorists might do something like that, if they had the time and were mad enough, but McComb sure hoped that American soldiers wouldn't.

And it hadn't been a gang war, either. Drug traffickers killed each other, sure, and they'd mutilate each other sometimes, whack off an ear for a souvenir, maybe even cut off some poor guys' balls to make a point; but they didn't skin people and hang them up to dry.

And even if some lunatic *had* decided to skin his competition, gang-bangers didn't kill eleven heavily armed people without putting any bullet holes in them.

Oh, there might have been bullet holes in the two on the roof—they were so chewed up no one could tell without a microscope. The eight inside the building, though, had been killed with blades.

They'd all been armed, they'd fired off thousands of rounds, and they'd been killed with blades.

And the forensics boys who had gotten a look before the feds chased everyone out said that it looked as if one of those eight had still been alive when he was skinned.

Even drug dealers didn't do that. Not even the crazy new bunch out of Jamaica.

Who the hell *did*?

Philips had contacted him the day before and told him there might be some kind of unusually vicious massacre about to happen, one that didn't seem to make any sense. He'd said it would probably be somewhere that wasn't air-conditioned, that the victims would probably be armed, that it would probably be well above street level.

And that's all he would say.

How had Philips known? What the hell was going on?

McComb didn't have any idea, but the more he thought about it, the more relieved he was that it was out of his hands.

Let Philips and his feds have this one—God knew that McComb didn't want it!

About 240 miles to the south, Philips stared at the phone.

Maybe he should have told McComb what was going on—but the reports on McComb, and Philips's own impression of the man, weren't encouraging about how he'd take it.

It wasn't as if it was easy to believe. Hell, Philips hadn't wanted to believe it himself when Dutch Schaefer had told him what had happened out there in the jungle eight years ago, even though Philips knew and trusted Dutch.

Eventually, though, he'd been convinced, and he'd convinced his superiors. The evidence had been there.

He wasn't sure McComb was the sort who'd believe the evidence.

And if he was, Philips wasn't sure he wanted McComb to know. This had to be kept quiet. If the news ever leaked out to the general public . . .

Nobody paid any attention to the tabloids when they raved about space aliens, but if the U.S. government was to announce that monsters from outer space were hunting humans in the streets of

New York—well, Philips wasn't sure how it would go over, but he knew he didn't want to find out. He imagined panicking crowds, crazed cultists, conspiracy theorists—half the people wouldn't believe the official story and would assume it was covering up something illicit, while the other half would probably see it as the end of the world.

And it wouldn't do any good. Unless Dutch had lied, the things, whatever they were, had technology that made good old U.S. know-how look like kids playing with sticks and pebbles. The aliens had invisibility screens, energy cannon, pocket nukes. They could do whatever they wanted to Earth, to the whole human race, and the best thing humanity could do was ignore it, bear up under it, and wait for the bastards to get bored and go away again.

They sure didn't want to get the aliens *angry*. People were no match for those things.

Sure, Dutch had fought one and killed it and lived to tell about it—but Dutch was about the toughest specimen the human race had ever produced, and he'd been damn lucky, as well. Philips had listened to the whole story several times and knew how much to adjust for Dutch's downplaying of his own talents—and even so, he knew Dutch had been lucky.

If the scientists could get their hands on some of those gadgets the creature had had, maybe things would be different, but so far that hadn't happened, and it didn't look as if it was going to anytime soon.

After they'd picked up Dutch and heard his report, Philips and his group had started studying anything and everything that had seemed as if it might be related. They had traced the legends in the area, had looked at everything from star charts to missing-pet reports, had gone looking for anything they could find.

They'd found plenty of evidence of the things, all right, had learned a little more about their habits and patterns—but nothing of their technology. The bastards were apparently very, very careful with their gadgetry—they didn't leave any cosmic equivalent of tossed beer cans lying around, let alone anything really important.

But there hadn't been any real urgency to the studies. The creatures had been coming to Earth to hunt people for centuries, and they always hunted in hot, harsh climates, in the back country, never in any place important.

Until now.

Now the things were loose in New York. The Air Force had picked up unfamiliar radar interference and had put word out to Philips's group in hopes of finding an explanation; he'd theorized it might be the radar equivalent of the shimmer effect the creatures' invisibility gadgets caused, and had asked where it had been found.

And the Air Force had told him.

New York.

Philips had had a whole platoon of radar analysts and stealth specialists put on it, and they'd confirmed the Air Force report.

If the radar was picking up what it appeared to be picking up, the things were in New York.

What the hell were they doing that far north? If

they wanted a city to play in, why not someplace like Rio, or Mexico City?

Maybe there was something special about New York, something in particular they wanted there—but what?

It hadn't seemed likely that they wanted something specific, something that could be found only in New York. And it hadn't seemed reasonable that after centuries of confining their hunts to hot places they'd suddenly go north.

Philips had considered all that, and he'd thought maybe it wasn't the intruders after all, maybe the radar signal was a false alarm, but he'd talked to McComb yesterday morning, just in case—and sure enough, the attack had happened, the hunt had come.

The hunters of men, the predators on human prey, were loose on the streets of New York.

And Philips didn't know why.

He still had some time before his flight; he pulled out the faxed report he'd gotten an hour before and began reading through it again, looking for some clue, some hint of what the things wanted in New York.

5

For the next few days the heat wave continued; the thick, hot blanket of tropical air that smothered the city showed no sign of going anywhere.

The investigation of the massacre at Beekman and Water showed no sign of going anywhere, either, as far as Schaefer and Rasche could tell—but they weren't on the inside. They were banned from the scene, and no one they spoke to knew who was handling the case. There were rumors that some special federal task force was involved.

Schaefer made it plain that he didn't like the sound of that.

"Hey, it isn't *necessarily* a cover-up," Rasche reminded him. "For all we know, the whole thing could be taped and ready to go. The feds do the job sometimes."

"Since when is this their job?"

"Since they said it is," Rasche answered. "Come on, Schaef, let it go."

"It's not their city," Schaefer said.

"It's not just yours, either."

"When some asshole comes in and massacres the punks I've been trying to nail for the past three years . . ."

"Schaef, you're not in narco anymore."

"You think that means it's over?"

"I think that means it's not our problem."

Schaefer was clearly not convinced of that, but he stopped arguing.

It wasn't their problem. The feds had taken over, and plain old NYPD homicide detectives were not welcome.

Rasche wasn't very happy about that either; for one thing, he knew that whenever something this weird and violent went down once and the cops weren't all over it, it was likely to happen again.

The idea of looking at another scene of carnage like the fifth floor of that tenement made Rasche sick to his stomach, and he had to admit that he didn't see much sign that the feds were doing anything. No G-men were combing the NYPD files, or questioning the cops who patrolled that beat, or talking to any of the guys in either homicide or narco.

He considered calling in the press, maybe making an anonymous call to *Newsday*, just to goose the feds a little—but reporters were a pain in the ass, pretty nearly as much his natural enemies as the feds were.

And it wasn't as if he had nothing better to do. He and Schaefer were keeping busy.

The day after the massacre, for example, a tourist from Missouri took a wrong turn, wound up on the Staten Island ferry instead of the boat to Liberty Island, and went berserk, taking three commuters hostage; one of the hostages knifed another, and Schaefer and Rasche got to clean up the mess.

Rasche got to spend the evening listening to lawyers argue over whether the tourist could be charged as an accomplice to attempted murder, while Schaefer tried to get the tourist's family back in Missouri on the phone and worked through a maze of cousins and friends.

The day after that the big event came when a complicated deal between Jamaican drug dealers, Somali gunrunners, and Serbian terrorists went bad in TriBeCa, of all places, when the Jamaicans decided to keep everything for themselves. After the dust settled and most of the participants were hauled away to either the lockup or the morgue, Rasche got to help haul a truckload of confiscated heavy weapons to the police lab on West Twentieth for investigation.

Rasche didn't even recognize some of the stuff. The plain old automatic weapons he knew, and the rocket-propelled grenades—though he had no idea why the Jamaicans would have wanted them—but some of the contraband looked more like spare jet parts than weapons.

And maybe, given the Serbian connection, it *was* spare jet parts.

Schaefer was ordered to stay away from the

scene on that one—apparently Captain McComb didn't trust him within reach of three tons of military ordnance. Instead, he spent his time interviewing survivors, trying to figure out just who had shot who with what.

That night two punks eager to impress someone tried to drop Schaefer from ambush; the first shot missed, and they never got a second. Both lived; one went straight to the Tombs, the other did a month in the hospital first.

All that stuff was ordinary enough—at least by the standards of NYPD homicide—but then the next day there was the police firing range.

Rasche and Schaefer weren't there when it happened; they hadn't had time to worry about their marksmanship.

Rasche probably wouldn't have bothered anyway, in this heat, even if his backlog of paperwork had vanished and the whole damn city had gone a week without so much as a jaywalking.

And Schaefer, Rasche sometimes thought, used the whole damn city as his firing range.

The range was in the basement of the police academy on West Twentieth, downstairs from the police lab. It was open to anyone licensed to carry a gun inside the city limits; officers were expected to practice there occasionally. Most of them did, including Rasche and Schaefer.

But neither of them was there when it happened.

It was late afternoon, and half a dozen assorted law enforcement personnel and civilian big shots were on the firing line, blowing away paper targets and griping about the heat whenever the noise level dropped enough to allow conversation. Fresh targets fluttered wildly in the breeze from the ventilators as they were cranked downrange, but the place was a steam bath, all the same. Tailored jackets lay in heaps on the floor at civilian feet, and none of the blue uniform shirts were buttoned all the way up.

Probation officer Richard K. Stillman rattled down the stairs from the street and marched happily along the basement corridor, untroubled by the heat. Life was good. He'd hit big at OTB yesterday, and he had a hot date lined up, with an hour to kill.

Something seemed to shimmer in the corridor ahead of him, but he paid no attention; he'd seen plenty of odd effects from the heat the last few days, and the air in this place was dusty enough for them.

He swung easily through the glass door and waved to Joe Salvati, who was manning the cash register. He glanced at the display cases and ammunition safe, and watched through the windows for a moment.

He didn't notice that the door took much longer than usual to close behind him.

"Hey, Joe," Stillman said as he pulled back his jacket, revealing the butt of a .45 in a shoulder holster. "How's it going?"

"Not bad," Salvati said.

Stillman drew the automatic. "Figured I'd get in a little practice," he said.

The other man smiled. "Can't hurt," he said.

Stillman hesitated; he wasn't in any hurry. He was taking it easy today.

The muffled sounds of shooting could be heard from the range; Stillman glanced at the windows again—just in time to see one of the doors to the range shatter spectacularly.

The firing suddenly stopped as everyone turned to look at this unexpected phenomenon.

Stillman's jaw dropped. "What in the hell did *that*?" he asked.

Then someone screamed, and blood sprayed across the carpeted shooting platform at one position.

"Hey!" Stillman shouted. He charged through the ruined door, pistol raised. "What the . . . ," he began.

He never finished that sentence—or any other sentence, ever again. He went down, blood spraying.

Salvati stepped back, startled, trying to see what was going on, but he couldn't find a clear view. He could hear screams, and he saw blood on one of the windows, but half the lights in the range seemed to have gone out suddenly, and all he could make out was frantic movement, he couldn't see who was doing what.

Was it some kind of brawl? Was someone going for the cash register? He couldn't imagine a stupider crime to attempt than robbing the police shooting range—but thieves could be amazingly stupid.

After all, Salvati thought, he was probably the only guy in there who wasn't armed.

He hesitated. He had his choice of several weapons, if he wanted one, but he hesitated. He couldn't see what was happening, but he heard shots now, and more screams, and loud thumping . . .

What the hell was going on in there?

The guys back there had guns, they were shooting, at least half of them were trained professionals—what could he do that they couldn't, except maybe walk into a cross fire?

But maybe something heavier than handguns would help. He turned to look at the display cases.

Something hit him on the back of the head, and Joe Salvati went down.

Down and out.

The next thing he knew was the sound of boots crunching on broken glass, flashlights moving in the darkness, and someone leaning over him and shouting, "This one's alive!"

And then they were all around him, telling him to lie still, the paramedics were coming, and had he seen what had happened?

He didn't know what to tell them. He tried to ask who was hurt in there, who was dead, but no one would give him a straight answer.

"This one's alive," the voice had said; he waited for the words to be repeated, for someone to say there was another survivor, but he hadn't heard anything of the kind by the time he was carried out.

He'd heard a man retching, he'd heard hardened cops saying, "Oh, my God," in shocked tones, but he hadn't heard anyone mention other survivors.

Detective Rasche had gone off duty at six o'clock that day, on time for once, and he was at home alone, relaxing. His wife Shari had taken the kids to a park concert; Rasche hadn't made it in time to go with them, but he'd found a note and a micro-wave dinner waiting for him when he got home.

He'd thought about going after them, but trying to find three people in the mob at the park just sounded like too much effort right now. Instead he'd decided to stay home and enjoy the quiet.

The quiet was good, but he'd really have pre-ferred seeing Shari. It seemed like weeks since he'd seen her for more than a few minutes over breakfast; even on his days off she was usually out doing temp work somewhere, doing her bit to help catch up on some of the bills.

When the heat wave broke and tempers cooled, maybe he'd be home more and get to see more of her—or maybe he wouldn't. Maybe it wasn't the heat; maybe it was just city living getting to every-one, the way it was getting to him.

He sipped tepid coffee and tossed the remains of a Healthy Gourmet herbs-and-chicken entrée into the trash.

Rasche had eight years to go till his pension—eight more years of living in New York City on a cop's pay, in a neighborhood in Queens that had been pretty decent when they'd bought the house but was now just the best they could afford, eight more years of microwaved dinners and mis-matched work schedules.

This evening was one of those times when he wondered whether it was all worth it. New York cops generally still had a pretty good rep, despite the latest round of scandals—not like some big-city departments he could name. If he decided to move out, he could probably land a high-ranking job with some small-town force or with the county mounties in one of those big square states out west.

The Pacific Northwest might be nice.

Shari evidently thought so, too, as the swarm of stupid plastic magnets on the refrigerator no longer held a display of the kids' homework; instead, they supported a growing constellation of real-estate ads and travel brochures from Alaska and Washington State.

The hint wasn't lost on Rasche, but he'd been in New York for so long, damn near his entire life, and he'd put so much into the job here, trying to save a little bit of the city from itself, that it was hard to think about giving it up, even for his family.

His family that he almost never saw.

At least he *had* a family, though; there on the fridge, in an upper corner that Shari hadn't yet got to with her brochures, a yellow plastic smiley-face held up a photo of Rasche and Schaefer, taken on the occasion of nailing a particularly vicious drug kingpin from uptown, a punk called Errol G.

In the picture Rasche was smiling so broadly his mustache looked as if it were upside down, but Schaefer was playing Old Stone Face as usual, standing stiff as a lamppost, his face like an undertaker's nightmare.

Schaefer didn't have a family, so far as Rasche knew, didn't have any close friends. He'd mentioned a brother once, but Rasche hadn't asked about him, and Schaefer sure hadn't volunteered anything. There were some buddies, mostly in the military or law enforcement, but none of them seemed close—certainly no closer than Rasche himself was.

And Rasche, after six years as Schaefer's partner, wasn't sure he knew Schaefer at all.

What the hell kept Schaefer going, anyway?

It wasn't a woman; Rasche had seen Schaefer's apartment once, and there wasn't any doubt that Schaefer lived alone. No other human being could have put up with that place—stained ceilings and cracked windows and the TV blaring from next door through paper-thin walls, but the bed was made with military precision and razor-sharp creases at the corners, the floor was spotless, everything was folded and sorted and filed away. The goddamn coffee cups in the kitchen cupboard had all had their handles pointing in the same direction, for Christ's sake.

Nobody but Schaefer could have lived there.

So what drove Schaefer? Why was he a cop? He could have landed a job somewhere else—there was always work for a big, smart, tough guy who wasn't afraid to tackle anything. So why was he still with the department?

He wasn't after any pension; Schaefer never gave a damn about money. If he'd wanted a pension, he could have stayed in the military instead of becoming a cop. So far as Rasche knew, it had been Schaefer's idea to switch.

Maybe he hadn't been seeing enough action in the army.

Or was it righteous anger that drove him, maybe? Outrage at the things people did to each other? He talked about New York as *his* city, but somehow Rasche couldn't see it as his motivation. He didn't think Schaefer meant so much that it was his city to protect, as that the city was his turf—the place where he was the boss male, and anyone else who showed up claiming to be tough was a challenge.

If that was it—it was pure macho dominance at work, not anger. Rasche and Schaefer had been partners for six years now, and Rasche wasn't sure at all that he'd ever yet really seen Schaefer get mad.

Which, when he thought about it, made him a little nervous. What kind of man could go through the crap that Schaefer went through without losing his temper every so often?

He'd got that far when the doorbell rang.

"Damn," he said, putting down the coffee.

The doorbell rang again.

"I'm coming, I'm coming!" he called as he trotted down the front hall.

The doorbell rang a third time.

"I'm *coming*, goddammit!" he shouted as he grabbed the doorknob.

Rasche yanked the front door open and found Schaefer standing on the stoop.

Schaefer's expression was exactly the same as in the photo on the fridge, and for a moment Rasche had an odd feeling of unreality, as if the past and present were tripping over each other.

Rasche had dumped his jacket and tie the moment he got in the door of his house, and was standing there in a sweaty undershirt; Schaefer still had the crease in his pants, the knot of his tie tight and perfect.

Rasche didn't think that was because Schaefer actually cared about his appearance; it was because the rules said what to wear, and that wasn't a rule Schaefer cared enough about to break.

"They hit again," Schaefer said in a growl, interrupting Rasche's thought. "The police range on Twentieth. The goddamn police academy! You want to go, or you want to watch *Green Acres*?"

"You *could* say hello," Rasche said. He didn't need to ask who Schaefer meant.

He was shaken and trying to hide it; he knew guys at Twentieth Street, and the image of dangling, skinned corpses with familiar faces was growing in the back of his mind.

Schaefer didn't bother to answer; he simply waited for Rasche to decide, in or out.

From that Rasche knew that he and Schaefer weren't supposed to be on this case. The feds probably wanted it kept quiet. The feds probably wanted to handle it themselves.

But those imagined faces of fellow cops weren't exactly encouraging Rasche to go along with the feds.

Rasche sighed. "Okay, okay. What the hell, *Green Acres* isn't on tonight anyway. Let me get my piece."

6

Forty minutes after ringing Rasche's doorbell, Schaefer marched over the yellow tape, past a protesting lieutenant, into the foyer of the firing range.

Rasche was close on his heels, saying, "Dammit, Schaef, the captain's going to suspend us if he . . ."

Schaefer interrupted.

"Good," he said. "I need a vacation."

The glass door at the entrance was smeared with blood, but unbroken; even so, as soon as Schaefer walked through it, glass crunched underfoot, and Rasche noticed that the display cases along the wall had been shattered.

"No bodies?" Schaefer said.

Rasche looked around.

The devastation was thorough enough, and the blood plentiful enough, that he hadn't even realized immediately that there were no corpses in sight.

Schaefer, of course, had never been one to let nonessentials distract him.

There were three forensics men at work in the lobby with cameras and tweezers; they were in civilian clothes, so Rasche couldn't tell if they were NYPD or feds. He didn't recognize any of them.

One of them looked up and said, "The bodies are in the range. We've ID'ed most of them. We had one survivor out here, Officer Joseph Salvati—he's on his way to the hospital with a concussion and a broken nose."

Schaefer nodded and studied the scene.

Rasche turned toward the firing range, peering through the windows, trying to ignore the cracks that hadn't been there the last time he was down here.

The lights were out in the range itself, but Rasche could see enough in the spillover from the foyer.

The bodies were hanging from the ceiling girders and the broken lights, swaying gently in the breeze from the ventilators, blood still dripping here and there. An unused target was clipped to one dangling finger, a touch of surreal grotesquerie that fascinated Rasche.

Schaefer stepped up beside him with a flashlight and pointed it through the broken door at the floor of the range; the beam glittered off the polished metal of assorted firearms and cartridge casings, and lit pools and streaks of blood a vivid red.

Rasche looked at the scattered arsenal. "They were packing enough hardware."

"Didn't do them much good, did it?" Schaefer replied.

Rasche had meant the attackers, but now he realized that Schaefer was right—the weapons on the floor matched up with the bodies.

Struggling to keep himself from screaming, Rasche said, "I think I knew some of these guys."

Schaefer glanced at Rasche. "So did I. This makes it personal." His tone was flat and dead, but Rasche was too stunned to notice.

"Last time, when they hit the gangs," Rasche said, talking to keep from screaming, "I figured maybe it was, you know, some sort of vigilante thing—but I guess not. This time it was our turn."

"Guess whoever it is doesn't like much of *anyone*," Schaefer said.

For a moment they stood there contemplating the situation; Rasche shivered. The firing range was about a hundred feet long, but the far end was completely lost in the darkness, so that it seemed to go on forever. A darkened room full of dangling, mutilated corpses, where whatever killed them might still be lurking . . . what was he doing in a place like this?

This was much too close to those monsters in the night that his mother had told him weren't real.

"Come on," Schaefer said. He took a step through the demolished door.

Just then the door of the gunsmithing room opened, and four men stepped out, one after the other.

One of them was Captain McComb.

Schaefer turned at the sound of the door, just as McComb saw the two detectives.

"What the . . . ," McComb spluttered. "Schaefer! Rasche! Who the hell let you in here? Who gave you authorization for this site?"

"Great," Rasche muttered, as he stood beside Schaefer, "just great."

"Come on, McComb," Schaefer said, "these were our own people here! Don't tell me you're going to turn *this* one over to the feds!"

"Don't you question me!" McComb bellowed. He glanced around for support, then shouted, "I want these two detectives removed from the premises *immediately*. If they won't go peaceably, then physically eject them!"

A quiet voice from somewhere behind the police captain said, "I wouldn't do that if I were you."

McComb turned. "Why the hell not?" he demanded.

A white-haired man in a rumpled army uniform and a bedraggled mustache stepped forward and said, "You called this man Schaefer?"

McComb glanced at Schaefer, puzzled. "That's Schaefer, yes," he said.

"Well, then," the soldier said, "you don't want to try ejecting him. Because if Detective Schaefer's anything like his brother Dutch, he'll probably *like* it, and you can't afford the damage. Especially not here."

Rasche threw a startled glance at Schaefer, then stared at this new arrival.

"You knew my brother?" Schaefer growled.

The white-haired man didn't answer; instead he addressed McComb.

"All that's left here is mop-up. Think your janitors can handle that, McComb?"

Rasche watched, amazed, as McComb nodded and said reluctantly, "Yessir."

McComb was a jerk, and could be relied on to kowtow to authority and side with civilians against his own men, but Rasche couldn't see why he'd be deferring so obviously to some old coot in fatigues, especially here on police turf. New York wasn't under martial law, and while McComb was always glad to cozy up to the feds whenever the FBI or DEA wanted something, he had never shown any great fondness for men in uniform.

He and Schaefer had known that the feds were involved in investigating the massacre—or rather, the massacres, plural, now—but they had assumed that "feds" meant the FBI, not the army.

What the hell did the army have to do with it?

And who the hell was this guy?

Rasche squinted, trying to see better in the dim light, and realized the army man had two stars on his cap.

Well, at least it took a general to impress McComb.

"C'mon, son, we've got to talk," the general said, pointing toward the passage that led back up to the street.

"Do we?" Schaefer asked.

The general nodded. He turned and started walking toward the stairs.

Schaefer followed.

So did Rasche. No one had invited him, but they hadn't told him to get lost, either, and he wanted to know what the hell was going on, who this general was and what he was doing in New York, and whatever else Schaefer might be told.

No one spoke in the corridor or on the stairs; on the street the general pointed east, and Schaefer nodded an acknowledgment. They walked on to Fifth Avenue, and uptown, still not saying a word.

Together, the three men got a booth in the back of a bar a few blocks away. Rasche and the general took one side, Schaefer the other—Schaefer was big enough to rate the whole bench for himself.

Rasche had seen the general's name on his shirt—Philips. It didn't tell him anything. The ribbons and other hardware didn't mean much, either. The guy had the weathered look of a field officer, not a desk man, and kept a cigarette clamped in his teeth.

What he was doing on the scene of a murder investigation—even one as bizarre as this—was something Rasche couldn't even guess.

For his part, General Philips was considering the two detectives.

Rasche didn't impress him. He looked good enough for a cop—a bit overweight and out of shape, but there was still some muscle in there, he hadn't gone soft, and if Dutch's brother had partnered with him for six years, the way the personnel files said, he had to be okay.

Still, it wasn't Rasche who interested Philips.

Schaefer, on the other hand, was about the same size as his brother—which meant big. And it was *all* muscle, same as on Dutch. The voice was deeper, but with the same trace of an accent.

And the look on his face . . . Maybe Dutch, tough as he was, was the gentler brother. Dutch had been able to relax and smile when he wasn't working; this Schaefer looked as if his expression had been carved out of granite.

Philips had been astonished, going through McComb's files, to find out that Dutch's brother was not just a cop, but a New York City homicide detective and the one who'd been first on the scene at the first massacre.

It had been Dutch who'd brought out the word on these things, these alien killers, in the first place. It was Dutch who had told Philips and his people everything they knew that was worth knowing about the hunters. If it hadn't been for Dutch, that squad would have just vanished into the jungles without a trace, and they'd never have known what happened to it.

Hell of a coincidence, running into Dutch's brother on this case—if it *was* a coincidence.

But what else could it be? Those things couldn't have known Dutch's brother was in New York—not unless they were mind readers, or something.

Of course, there was no way to be sure they *weren't* mind readers. Or they might have mind-reading machines. They might have any technology he could imagine, and probably some he couldn't.

Or maybe they could just *smell* the Schaefers, somehow. Who knew?

"Bourbon," he told the waitress who had arrived by the table. "Straight up."

He waited until the woman had left, then leaned across the table.

"Look, Schaefer," he said, "I know you think McComb's being an asshole about this, and maybe he is, but he's following orders. We *told* him to keep you out of this."

"And who are you?" Schaefer asked.

"I can't tell you that," Philips replied. "And you probably guessed that. I can tell you that your brother used to work for me, back in the eighties—and you probably guessed that, too. I don't know if you're as smart as your brother, but you aren't stupid, you're a detective; you can probably guess at least half of what I could tell you, and the rest you're better off not knowing."

The waitress returned with the drinks; again Philips waited for her to depart.

"I'll tell ya, Schaefer," the general said, sitting back, trying to relax the atmosphere a little, "Dutch saved my ass on more than one occasion. He was a good man—a *hell* of a good man." He swigged bourbon. "He used to talk about you sometimes, brag on his brother back in the States."

"Where is he?" Schaefer asked. He wasn't drinking. Rasche had ordered a beer to be sociable; Schaefer hadn't bothered. He sat stiff and straight, staring at Philips—though he had gone so far as to loosen his tie.

"Where is he?" he repeated. "What happened to him?"

Philips didn't answer. He looked down at his drink, took a puff on his cigarette, then looked back at Schaefer.

Schaefer had that same stubborn streak Dutch had always had, no doubt about it.

"This meeting is off the record," he said. "It never happened. You got that?"

Schaefer didn't answer; his expression made it

plain that he was still waiting for an answer to his question and didn't give a shit about any record.

"I'm not here, I'm not telling you this, you never saw me, all that crap," Philips said, "but I owe you this much, for Dutch's sake. Drop this one, son. Just back away from it. Forget about it."

"I can't do that," Schaefer said. "You saw that shooting range. Those were cops. Those were my men."

"You've *got* to drop it," Philips replied. He reached for his hat. "You've got to, understand?"

He didn't dare stay any longer; he'd let something slip if he stayed.

He was tempted to tell Schaefer all of it, but he didn't dare.

So he had to leave, and leave quickly. He didn't trust himself if he stayed—and he didn't trust Schaefer. He'd read about some of Schaefer's stunts.

Schaefer studied Philips. "You already know who these killers are, don't you? You know who was behind both those slaughters. You came to New York to check them out, maybe to cover them up, didn't you? And you know Dutch, he worked for you—there's some connection there? These killers are somehow connected to Dutch?" He started to rise. "Who the hell *are* they?"

Philips was on his feet, straightening his hat. He didn't answer.

"Who are they?" Schaefer demanded. He stood, clenched fists at his sides, towering over Philips. "What the hell are they doing? What do they want in New York?"

Philips shook his head. "I can't tell you anything, Schaefer. Drop it."

"Why now?" Schaefer asked. "Dutch has been missing for years—why are these murders happening *now*? Who is it killing both cops and punks? *What* is it killing them?" He started to reach for Philips.

The general stepped back, out of reach.

"I can't tell you," he said.

"What the hell *can* you tell me? Don't say you can't tell me anything, Philips—give me *something*."

Philips hesitated. "They like the heat, dammit," he said uneasily. "They want the *sport*. Look, leave 'em be, and in two, three weeks they'll be gone. Mess with them, and God only knows what might happen." He hesitated again, then added, "And that's all. I've already said too much."

He turned and walked toward the door.

Schaefer stood, his hands still clenched into fists, and watched.

In the doorway Philips turned.

"Believe me," he called, "it's got to be this way."

Then he was gone.

Rasche stood up; he hadn't said a word the entire time. Whatever was going on, it was obviously between Philips and Schaefer.

He almost missed Schaefer's muttered, "It's got to be this way? The hell it does."

7

They couldn't get back into the firing range, and Rasche figured there wouldn't have been anything to see there anyway. They couldn't get anything more from Philips, even if they'd followed him. Rasche figured that was the end of it, at least for the moment.

But when they were rolling again, Schaefer didn't take the turn for the bridge to take Rasche back home to Queens; instead he headed straight downtown.

Rasche looked at the expression on Schaefer's face and decided not to argue. He remembered how he had been thinking earlier that he'd never seen Schaefer really angry, and suspected that that was in the process of changing.

"So," he said, in hopes of lightening the atmosphere, "just what kind of . . . of work did your brother used to do for this General Philips?"

"Rescue operations," Schaefer said. "Covert stuff. Their dirty jobs, the stuff they couldn't do themselves. When they fucked up and needed someone to pull their asses out of the fire, they called Dutch."

Rasche didn't need to ask who "they" were.

"He kept it as clean as he could, though," Schaefer said. "That was why he worked freelance, so he could turn down jobs he didn't like. He'd had enough of that 'do as you're told' crap in 'Nam. Worked his way up to major and still had to put up with it until he went out on his own."

Rasche wondered where Schaefer had got *his* fill of that "do as you're told" crap—he pretty obviously wasn't any fonder of taking orders than his brother had been, even though he'd stayed in the army longer.

"There were still screwups sometimes," Schaefer said. "He told me about a bad one in Afghanistan once."

"Afghanistan? Did it have anything to do with these killers?"

"No."

For a moment Schaefer drove on silently.

Then he said, "There was another thing, though."

Rasche waited.

"Last I heard from Dutch," Schaefer said at last, staring straight ahead as they left the avenue and turned into the narrow streets of lower Manhattan, "was when he was passing through, on his way from nowhere in particular to somewhere else. He and I went out drinking. You have any brothers, Rasche?"

"No. Two sisters."

"That wouldn't be the same. Dutch and I, we didn't need to talk much."

Rasche nodded.

"So I wasn't expecting him to tell me all the latest shit about what he was doing or anything. It was enough to be sitting there with him drinking, watching the TV over the bar—you know. But that last time it was kind of weird. Something was different."

Rasche knew what Schaefer meant; he also knew he didn't need to say so.

"We sat there drinking for a long time," Schaefer said, "and he started in telling me stuff after all—not in any particular order, you know, we were both feeling the booze by then, and he just said whatever he was thinking about, whatever was bothering him, as he thought of it."

"What'd he say?" Rasche asked.

"He told me about this job he'd had," Schaefer replied, "leading his squad into Central America on another rescue mission where some half-assed CIA stunt had gone wrong somehow. He didn't tell me any details of what it was about or what he did there—he never did. Wasn't supposed to, it was all top-secret bullshit, and besides, who cared? Anyway, he told me that this time it had gone bad, he'd lost his whole team. That was rough, and I figured that was why he'd been weird—they were good men, all of 'em."

"Yeah," Rasche said, to show he was still listening. He'd never met Dutch or any of his men.

"Then he stopped talking about that and started talking about hunting," Schaefer said. "Just a bunch of crazy stuff. Talked about when we hunted deer as kids. Asked if I'd ever thought about what it would feel like to be hunted. Talked about how if you and your equipment were good enough, it'd take the sport out of it, and you'd want to make things harder for yourself sometimes, to give the prey a chance—but not much of one, you'd still want to kill it in the end, that the whole point is to show you're better than it is by killing it. But you might take on a whole pack at once. Or you'd only tackle the ones that could fight. You'd find the toughest game you could. You'd want a *challenge*. I mean, you don't go after squirrels with an elephant gun.

"And then he started talking about stuff a hunter might have someday—some sort of camouflage that would make you damn near invisible, say. Guns and knives, faster reflexes, be able to mimic sounds.

"I didn't know what he was talking about, I thought he was just drunk."

"You think you know now?" Rasche asked.

Schaefer shook his head. "No. But maybe there's some connection. That was the last time I saw Dutch, seven years ago. I haven't heard from him since. No one has. He disappeared. Never heard another word, from Dutch or anyone else."

"Shit," Rasche said. He tried to imagine what that would be like, losing the guy who was practically your whole family like that—just one day he's gone, and nobody ever mentions him again. . . .

No wonder Schaefer had an attitude.

And maybe there *was* some connection. Maybe the berserk killers loose in New York were the same ones that had taken out Dutch's squad in Central America. Maybe Philips knew that, maybe he'd tracked them here.

And maybe these people killed for sport, like big-game hunters. The skinned bodies seemed horribly appropriate for that theory.

But who would do that? Why? And if they had this super hunting equipment Schaefer said Dutch had talked about, where'd they get it?

Had some secret operation of one of the government organizations that weren't supposed to exist gone wrong somehow? Were the killers Philips's own men, maybe, gone rogue?

But what did that have to do with the heat? Why couldn't Philips send out better men and better equipment to stop them, instead of just covering up after them?

It didn't make sense.

But there almost had to be some connection. Schaefer had seen it right away.

Were the killers after Schaefer? Had they gotten Dutch, and come after Schaefer in case Dutch had told him too much?

But so far they hadn't tried for him—those two amateurs the other night couldn't be related to whoever had taken out Lamb and his crew.

Were they *taunting* him, somehow?

It didn't fit together right. There was some piece of the puzzle still missing.

"So where are we going?" Rasche asked a moment later.

"Here," Schaefer said, pulling over to the curb.

Rasche looked up at the abandoned tenement, at the hole in the wall on the fifth floor.

"Oh, great," he muttered to himself. "This place. Here we go again."

He'd had nightmares about the place.

Of course, he would probably have nightmares about the police firing range, too. At least this little side trip wouldn't be adding any new scenery to his bad dreams.

And after all, where else was there to go, with the firing range off-limits?

But there wasn't going to be anything left to find here; there couldn't be.

Schaefer was already out of the car, adjusting his shoulder holster; Rasche scrambled out of the passenger side as quickly as his incipient paunch would allow, and said, "Schaef, McComb must've had his forensics people go over this place with *tweezers* by now. . . ."

"McComb's people," Schaefer interrupted, "couldn't find their asses with both hands in their back pockets."

"But the feds . . ."

"Screw the feds." He marched up to the building.

The door was chained and padlocked, and crisscrossed with yellow police-line tape. For a moment Schaefer stood, fists at his sides, and stared at it.

"Whoever's doing these killings," he said, "they've messed with my city, they've messed with my people, they've messed with the cops, and maybe, just *maybe*, they've messed with my brother." He raised one foot. "I *want* them."

He kicked, hard; the chain snapped, and the rotted wood of the door shattered.

Schaefer stepped through the ruins.

"You wait outside," he told Rasche without looking back. "Anybody tries to come after me—shoot 'em."

Rasche watched Schaefer vanish into the gloom.

Yeah, he thought, I've finally seen him angry.

He wished he hadn't.

8

Schaefer didn't waste any time poking around on the lower floors; he went straight up to the room where the corpses had been strung up like so many slabs of beef.

The bodies were gone, of course, carted away by either the feds or the cops; so were the guns. Some of the debris had been cleared away as well, or shoved aside.

The bloodstains were still there—some of them, anyway. They weren't red anymore, of course; they were dried to rusty brown or powdery black.

And no one had bothered to clear away all the spent cartridges; Schaefer suspected there were just too damn many of them.

The holes in the walls and ceiling were still there, too—and that was what Schaefer wanted a good look at, at least to start.

Most of them were bullet holes, of course—automatic weapons had stitched back and forth across the room in every direction during the fight.

There were three holes, though, that weren't right. He'd noticed them immediately when he'd come up here before—he'd mentioned them to McComb; they weren't *right*.

For one thing, they were far too big for bullet holes—each was as big as a man's head.

Each was about eye level for Schaefer—he figured that would be just above head height for most people, including the gang members who had died here. Nobody was going to be throwing punches that high up.

If someone had picked up a man, raised him over his head like a wrestler doing an airplane spin, and then rammed him against the wall . . .

No. These holes punched right *through* the wall. Do that with a man's head, and when you pull him back out, he'll be a bloody mess, and probably dead. The bodies, mangled as they were, hadn't shown that particular sort of injury—Schaefer had managed to read the autopsy reports before McComb made them vanish.

Some kind of weapon? Something like a mace?

No. The holes were wrong for that. For one thing . . .

Schaefer stepped back out into the corridor and around into the next room, where the hole came out, and looked at it.

Then he turned and looked at the far wall.

There was another hole there; he'd thought, when he'd looked through from the other side, that he'd seen one.

And yes, the two lined up—but the second, smaller hole was below the first one.

That meant that whatever had made them had been angled downward.

Schaefer strode back to the bigger room, the room where the massacre had taken place. He looked through the opening, judged the angle, tried to guess where the killer had stood, and then estimated the height of whatever had made that hole.

It looked to him as if some son of a bitch must have been wearing a cannon on his hat, and had neatly collected the cannonballs when he was done.

Or did McComb have those cannonballs locked away somewhere? Schaefer wouldn't put it past him.

He reached out and touched the edge of the hole.

It was charred. That wasn't just powder burns or soot; whatever it was that had punched the hole had charred the lath for a good half inch around the opening. That had been something *hot*. A bullet wouldn't do that, nor would a cannonball.

Incendiaries of some kind?

But then why was the building still standing?

This was something different, something *strange*.

Schaefer remembered that last conversation with Dutch, remembered some things Dutch had said that he hadn't mentioned to Rasche in the car, about how a good enough hunter wouldn't want to bother hunting anything as stupid as a mere animal.

He remembered Dutch talking about weapons

such a hunter might use, stuff that didn't exist yet anywhere on earth, so far as Schaefer knew. He'd thought Dutch was just rambling drunkenly.

He didn't think so anymore.

If the killers had a weapon that would punch holes through walls like this, maybe they had the other things Dutch had talked about—perfect camouflage that made them effectively invisible, something that protected them from bullets.

Schaefer began to see why the army, or whoever General Philips worked for, might be involved.

He began to feel something else, as well—something he had felt before, something he'd been feeling off and on for days, but never as strongly as this. It was a prickly feeling of something indefinably wrong, a feeling like something brushing the hairs at the back of his neck.

He remembered Dutch asking if he'd ever wondered what it felt like to be hunted. Right now Schaefer thought he knew *exactly* how it felt.

He turned; the room was empty.

He looked through the hole, and the room on the other side was empty, as well.

He stepped slowly away from the wall and turned a full 360 degrees, ending up facing the hole again.

He didn't see anything—but the light was poor.

And a good hunter used camouflage. The prey wasn't *supposed* to see him.

And these hunters might have *perfect* camouflage.

He started to turn again—and all of a sudden it was *there*, just at arm's length.

Schaefer knew this was the killer, or at least one of the killers, and that he couldn't afford to play nice. He snatched at his automatic and pulled it from its holster as he said, "Figured you might show up. I could *feel* you. Can't say I'm that impress—"

He was talking to distract it, but it wasn't working; he was in the middle of a word, his pistol halfway drawn, when a huge yellowish fist slammed across his jaw and sent him reeling backward.

The pistol flew to one side, and Schaefer's mouth filled with blood; the lower teeth on one side suddenly all felt loose. Blood spurted from his nose.

He landed on his hands and knees, facing away from the thing that loomed over him, outlined against the gaping hole in the wall.

"Lucky punch," he said.

It wasn't human. It stood on two legs and was shaped more or less like a man, but it was too big, and too fast. As he knelt, half-dazed for a fraction of a second, he saw its feet in their heavy silver sandals, saw the four toes with their curving black talons. He started to turn and saw the grayish-yellow legs, the gleaming metal greaves, the black netting that covered its body.

This was the hunter Dutch had talked about, it had to be—the thing that had killed Dutch's squad.

It wasn't any gang of terrorists that had done these killings—it was *this*, this monster, this hunter, whatever it was.

But it didn't matter what it was, or what it looked like; he had to take it down. This killer had invaded his city, his turf. This thing had attacked him. It was big and strong and fast, it had him down, but he had to beat it.

He couldn't afford the time to look at it, not when it was as fast as it was.

Schaefer threw his weight forward onto his hands and dove a boot upward at the thing's belly—and if he fell short and caught it in the crotch, he wouldn't mind that, either.

He didn't catch it anywhere; a clawed hand caught him, instead. Black talons locked around his ankle before his foot had covered half the distance he had intended, and the glow of the streetlights outside sparkled off jagged-edged blades that projected from the complicated band of gadgetry on the thing's wrist.

Before Schaefer could even begin to twist, to struggle, to try to escape, the thing picked him up by that one leg and flung him away.

It moved impossibly fast, but with casual ease and grace, as if this was nothing for it, as if it wasn't even trying.

Then Schaefer slammed into the wall and stopped noticing details; he heard plaster and lath crunch on impact, and for a millisecond or so he hoped that he hadn't heard any of his bones breaking.

Then his head snapped back and hit an exposed stud, and he wasn't able to hope anything.

He tried not to pass out, tried to force himself back to full alertness. He was on the floor, looking up through a haze, and he saw those yellowish claws reaching for him, that blank thing that wasn't a face looking down at him . . .

It *wasn't* a face. It was metal. The thing was wearing some kind of mask.

Then its fingers, or claws, whichever they were,

closed on Schaefer's bruised jaw and wrenched his head sideways, exposing his neck, turning his eyes away so that he couldn't see anymore, and Schaefer tried to force defiance out through the blood in his throat.

"Asshole," he said as he tried to bring himself to fight, force his hands to strike at the thing.

Then something bit into his flesh below his left ear, and Schaefer screamed, not so much at the pain—it hurt like hell, like three hot knives had just punched into his neck—but he could handle pain. He screamed at the violation. The thing wasn't killing him, it was doing *something else*.

"What the hell . . . ," he gasped as the thing stood up and stepped back, ". . . did you do . . ."

Schaefer's hand closed on a broken two-by-four, and his anger gave him strength.

". . . *to me!*" he shouted as he came up swinging.

The blow of the two-by-four caught the thing on the side of its head, and the mask wrenched to one side. It reached up to straighten it, but Schaefer was there first, following up his attack.

The crooked mask, or helmet, or whatever it was, was blocking the thing's vision. It was blinded.

If he could keep it blinded, he might have a chance.

He grabbed for the metal mask and got both thumbs under the edge.

The thing reached up and ripped him away, but his grip held, and the mask tore free as well.

Something sparked, and Schaefer heard a hiss like escaping gas, but he didn't have time to worry about that; he was falling backward, toward the hole in the wall where the windows had once been.

The mask was in his hands, and he was staring at a face straight out of a nightmare, a huge mottled face framed in black snakelike locks, a face with great baleful eyes and a fang-rimmed mouth that worked in layers, like that of some unspeakable deep-sea horror.

The fangs flexed, as if reaching for him.

Schaefer landed on his feet this time, caught his balance by slamming the mask against the floor with a ringing clang, and stared at his foe.

Those mouth parts moved again, the outermost ring of fangs opening like some ghastly flower, an inner membrane vibrating, and the thing spoke.

"Trick or treat," it said in a voice Schaefer knew, in Carr's voice, amplified to deafening volume.

Then it came at him again, and even Schaefer knew better than to charge the thing or to stand his ground; he took a step backward, trying to dodge, and his foot landed on something hard, something that shouldn't have been there, something that went out from under him, and as he tumbled backward out the hole in the building's wall he realized that he'd tripped over his own dropped pistol.

And then he was out the window and falling, falling headfirst toward the street five stories below.

9

Cops in New York tend to get used to things, Detective Rasche thought. There isn't much that can faze a person after a few years on the city payroll.

The muggers, the everyday crazies, the street people, they were nothing; even the civilians were used to them. Cops got to handle stuff civilians never thought about.

Like the time some live wire tied a cow to the chairman of Federal Beef and pitched 'em both off the Chrysler Building. It was supposed to be some sort of protest against fattening up beef with antibiotics, but when that Jersey had pancaked onto Lexington Avenue, all anyone cared about was cleaning up the mess.

City sanitation must have gone through a dozen mops, but they didn't care—it meant free steaks for

Christmas. Sure, it was a mess, but they dealt with it.

It was just part of the job. When weird stuff went down, you couldn't let it get to you. You just had to learn to deal with it.

When the real crazies were running loose, you couldn't let it throw you, couldn't waste time getting upset; you just had to deal with it before it got too far out of hand, and worry about what the hell it all meant later.

And when you hear a yell and you look up to see your partner come flying backward out of the fifth floor of an abandoned building, arms flailing, looking for something, anything, that would break his fall, you don't waste your time wondering how it happened, you deal with it.

Rasche had been standing out on the sidewalk, wiping sweat from the back of his neck, trying not to smell the garbage, wondering how long Schaefer was going to be in there, thinking that he wasn't going to find anything and that was going to make him madder than ever—and Schaefer had sailed out through that hole Carr and Lamb and the others had blown in the wall, shouting Rasche's name.

Rasche's mind kicked into high, and he was thinking three or four things at once the instant he saw Schaefer, up there in the sky, catching the light from the streetlamps so that he seemed to glow against the night sky.

There had been someone in there, one of the killers, which was crazy—why would anyone come back here?

But it had to be one of the killers; who else could it be?

Maybe it was a guard the feds had posted, but why would a guard throw Schaefer out of the building?

For that matter, who the hell *could* throw Schaefer out of the building?

And in any case, Rasche thought, he had to do something right now if he didn't want to see his partner splatter on the sidewalk. This wasn't exactly the Chrysler Building, but a five-story fall was more than enough to kill a man.

As Schaefer fell he grabbed for an old wire that stretched across the alley at third-floor height. Rasche watched as he caught it, but couldn't hold on—the old phone line, Rasche thought, this building was old enough it wouldn't have always been buried, and they'd never cleared the old one away.

Even as he saw Schaefer reaching for the wire, Rasche was moving, he had already grabbed up garbage bags with both hands; now he heaved them under Schaefer, then snatched up two more, thanking God for the latest garbage strike.

He had a third pair in his hands when Schaefer hit, but wasn't in time to use them.

Black plastic exploded with a gigantic pop, and half-rotted garbage sprayed everywhere; Schaefer slammed through the trash onto the pavement.

Rasche dropped the last two bags and ran to Schaefer's side, calling, "Schaef! Jesus! Are you all right?"

Schaefer was obviously not all right, but he was breathing—sort of—and he was still conscious.

"Just dandy," Schaefer wheezed, spraying blood with each word.

Rasche didn't stay to argue; he ran for the radio in Schaefer's car.

Two minutes later he was back at Schaefer's side, leaning over. Schaefer was unconscious, but Rasche said, "Hang on, the ambulance is coming, hang on."

He looked up anxiously, and when he looked back, Schaefer's eyes were wide open again.

"I *slipped*," he said. "On a banana peel." He coughed out a mouthful of blood. "You hear me? Wasn't anyone up there. I slipped. It was an accident!"

Rasche nodded.

"I hear you, man. It was an accident." He noticed for the first time that Schaefer was clutching something in one hand, something strange. "What the hell is this?" he asked, reaching for it.

Schaefer released the mask and gasped out, "I stole . . . the son of a bitch's hat. . . ."

Then he was out again.

Rasche looked at the "hat."

It could be a mask or helmet of some sort, all right, but if so, it was too big for anyone but a giant. It was metal, with a smooth, dull finish; inside Rasche could see gadgetry. There were little tubes along the sides, and oddly shaped plastic fittings here and there on the inside. The eyeholes were not open, but covered by multicolored lenses of some kind.

Rasche couldn't imagine what the hell the thing was for; the closest guess he could come up with was that it was some kind of high-tech night-vision equipment, but even that didn't seem very likely.

Whatever it was, Schaefer wouldn't be able to

hang on to it in the hospital, but somehow Rasche didn't think he'd just want it turned over to McComb and the gang.

If the feds got it, it would probably wind up in a warehouse somewhere, right next to the Ark of the Covenant.

Rasche didn't know what the thing was, or what use it might be, but he didn't think it would do anyone any good locked in a drawer somewhere.

He wrapped the mask in his jacket, and when the ambulance arrived a moment later, he had it tucked securely under his arm. It stayed there as Rasche watched the paramedics strap Schaefer to the stretcher and load him aboard the ambulance.

Even McComb would have trouble believing Schaefer had slipped and fallen out a window, but that was what Schaefer had said his story was, and Rasche would stick to it. He'd seen the look in Schaefer's eyes. He'd seen what Schaefer had looked like when he'd gone charging in there.

Whatever the hell was going on, Schaefer intended to deal with it, and Rasche was sure that Schaefer didn't give a damn what McComb or Philips or anyone else—including Rasche—had to say about it.

McComb might try to stop him, but Rasche knew better. You couldn't stop Schaefer when he got set onto something, not without killing him, and no one had ever yet managed to kill him. The best thing to do was to help him when you could, and stay out of the way the rest of the time.

Philips couldn't stop him, McComb couldn't stop him, and whoever just threw him out of the building couldn't stop him, not without killing him.

Rasche didn't think Philips or McComb was ready to kill Schaefer over this; he wasn't so sure about whoever was in the building.

He'd stashed the mask and was back at Schaefer's side when the ambulance pulled up.

The crew wouldn't make any guesses about whether Schaefer would live, or whether anything was broken. "No offense," one of them said, "but we don't need any malpractice suits, so we just do our jobs and keep our mouths shut."

They wouldn't let him ride in the ambulance with Schaefer, so when it pulled away, lights flashing, Rasche looked around, thinking.

He could go up in that building, looking for whatever "banana peel" Schaefer had slipped on, up there in the room where Lamb and the others had died, where the bodies had dripped blood in graceful spirals across the plaster dust—the room he'd had nightmares about.

Schaefer's pistol was missing, and he should look for that, too.

Rasche didn't like to think of himself as a coward; hell, he knew he wasn't a coward, not really. All the same, he wasn't about to go into that building again alone. Maybe if he had some serious backup—but how could he call for backup when his partner had slipped and fallen?

He should do something, when your partner was beaten, you were supposed to do something, but he just couldn't.

Besides, he had to know what was happening to Schaefer. How badly was he hurt?

He stopped at a pay phone to call Shari and tell

her enough to keep her from worrying too much; then he headed for the hospital in Schaefer's car.

They told him they didn't think Schaefer was going to die right away, though they wouldn't put it in writing, and no, he couldn't see the patient, but he could wait if he wanted, and there was some paperwork he could take care of . . .

After that it was all waiting and filling out reports and forms and applications.

Rasche hated waiting. He hated hospitals, thought they all smelled like death mixed with linoleum.

Ordinarily he hated filling out reports, too, but at least it made the waiting a bit less tiresome, and gave him something to look at other than blank walls and human misery.

He was pacing the floor for the hundredth time when a young doctor in wire-rimmed glasses and a neatly trimmed beard asked, "Are you Detective Rasche?"

Rasche looked up and didn't bother to answer. The doctor's firm belly and tidy appearance made Rasche uncomfortably aware that his own gut was bigger and softer than he liked, and his mustache was long enough to chew on—he hadn't had time lately to worry about trimming it.

How the hell did this guy look so tidy at this hour of the morning?

"I read your preliminary report," the doctor said as he took Rasche by the arm and marched him toward Schaefer's room. "So Detective Schaefer *tripped*, huh? I haven't seen an explanation that lame since third grade."

Rasche shrugged. He allowed himself to be led—

after all, he wanted to see how Schaefer was doing, and if the doctor wanted to show him something, so much the better.

"Look," the doctor said as they reached the door of Schaefer's room, "I don't care what you tell your superiors. I'm not a cop, and it's not my business what you say officially, but I want some answers. I can't do my job properly if you lie to me. So what the hell happened?"

"What does it matter?" Rasche asked nervously. "Look, the guy's banged up, but a few stitches, a little rest, and he'll be good as new, right? He's not gonna die and make you look bad or anything." They stepped into the room. "I *know* Schaefer, Doc," Rasche insisted. "He carries liability insurance in case cars run into *him*. This isn't anything."

He hoped, very much, that it wasn't anything, that Schaefer wasn't going to die.

"Look, enough of the bullshit," the doctor said wearily, pulling aside the curtain around Schaefer's bed and revealing Rasche's unconscious, but still breathing, partner. "It's late, I'm tired, and you don't get something like *that* from falling out of a building."

He thrust out a finger and pointed to Schaefer's neck, just below the left ear.

Rasche had been taking in the monitors, the tubes up Schaefer's nose, the bandages across his nose and forehead and around his jaw—even though he'd landed on his back when he hit the pile of trash. Now he looked where the doctor's finger indicated.

It was a lump of dully gleaming metal, about the

diameter of a nickel, but rounded like a beetle or the head of a bolt—Rasche had a sudden mental image of Schaefer as a Frankenstein's monster, with electrodes on either side.

By now he probably had about enough stitches for the part, too.

The metal thing was rimmed with blood—*fresh* blood, from the color; everywhere else the blood had either been wiped away or dried to an ugly red-brown, but here was a circle that was still bright, bright red.

As Rasche watched, a thin red trickle ran down Schaefer's neck and dripped onto the pillow.

This wasn't anything Rasche had seen before; either Schaefer's shirt collar or the scattered garbage had hidden it when he had knelt over Schaefer on the pavement of Beekman Street.

Rasche looked questioningly at the doctor.

"We can't get it off without surgery," the doctor said. "Maybe not even then. It's got these barbed claws dug into the carotid artery, and any time we pull at it, they start moving. If we tear it off, maybe even if we cut it off, it'll chew the blood vessels to pulp, and he'll bleed to death before we can repair them."

"Jesus," Rasche said, looking back at Schaefer.

"We've x-rayed it, looked at it every way we know, and we can't see inside it or get any idea how it works. Now, Detective," the doctor said, "would you mind telling me what the hell that thing *is*?"

"I'd like to, Doc," Rasche said honestly, "but I swear to God, I don't know."

10

It took fifteen minutes to convince the doctor that Rasche didn't know what the thing on Schaefer's neck was, or how it got there.

It took another fifteen minutes to finish the paperwork, and forty more to get home. Even though the sun wasn't yet showing more than a faint glow in the east, the morning traffic had begun.

Rasche didn't bother cursing as he drove, or trying to make time. It wasn't as if he was in any hurry. He needed sleep, but he knew he wasn't going to get any right away, not while the image of that gadget on Schaefer's neck was stuck in his mind, not while he kept imagining those claws the doctor had described . . .

The drive gave Rasche him to think, but he

didn't think of anything useful. He just kept seeing that ring of blood, or Schaefer's body falling, or the dangling, mutilated corpses at the police range.

He left Schaefer's car at the curb and hauled himself wearily into his darkened house.

Shari and the kids were still asleep, Rasche figured. At least Shari hadn't tried to wait up for him—she wasn't lying on the living-room couch with the television still on.

For a moment he was tempted to take a quick look upstairs, make sure they were all right, but that was crazy, he'd just risk waking them up.

They were safe here—as much as anyone was safe anywhere in New York.

He trudged into the kitchen, where he hung his holstered gun on a door handle while he found a bottle of bourbon—he was acting on the theory that a good stiff shot of booze might help him sleep.

Bourbon. General Philips had been drinking bourbon. Just who the hell was Philips, anyway? Who did he work for? He knew what was going on here, or at least part of it—what was his connection with the killers?

Schaefer's brother, Dutch, was connected to it somehow, too—and so was Schaefer. It couldn't just be a coincidence. The killers had taken out a bunch of Schaefer's enemies, then a bunch of Schaefer's allies—they hadn't touched anyone in New York that Schaefer didn't care about, one way or another.

And they'd been waiting for him at that tenement—or *someone* had. They must have guessed Schaefer would go back there after the massacre on Twentieth Street.

What *had* happened to Schaefer up there? Rasche had never seen him take a beating like that, with his nose and jaw both smashed *before* he went out through the hole in the wall.

And that thing stuck on his neck—did Philips know what that was?

What was it Philips had said? "They like the heat . . . They want the *sport*."

Sport?

"Makes it sound like the America's Cup or something," Rasche muttered.

"Did you say something, hon?" Shari asked him from the doorway.

Rasche started and almost spilled the whiskey.

"I heard you come in," Shari said. She was wearing her old pink terry-cloth bathrobe.

"Sorry," Rasche said. "I didn't mean to wake you."

"I'd be getting up in fifteen minutes anyway. So did you say something?"

"No, no," Rasche said. "It's nothing." He gulped bourbon and glanced at the clock, and saw that Shari was right about the time.

"Isn't it kind of early to be drinking like that?" she asked.

"No," Rasche said, "it's late. Very late." He swallowed the rest of the whiskey.

"Do you want some breakfast?" Shari asked, reaching for a cupboard door.

Rasche shook his head. "I'll be going to bed in a few minutes."

"You've got the day off?"

"I'm *taking* the day off. I've been up all night." He looked at the empty glass and the half-full bottle, then put the cap back on the bottle, and the glass in the sink.

There was someone or something out there in the city, something that had thrown Schaefer off the fifth floor, something that had butchered a dozen armed men—and according to Philips, it had done it for sport.

For *fun*.

Whatever it was, he didn't want to be drunk into a stupor if he ever had to face it—and it could show up anytime.

"Did you eat anything?" Shari asked.

"Yeah," Rasche lied.

He sat and watched as his wife got her own breakfast—cornflakes and milk. She didn't bother cooking if he wasn't going to eat.

Sometimes he wished she didn't care so much for him; if he ever did get himself killed, she'd suffer for it, and he hated thinking of that even more than he hated thinking of his own death.

He knew he should get some sleep, but he wasn't ready yet. He wasn't sure why not. He sat there by the table as if waiting for something—but he didn't know what.

He was still sitting there when someone began pounding on the front door.

Rasche was on his feet in an instant, grabbing his gun and shouting, "Shari, get upstairs with the kids, *now*!"

Shari threw him a terrified glance, then scampered for the stairs.

Pistol in hand, Rasche crept down the front hall.

Whoever it was was still knocking—but just knocking. No one had broken in the glass panes in the door, no one had kicked at the door, no one had picked or smashed the lock, no one had come in through the windows. That was promising—but Rasche still kept his gun ready.

"All right, all right, I'm coming," he called as his hand closed on the knob.

He could see the outline of two men through the white curtain that covered the glass; carefully, he nudged the fabric aside with the barrel of the revolver and peered out at the faces. One was out of his line of sight, but the other he recognized.

Schaefer.

His face was half-covered with bandages, but there was no question—it was Schaefer.

For a moment Rasche's weary mind went blank—what the hell was *Schaefer* doing there?

The pounding continued, and eventually that penetrated Rasche's confusion. He opened the door, pistol still in his hand.

" 'Bout time, Mac," the stranger said.

He was a young black man of undistinguished size, and he was struggling to keep Schaefer upright with one arm while he knocked with the other.

Schaefer was barefoot, still wearing his green hospital gown. He coughed. "Hey, Rasche," he said, "pay this creep, will you?"

Rasche looked past them both at the city cab waiting at the curb.

Schaefer had gotten out of the hospital and found a cab. He didn't have any money, didn't have his goddamn *clothes*, but he'd gotten a cab.

"Let's get him on the couch," Rasche said to the stranger, ignoring Schaefer.

Together, Rasche and the cab driver got Schaefer onto the sofa in the living room, his head propped up on a throw pillow, Shari's crocheted afghan thrown across his bare legs. A twenty from the housekeeping money covered the fare and a tip—Rasche didn't want to keep the cabbie around long enough to worry about change.

As he showed the driver out, Rasche saw Shari at the top of the stairs and signaled to her that everything was okay. She crept down the steps and saw their guest. She relaxed slightly upon recognizing him, but his condition was enough to keep her nervous.

"I'll get you some tea," she said.

Rasche pulled a chair up beside the couch and sat, looking down at his partner.

Schaefer was still in bad shape—that had been obvious at the door. He was bandaged half a dozen places, and couldn't speak without coughing—Rasche guessed that came from pressure on his lungs from a broken rib.

He was conscious, though.

"How did you get out of the hospital?" Rasche asked. "The doctor said—"

"Screw the doctor," Schaefer interrupted.

Then he went into a brief fit of coughing.

Rasche waited for it to pass.

"So what're you doing here?" he demanded.

Schaefer held up a bandaged hand. "I'm going to need some help for a few days," he said.

"Help?" Rasche asked. "Help doing *what*?"

Schaefer coughed. "I need a place to stay where

I can do some thinking, get some things done. Can't do shit in that damn hospital. Besides, the feds can watch me every goddamn minute there."

"But, Schaef, you're all busted up. . . ."

"That's why I didn't fucking go *home*, Rasche," Schaefer said, lifting his head. "I can't manage by myself yet. Come on, give me a break."

"Right, you can't go home like this . . . ," Rasche agreed uncertainly.

"So can I stay, or not?"

"You're welcome to stay, Schaef, but what is it you want to do that you can't do in the hospital? I mean, you're in no shape to . . ."

"I'm going to find the ugly son of a bitch that did this . . . ," Schaefer interrupted, before being overtaken by more coughing. Again Rasche waited for the coughing to stop.

"I'm going to find him," Schaefer said, "and I'm going to kick his ugly ass from here to Jersey."

Shari appeared in the kitchen doorway, holding a cup. "I . . . I made you some tea, Schaef. I . . ."

Schaefer, already sitting up to ease the coughing, turned slightly and accepted the cup.

"Thanks, Shari," he said.

A voice spoke from the hallway.

"Wow, just look at his neck!" the boy said. "It's all bloody!"

"Cool!" another voice answered.

Rasche looked up and saw his two sons standing in the doorway, staring at Schaefer.

They were right; the thing on Schaefer's neck was oozing fresh blood again. The coughing had probably done it.

"Honey, please," Rasche said, "could you get the boys out of here?"

Shari obeyed, dragging the pair of them to the kitchen for breakfast.

When they were gone, Rasche asked, "What about that thing on your neck? We've got to get it off before it kills you."

"I don't think it's there to kill me," Schaefer said. "At least not yet."

"So what *do* you think?"

"I think I've been tagged, like some kind of baby seal," Schaefer said. "Guess he wants to keep tabs on me." He grimaced, coughed, then added wryly, "I guess the bastard *likes* me."

11

Schaefer, Rasche thought, was one tough hombre.

If *I* had been beaten up and thrown off the fifth floor, he thought, I'd spend the next few days sipping chicken soup and watching *Love Boat* reruns.

Schaefer just wanted to get back to work.

Oh, they'd both slept most of the day and taken it easy that evening; Rasche had made a run down to the hospital and talked the nurse into turning over Schaefer's clothes and wallet, made a stop at Schaefer's apartment for a fresher outfit, then come home and tried to coax a coherent description from Schaefer of just what he had fought in that tenement.

They'd talked over what it was, where it came from, what it was after—all of it guesswork, of course, but Schaefer had that last chat with Dutch to help him.

He thought the thing was a hunter, the kind Dutch had talked about—probably the one Dutch encountered; after all, how many could there be?

Schaefer told Rasche the thing wasn't human, but he admitted he hadn't gotten that good a look at it, had only been in the same room with it for a few seconds in poor light; Rasche didn't comment on that.

But Dutch had run into it in Central America, and this one was in New York.

Well, it had had seven or eight years to find its way north. Maybe it had already gotten Dutch and was going on after his family. Or maybe Dutch had gotten away, and it had mistaken Schaefer for his brother.

In any case, Schaefer figured that it was toying with him, playing cat-and-mouse games, killing Schaefer's own natural prey at the downtown tenement, killing Schaefer's allies on Twentieth Street, marking Schaefer.

Schaefer didn't think it had intended to knock him out of the building; that had been an accident. And it hadn't bothered coming down after him because it wanted the chase to continue a bit longer, it didn't want to kill him while he was helpless.

It wanted the *sport* of hunting him.

It was all guesswork, all just talk, and that was all Schaefer and Rasche did that first evening.

But the next morning, bright and early, they were in Schaefer's car again, driving back to Manhattan.

Schaefer planned strategy on the way as Rasche negotiated New York's traffic.

"We can't let that thing call all the shots," Schaefer said. "We have to track it down, get at it when it isn't ready, catch it off guard."

"How the hell are we supposed to do that?" Rasche asked.

"We need to find out more about it," Schaefer said. "We've got to backtrack Philips. He knows a lot more than he's telling—he's plugged into this somehow. He knew that thing was in town. And he's hiding something about Dutch, something more than I know. I can *feel* it."

"*I* can feel that we're going to be canned if we don't bring McComb in on this," Rasche replied. "Look, Schaef, I haven't pushed you because I figure you have your reasons, but I've got to know what we're really up against. You saw that character up there, I didn't—you must have some idea what's going on. Okay, so it's some kind of superhunter—who sent it? Why was it after your brother? Who'd he piss off, the mob? Terrorists? Some foreign government? Sinatra's bodyguards?"

"How about, 'None of the above'?" Schaefer said. "You want the truth, Rasche? The truth is, I just don't know. It could be some kind of mutant monster on the rampage for all I know; it could be from outer space. Maybe Philips is involved because it's some kind of biowar experiment gone wrong. I just don't *know*."

Rasche started to ask another question, then dropped it. If Schaefer didn't know, more questions wouldn't help.

At Police Plaza they didn't need to go looking for

McComb; they were scarcely inside the building when he spotted them and came charging down the corridor at them, fists clenched.

"There you are!" he bellowed. "About time you put in an appearance!"

"You could've called—" Rasche began.

"You should've stayed in the goddamn hospital where you belonged, Schaefer! I *warned* you! I've got the chief crawling up my ass, wondering why one of my homicide detectives was pissing around a federally sealed crime scene—"

"Give it a rest, McComb," Schaefer interrupted.

"That's *Captain* McComb, Detective," growled McComb. "In my office. *Now*."

Neither of them paid any attention to Rasche— and that suited Rasche just fine. The order to McComb's office was directed at Schaefer, and as far as Rasche could tell, he wasn't wanted.

He was just as glad not to get caught in the cross fire in there. He headed for his own desk, ready to turn if either McComb or Schaefer shouted at him.

Neither of them did; instead, the two men marched into McComb's specially soundproofed office.

McComb slammed the door behind them, then turned to the detective.

"Lemme make it simple," he said to Schaefer, "since you don't seem to listen real good. I'm telling you, you keep messing with me and I'll have your job. Hell, I'll have you up on charges—"

"I want to talk to Philips," Schaefer said, cutting McComb off. "I want to confirm—"

"You're not *hearing* me, Schaefer!" McComb shouted.

Schaefer stopped talking, and McComb continued. "This isn't an official investigation. There are no feds involved here, as far as you're concerned. Philips doesn't exist. Nobody's going to confirm shit."

"And those dead bodies . . . how are you explaining those?" Schaefer demanded. "Suicide? They all fired off all their ammunition, then skinned themselves?"

"It's *not your problem*, Schaefer," McComb bellowed, "or mine either. It's a federal matter, and you just keep your fucking nose—"

"Look, McComb," Schaefer interrupted. "I want to talk to Philips. It's personal, all right? Maybe it's nothing to do with this case—it's about my brother."

"I told you, Philips doesn't exist," McComb replied, glaring.

Schaefer stared back silently for a moment, then said, "Fine, he doesn't exist. So let me talk to a figment of my goddamn imagination!"

"You want to talk to anybody on personal business, Schaefer, that's your business, you do it on your time—I'm not going to bother the general on your behalf."

"You're my only contact with him, asshole!"

McComb stared at Schaefer.

"What did you call me?"

"Look, McComb, I've got to talk to him!"

"Fuck off, Schaefer," McComb replied. "Listen, you shut up right now, you give me your word you'll stay the hell away from the feds and from Twentieth Street and from that tenement, and you can go—"

"You can go to hell, McComb," Schaefer said, cutting him off. "Where do I find Philips?"

"All right, that does it," McComb said. "You're history, Schaefer—you're going down, you're out of the department." He snatched up his phone and bellowed, "Give me the desk sergeant, I want—"

Before he could finish the sentence, Schaefer's fist came down on the phone's base, smashing plastic and circuitry.

"Bad connection," Schaefer said.

For a moment McComb stared down at the broken phone, the receiver still clutched in his hand.

Then Schaefer grabbed him by the front of his shirt and picked him up and slammed him against a bookcase; law books and old reports tumbled down around him.

"Listen," Schaefer said calmly. "You probably *could* have me fired, just the way you think, despite the union. I might even do a little time. Lose my pension, six months behind bars, and you know what would happen then?"

He waited while McComb stared down at him in terror; then Schaefer answered his own question.

"*Then* I might get *mad*," he said.

McComb managed a glance at the door and saw no sign of approaching rescue. He had had this office rebuilt to his own specifications, to ensure complete privacy—he hadn't wanted officers eavesdropping on confidential business.

He regretted that now.

Then he looked back at the expression on Schaefer's face. He saw the bandages on the nose and jaw, but most of all he saw those cold blue eyes.

Something in them looked dead, McComb

thought—and Schaefer had told the truth. He wasn't angry.

Not yet.

"Jesus," McComb said. "Look, I'm telling you the truth—you'll never find Philips. He's not regular army or special forces or even CIA, he's some kind of army freelance that isn't supposed to exist. And I swear, Schaefer, I don't know what's really going on, he wouldn't even tell *me*, he just ordered us to keep everybody out, to go through the motions and then forget it all. He wouldn't tell me a thing!"

"No?" Schaefer dropped McComb; the captain flung out an arm and spilled a shelf to the floor in a useless attempt to catch himself, and landed sitting, sprawled on a pile of ledgers and reports.

"Can you reach him?"

"Not anymore," McComb said. "I had a phone number, but it's been disconnected."

"So he doesn't trust you. Smart man, Philips," Schaefer said. "I guess I'll have to try something else."

He marched out before McComb could move to stop him—not that McComb had any intention of stopping him.

He marched on out through the squad room.

Rasche jumped up and followed him.

At the curb outside Schaefer turned and saw Rasche.

"Good," he said, "you can save me the cab fare."

Rasche had just wanted to ask what had happened with McComb, whether they still had their jobs, but the expression on Schaefer's face wasn't anything he wanted to argue with; he went to get the car.

After all, they could talk while he drove.

A moment later he pulled up at the curb; Schaefer climbed in, slammed the door, and said, "Kennedy."

"Kennedy?" Rasche turned to stare at him. "Christ, Schaef, you mean this has something to do with the assassination? Was the CIA in it, after all? I always thought that was just another crackpot conspiracy theory—"

"Kennedy *Airport*," Schaefer said.

"Oh," Rasche said. He put the car in gear, pulled out into traffic, and headed for Queens, too embarrassed to say anything more right away.

They were crossing the Williamsburg Bridge when he asked, "So what'd McComb say?"

"Nothing," Schaefer said, staring out the window.

"He didn't fire us?"

Schaefer shrugged. "Not you, anyway," he said.

Rasche considered that as he turned onto the Brooklyn-Queens Expressway.

"So you're going to the airport?" Rasche asked.

Schaefer didn't bother to answer.

"No luggage?"

"It's in the trunk. I keep a suitcase there."

Rasche grimaced. They were still using Schaefer's car, and that was just like Schaefer—always ready for disaster.

And of course he hadn't mentioned it sooner and saved Rasche that side trip to his apartment.

Rasche drove on, made the turn onto the Long Island Expressway, then asked, "So you're flying somewhere?"

Schaefer didn't bother to answer that, either.

"Washington?" Rasche asked. "Did you get an address for Phillips?"

Schaefer shook his head. "Central America," he said.

Rasche slammed on the brakes. "*Central America*? Are you out of your mind?"

Horns blared behind him; he pulled to the shoulder.

"Keep driving," Schaefer said.

"You tell me what you're doing, or I stop again," Rasche said as he pulled back into traffic.

"Dutch told me the rescue mission where he lost his men was in Central America, and I think I remember enough of what he said to figure out just about where," Schaefer said, ticking off the first of three raised fingers. "So if we're right that it's the same one, then the killer was there once, right?"

Rasche nodded reluctantly.

"Philips said the killer likes the heat—and Central America's hotter than hell. Maybe it's home for whatever we're up against." A second finger came down.

"That's pretty weak, Schaef," Rasche said.

"And finally, Carr and Lamb were meeting in that dump, and why would they be doing that? Because they were making peace, maybe? Why would they do that? Because they had a common enemy. And who could that be? That could be the Cali cartel, or the La Costa, trying to pick up where the Medellin used to be. Carr and Lamb were cutting out the Colombians, and the Colombians didn't like it— that's the first motive we've got for that massacre that makes any sense. So the Colombians run a lot of their stuff up through Central America—the

Cali, especially. So maybe there's a connection. Maybe they hired this killer there. Or if he's not someone they hired, maybe they found him there—or he found them." Schaefer held up a clenched fist.

"And maybe this is all coincidence!"

Schaefer almost shrugged. "Maybe. But it's the best shot I've got, without Philips. Something happened down there eight years ago that ties into Dutch's mission, the murders, Philips, that thing I fought—*all* of it. It's the only thing that makes sense."

"It doesn't make sense to *me*," Rasche protested. "That killer isn't in Central America *now*, it's here in New York!"

"Yeah," Schaefer said, "but where? It's a big city, Rasche—you know that as well as I do. If we're going to find that thing, we need a lead of some kind."

"And you think you'll find one in fucking *Central America*?"

Schaefer didn't bother to reply.

They were halfway down the Van Wyck Expressway when Rasche said, "We ticked off some heavy players down there when we worked narcotics, you know—some of those Colombians you mentioned. If any of our *compañeros* catch you, they'll peel your tan with a straight razor."

"Screw 'em," Schaefer said.

It was Rasche's turn not to answer; he drove into the airport and looked for an appropriate terminal.

He eventually decided that American would do.

"How are you going to pay for this?" he asked as

he looked for somewhere to pull over. "Is McComb going to okay departmental funds?"

"Hell, no," Schaefer said. "I've got credit cards. I'll put it all on plastic and worry about paying when the bills come."

"Schaef, that's—"

"That's *my* business, Rasche."

Rasche couldn't argue with that, so he didn't.

As Schaefer pulled his suitcase from the trunk, he said, "Listen, Rasche, get Shari and the kids away from the city until this is over. Have them stay with your parents or something—tell them it's a vacation. Tell them anything, just get them away."

"It's a big city, Schaef. . . ."

Schaefer shook his head. "I've got a feeling something ugly's coming down here," he said, "something that's going to make our Colombian friends look like something out of a Dr. Seuss book. I saw that thing, you didn't." He touched the bandaged lump on his neck. "If it picked me because I'm Dutch's brother, and it's not just a coincidence, then maybe it went after Lamb and Carr because I wanted them, maybe it hit Twentieth Street because I'm a cop. If any of that's true, then it might decide it'd be fun to go after *you*, too—partner. And like you said, I may be going to Central America, but the killer's still here in New York. So get out of the city, Rasche, you *and* your family. Go somewhere cool."

Then he turned and almost jogged into the terminal.

Rasche watched him go. Schaefer's nose and jaw and one hand were all still swathed in bandages, but he moved as if nothing had happened.

When he was out of sight in the airport crowds, Rasche got back into the car and started the engine.

He sat thinking for a moment before he pulled out into traffic.

He had some vacation time saved up. He hadn't planned to use it this soon, and McComb might not like it, the department wasn't real fond of short-notice vacations, but maybe a vacation would do Shari good, he thought.

Maybe, it would do them *all* some good.

And, he thought, wiping at the sweat on his forehead, it *would* be nice to go somewhere cool.

12

General Philips looked over the latest weather reports and frowned.

The heat wave was still hanging on. Summer was slipping away, but the hot, humid air was holding steady over the city, and temperatures were staying in the nineties or above.

The pollution count was well into the unhealthy range, but New York's unwelcome visitors wouldn't give a shit about that; hell, according to Dutch they wore those masks—they probably didn't breathe the local air in the first place.

Though they apparently could if they wanted to.

They could do just about any damn thing they pleased, it seemed.

The radar reports showed that faint, unnatural interference was still there—not that he really needed that; he could just turn on a TV that didn't have cable and see if reception was still lousy. Philips was pretty sure, despite all the fumfering from his scientists, that that interference came from those damned alien ships.

The police reports were the only encouraging sign—there hadn't been a third massacre yet.

At least not that anyone at the NYPD knew of, but who knew what sort of slaughterhouse scenes might be lurking undiscovered in some attic somewhere? It was a big city, and it had been a long time since most New Yorkers could be bothered to be their brothers' keepers.

Of course, usually those things let their victims get a few shots off, just to make it interesting, and that might still draw attention in most neighborhoods.

So maybe they really hadn't struck again.

But if that was the case—why hadn't they? What were they waiting for?

Philips read down past the summary, into the body of the report—usually he left that for underlings, but he didn't want to risk missing anything on this one.

Sealing off the scene at Twentieth Street had made some trouble—that was no surprise. He'd tell his boys to hurry it up and get that place reopened. The local cops were never going to stop hassling about it as long as there were reminders there in their own basement.

And hassling those things would just get more good men killed. The only way to deal with the creatures was to leave them alone, let them have their fun; when they'd had enough, they would go home.

That reminded him of Dutch, and Dutch's brother; he began flipping through the report, looking for some mention of Schaefer. *That* stubborn son of a bitch wouldn't leave anything alone, Philips was sure.

He spotted Schaefer's name and paused, then stared.

"Goddammit," he said.

Captain McComb had ordered Detective Schaefer dismissed from the NYPD. The union was fighting it, but for the moment Schaefer was off the force.

That would just make Schaefer more determined than ever to get whatever had trashed the firing range, and now he'd have all the time he needed for it, without any paperwork or office politics to worry about.

That asshole McComb . . .

He punched a button.

"Perkins," he said, "get a squad together and send them to fetch Detective Schaefer."

"Yessir," the radio replied.

"Make sure they're armed—he may not want to come. Warn 'em who they're dealing with."

"Yessir."

Philips turned back to the report.

Detective Rasche had put in for his annual vacation, and McComb had agreed—after all, Rasche's partner was gone, and he might as well take some time off before they found him someone new.

Was Rasche helping Schaefer? Were the two of them up to something that might stir up trouble?

"Damn," Philips muttered. He took the stub of

cigar out of his mouth and threw it at the waste-basket.

He spent the next hour going through reports, reading a summary of every unsolved murder that had taken place in New York City or northern New Jersey since the heat wave began.

He was just finishing up when his aide, Perkins, appeared in the door of the office Philips was using.

"Sir?" he asked.

Philips tossed the report aside.

"We can't locate Detective Schaefer," the aide said. "He hasn't been seen anywhere in the NYPD since McComb fired him—not at One Police Plaza, not at the academy on West Twentieth, not anywhere. He isn't at his apartment, and his mail hasn't been picked up for at least the past two days. He's not at Detective Rasche's home in Queens, or if he is, he's not answering the door or the phone."

Philips stared at him for a moment.

"Shit," he said.

He thought it over, then said, "All right, put a trace on him—get a search warrant. When they ask for probable cause, tell 'em flight to avoid pros-ecution for assault, and that he's wanted for ques-tioning in a murder investigation. Search his apartment. Check phone records, bank records, credit-card records, everything. Find him. And find Rasche, too—if anyone knows where Schaefer is and what he's up to, Rasche does."

"Do you want Rasche brought in?"

Philips chewed his mustache.

"Yeah," he said. "If we ask questions and then don't bring him in, he'll warn Schaefer."

Perkins nodded. "And if he doesn't want to cooperate with us?"

"Shit," Philips said again. "Look, bring Rasche in, but don't rough him up; we want him to cooperate, and maybe he will eventually if we play nice."

"Yessir." Perkins saluted, turned, and left.

Philips stared morosely after him.

This whole setup stank. This wasn't how it was supposed to work. There were monsters loose in the city, and Philips wasn't trying to stop them; instead he was trying to stop a couple of good men who were just trying to protect their homes and families.

But it had to be like this. The monsters couldn't be stopped. The best he could hope for was not to make them angry, and to keep their presence a secret, so there wouldn't be any panic, wouldn't be any harebrained attempts to fight them, wouldn't be a lot of endless recriminations about who didn't prevent what, wouldn't be congressional investigations and independent prosecutors and reporters prying into every nook and cranny of the government operation, investigations that wouldn't do a damn bit of good as far as stopping the aliens, but would blow the lid off every secret the government had left in covert operations.

Maybe it would have been smarter to have built up a whole separate operation to deal with the alien hunters right from the start, instead of using the existing structures at first; but at the time, eight years ago, no one had known how fast they'd have to act, or what they might need to do. It had seemed better to take a little piece of everything that was already up and running—CIA, FBI, NSA, everything.

Which meant that if the shit hit the fan and the reporters began turning over rocks to see what they could find, they'd expose the dirty laundry in every branch.

A single all-new black operation would have been better, all right.

Hindsight was always twenty-twenty.

"Sir?"

Perkins was in the door again. Philips looked up expectantly.

"The radar-analysis group reports they've found something anomalous—a reading for something splitting off from the main group and heading south."

"Christ, now what?" Philips stood up. "Show me what you've got."

He followed Perkins out.

Twenty minutes later he was studying a fax of a chart showing a radar signature of something that looked like a small swarm of insects, something that wouldn't even have registered on any ordinary equipment, something that would ordinarily have been dismissed as a bit of cloud, or a bunch of bees, if it was noticed at all.

Except this particular swarm of bees or bit of cloud had apparently been moving south at roughly six hundred miles per hour.

Philips glowered at the fax.

"Six hundred," he said. "Since when are space-ships subsonic?"

"Since never, sir," a technical sergeant replied.

"Our previous tracks were all at hypersonic speeds."

"So what the hell was *this* one doing?"

"We don't know, sir," the sergeant replied. "Except . . . well, commercial airliners cruise at about that speed."

Philips looked up from the paper. "So is this a goddamn airliner?"

"No, sir, it's not," the sergeant said, "but . . . well, it might be a shadow of some kind, or an echo. We're dealing with stuff right on the edge here, sir—right at the limits of our equipment."

"So it may not have anything to do with our unwanted visitors?" Philips asked.

The sergeant shrugged.

"I wish I knew, sir," he said. "I really wish I knew."

"I wish, too," Philips said, flinging the paper aside. "I wish to God *somebody* knew what those things are doing!"

13

Rasche turned into the drive and pulled the family car into the motel parking lot.

"Here we are again," he said cheerfully. "Our home away from home."

"Can we go swimming in the pool now?" Steven asked from the back.

"Later," Shari answered.

Rasche parked the car neatly in front of room 112; a space was open in just the right spot.

The boys immediately jumped out on either side, but Rasche sat behind the wheel for a moment and looked over the white-painted concrete walls and the flat-pink doors. "This place is a bit tacky, isn't it?"

"It's fine," Shari said. She leaned over and squeezed her husband's arm. "Thanks."

Rasche turned, startled. "Thanks for what?"

"For bringing us here. For taking a vacation."

"Hey," Rasche said, "I figured we were due. And it was about time the boys got to see the falls."

"I thought so, too," Shari agreed. She hesitated. "This didn't have anything to do with, you know, Schaef getting beat up, did it?"

"He wasn't exactly . . . ," Rasche began, then stopped.

"Honey, I've been a cop's wife for a long time. I didn't listen in or anything, I don't want to know all the details, but I saw what Schaef looked like— something bad happened to him." She shuddered. "There must've been a lot of them, to beat *him* up like that!"

"He wasn't beaten up, he fell out a window," Rasche said. "Fifth floor."

"And then he left the hospital and came straight to our door and spent a day talking to you," Shari said, "and then you went into work with him and came home early without him and said we were taking a vacation, and how did Niagara Falls sound . . . Honey, are you in trouble?"

Rasche looked her in the eye and admitted, "I don't know."

"Is Schaef okay?"

"I don't know that, either. I swear, Shari, I wish I did." He leaned over and kissed her cheek. "Look, don't worry about it," he said. "We'll all be fine. Just relax and have a good time."

"Are you sure?"

"Absolutely."

Someone rapped on Rasche's window, and he turned to find their younger son's face pressed up against the glass. "Come on, you guys!" he shouted.

Rasche smiled and opened the door.

An hour later Shari and the boys were splashing in the motel pool, but Rasche didn't feel like staying in the water. Despite what he'd told his wife, he couldn't really relax; he was still thinking about his work.

He got up and dried himself off, then headed back to the room.

There was some kind of superhuman killer loose in New York, and he was up here on vacation with his family, and that just didn't feel right.

And Shari's questions were nagging at him. *Was* he in trouble? How much?

Was Schaefer okay?

Schaefer was off in Central America somewhere, and Rasche hadn't heard a word since he left.

Rasche had left word with the department of where he was going, of course, and after they'd arrived and gotten settled in, he'd phoned back and given the desk sergeant their room number and the name and phone number of the motel; if anything came up, they'd call him. . . .

Wouldn't they?

Well, no, they wouldn't. It wasn't his case. It wasn't Schaefer's case, either. And if Schaefer called and asked for Rasche, the desk man would probably just tell him, "I ain't your goddamn answering service," and hang up.

Rasche frowned as he dressed. Maybe, he thought, he should head back to the city, just in case Schaefer did call. Shari and the boys could stay up here, where they'd be safe, or go to her mother's place in Elmira.

Of course, they had only the one car, and Shari didn't like driving—she'd lived in the city for a long time. She drove well enough when she had to, but she didn't *like* it.

As he buckled his belt, he shook his head. This was ridiculous; he was being paranoid, worrying about nothing. The feds would get the killer, whoever and whatever he was. They obviously knew what was going on; Philips had said to wait a couple of weeks and it would all be over, and Rasche had to admit Philips was probably telling the truth. Schaefer was on a wild-goose chase; he'd poke around the jungles for a while, then come home.

And by then, when everything had blown over, Schaefer could sue for reinstatement and the union would back him up and he'd get his job back, and everything could go on the way it was before, and in eight years Rasche would retire and collect his pension and he and Shari would pack up and head out to Portland or Anchorage or somewhere.

He was sitting on the bed and had just tied his shoes when he heard footsteps outside; he glanced up.

The shadows of two men—two *big* men—were visible on the drawn curtains, passing by the window.

Then the footsteps stopped, and Rasche judged that the two men were just outside the door of his room.

Suddenly nervous, he reached over to the lower shelf of the rickety little nightstand and found his pistol—he'd brought it with him, of course, but he hadn't expected to touch it while he was here.

"One-twelve," one of the men said in a low voice, barely audible through the paper-thin door, and Rasche froze. "Do we knock?"

"He's probably out somewhere," the other said. "Maybe we should just wait."

"Let's see if he's in there first."

The men couldn't have realized how thin the door was, that Rasche had heard them.

They were after him.

Who were they?

If this was something legitimate, if the department needed to reach him, they'd have phoned, they'd have left a message—so this had to be somebody else.

Like whoever was behind the two massacres.

They just looked like ordinary men through the curtains, not like the eight-foot-tall monster that Schaefer had described, but that monster couldn't be operating alone, could it? And maybe Schaefer had been hallucinating, maybe he'd been drugged somehow, and why hadn't Rasche thought of that sooner?

For an instant he thought about his choices. He could sit here and let them come in, but if these were the killers, come to skin him alive because he was Schaefer's partner, that would be suicide. He could shoot it out with them—he checked, and yes, his weapon was loaded—but if they *weren't* the killers, that would be a disaster.

The best thing to do was not to be here at all.

He headed for the bathroom, praying the window there would open.

It did; by the time the knock sounded on the door, he was hauling himself up and through it, wishing he'd stayed in better shape. This shouldn't have been such a struggle; he really did need to lose some weight.

A moment later he was standing on a strip of poorly maintained asphalt between the back of the motel and a tall wooden fence; to one side sat a big blue Dumpster, and Rasche could smell something rotting. Flies were buzzing over the Dumpster.

He wrinkled his nose in disgust. It wasn't anywhere near as hot here as it was down in the city, but it was hot enough that something in the trash had gotten very ripe.

He ducked below the window and listened for a moment, but heard nothing—apparently the men hadn't heard him and thought the room was empty. They hadn't broken in to check; maybe they didn't want to be that obvious.

He turned and hurried—not running, but walking fast—the other way, toward the motel office.

He had to make sure of what was happening—and he had to protect Shari and the boys.

And then he had to get back to New York, because obviously, running away from whatever was going on wasn't working.

He reached the back door of the motel office and walked in, trying to look casual.

"Any messages for me?" he asked. "Rasche, room one-twelve?"

The clerk looked up, then glanced down at the desk.

"No, sir," he said.

Then it wasn't McComb who sent those two. McComb would have called.

But they'd known his room number, and they hadn't had to ask here at the office, either. They must have gotten it from someone at the department, but no one had phoned, so this wasn't a friendly official visit.

Rasche leaned over and looked out a window, along the row of rooms; the two men were still there, one standing alertly, the other lounging against the wall.

They wore dark suits that looked completely out of place in this pastel tourist trap, especially since even up here the weather wasn't exactly cool—no sane person would be wearing a jacket.

At least not unless he wanted to hide something, such as a shoulder holster.

They were obviously not just a couple of locals here to award him a free pizza or something.

They might be feds—but if so, it wasn't a *friendly* visit, if they were coming to get him instead of phoning him to come in and talk.

Rasche had to get away, get back to the city to straighten this out—but he also had to make sure that Shari and the boys would be all right, whoever those men were. And he hated to leave all the luggage that was back there in the room.

"Thanks," Rasche told the clerk. "Can I use the phone?"

The clerk pointed to a pay phone on the far wall.

Rasche pawed through the yellow pages below the phone, then dialed the number of the local Budget car rental.

When he got an answer, he said, "I need to rent a car—can you drop it off for me?"

"When would you need it, sir, and where are you?"

"I need it right now, and I'm at the American Maid Motel on Route Thirty-one."

The rental agent was dubious, but Rasche argued. The agent insisted he didn't have any cars right there on the lot just now, but eventually conceded that there was a van available, and after further negotiation it was agreed that the van would be at the motel in twenty minutes.

That settled, Rasche went back out to the pool.

Shari waved to him, and Richard, the older boy, tried to splash him; Rasche was a foot or two out of range.

"Shari!" he called, beckoning to her.

She swam over and hung on the side of the pool; he knelt down.

"Listen, honey," he said, "something's come up. Remember you asked me if I was in trouble?"

She nodded.

"It looks as if maybe I am. So I'm heading back to New York to see what I can do about it—I'm renting a car, I'll leave ours here for you. And I think it'd be a good idea if you and the boys packed up and went somewhere else—another motel, or maybe down to Buffalo, or go visit your mom, whatever. Stay another two weeks—I hope that'll be enough."

"Are you . . ."

He held up a hand. "I'm fine, I'm just being extra careful, okay? But there's one other thing. If there's a guy in a suit anywhere in sight when you go back to the room—*don't* go back to the room. Go to the motel office and call the local cops, tell 'em the guy's been harassing you, and you think he's dangerous, and then don't go in the room until the cops get here. You understand?"

"Of course I do . . . but are you sure . . . ?"

"I'm sure. I love you; you be careful, okay?"

He stood up and looked around.

No sign yet of his rental van; no sign that the men in suits were watching. The pool was on the far side of the office, out of sight of Room 112, fortunately.

He strolled out toward the road, glancing casually toward the room, then wandered back, out of sight.

The two were still there, still waiting.

He had to lead them away, so that Shari and the kids could get out.

Five minutes later a white van turned into the parking lot and pulled up to the office. Rasche trotted over.

The driver was a pimply teenager. "Mr. Rasche?" he asked hopefully.

Rasche nodded.

A moment later the paperwork was done and the teenager was settled in the office, waiting for his ride back into town.

Rasche accepted the keys, went out to the van, and headed it over toward Room 112. Deliberately parking farther away than necessary, he got out, but left the engine running.

Then he walked casually toward the room.

The men spotted him almost immediately; Rasche heard one of them say, "That's him!"

Rasche didn't wait for anything more; he stopped, stared, and turned and dashed for the van.

The men dashed after him, as he had thought they would.

They were still a dozen feet away when he put the van in reverse and pulled out.

He watched in the rearview mirror as they turned and scrambled for their own car—a blue sedan, down at the end of the row.

He didn't wait, though—he wasn't any Hollywood stunt driver. If he wanted to lose his pursuers, he needed all the lead he could get.

Lose them he did, by dodging into a suburban shopping plaza a few blocks away and pulling out onto a different road. After a few more twists and turns he was able to double back past the motel.

Steven was standing in the door of Room 112 and spotted Daddy's van as it went by; he waved, and Rasche waved back.

Shari was already loading suitcases into the trunk of the family car, and there was no sign of the men in suits; Rasche drove on toward the east, back toward New York, fairly confident that he'd pulled it off, that Shari would get away, that everything would be fine.

At least for the moment.

14

P erkins's expression was wary as he waited for the general to notice him. Philips saw that as soon as he looked up.

He wished Perkins wouldn't do that; sure, it let him know there was bad news coming, but it made it look as if Perkins were scared of him. He didn't like to think he'd take out his annoyance at bad news on the messenger, or that Perkins would think he might. He wanted his men to respect him, not be scared of him.

"What is it?" Philips demanded, annoyed.

"It's Detective Rasche, sir," Perkins said.

"What about him?"

"Something spooked him," Perkins said. "He took off before our men could talk to him, and while they were chasing him, his family checked out of the motel and disappeared. We've lost him, and them, completely."

Philips shrugged. "Doesn't matter," he said; Perkins relaxed visibly, annoying Philips further.

"I thought you needed Rasche—"

"We just wanted him to tell us where Detective Schaefer went," the general said. He gestured at the faxes on the desk. "I think we've figured that out on our own. His credit cards show that he charged an airline ticket for a flight to Panama City, and the flight schedules match that radar trace we couldn't explain—it looks like one of those things followed him somehow, matched speeds with the airliner."

"I don't understand," Perkins said. "Why would Schaefer fly to Central America?"

"Dutch must have told him something about the mission there," Philips explained, "and he's put two and two together and gone off to find out what happened to his brother, to see what it has to do with our friends here in New York." Philips sighed. "And that radar trace means that one of the aliens went after him." He shook his head. "So now it looks as if our friend Detective Schaefer is dead meat. Out in the jungle that thing'll be right in its element, and a New York City cop'll be as out of place as a priest in a whorehouse. It's a damn shame, Perkins."

Perkins hesitated. "Shouldn't we do something about it, sir?"

"Not much we can do, son," Philips said. "Maybe send someone out to keep an eye on the situation, make sure nobody else gets caught in the cross fire—guess we should give that a shot."

"Couldn't we . . ." Perkins hesitated. "I mean, he's Dutch's brother. Shouldn't we do something to give him a fighting chance?"

Philips shook his head. "No, son," he said gently. "We can't do that. Think it through. One of the aliens *followed* Schaefer from New York. That means they want *him*—not just anybody, but Detective Schaefer specifically. So they're going to get him sooner or later; we can't stop them. It's a safe bet they've got the technology to take out that whole goddamn country if they want to."

"But you said there was just one that went after him . . . ," Perkins protested.

"That's one *ship*," Philips pointed out. "We don't know how big the ships are, how many of those creatures are on each ship—we've never actually *seen* a ship, remember, just picked up the radar traces. Besides, even one of those things is enough to kill anyone. And you aren't going to stop it short of killing it."

"Well, sir, if we armed Schaefer and told him what he was up against . . ."

"Then it's just barely possible he might kill it, yeah," Philips acknowledged. "And if he did, then we'd *all* be in deep shit. How do you think the others would react if Schaefer killed one?"

"I don't know, sir, but . . . well, Dutch killed one eight years ago, and nothing came of it."

"Dutch killed one that as far as we can determine came to Earth all by its lonesome," Philips said. "Dutch killed one that proceeded to blow up about a square mile of jungle while it was dying. Any of the others that might have been around, or that came to check on their buddy, must have thought Dutch was caught in the explosion and killed—hell, he damn near was. Or maybe they figured their buddy tripped over his own feet and broke his neck, maybe they didn't *know* who killed him."

"But then why would . . ."

"Why would they be after Schaefer? Okay, they figured out something somehow, and they came to get the mad-dog human that was able to notch one of their people, and they got it a bit wrong and went after his brother instead. Fine. Think that through, Perkins—*they knew who did it*, out of five billion humans on this planet, even though they didn't see what happened, and they were able to *find* a close approximation of the right one. Think about the kind of technological sophistication that implies.

"And this time, judging by the radar reports, they didn't just send one lone hunter out for a good time; they sent a whole goddamn *fleet*.

"Are you beginning to see my point?"

"I'm not sure, sir."

"Well, think about it. Think about what happens if we help Schaefer defend himself. *They'd know it.* I don't know how, but if they could find Schaefer, then they must have ways of finding these things out that we can't imagine. To them Schaefer's a murderer, a man-eating tiger loose in the game park. *We* know he's the wrong man, but how could we convince *them* of that? They can't be bothered to talk to us—we've seen that. They treat us like animals, they hunt us for sport, but if we start organizing against them, then we start to look dangerous, maybe *too* dangerous. They'd wipe us out."

Perkins considered this unhappily.

"I'm not sure about this, sir; seems to me you're making a lot of assumptions—"

"Damn right I am," Philips agreed. "I know it. But it hangs together, it works—and are you willing to bet the whole goddamn planet that I'm wrong?"

Perkins didn't answer that. He stood silently as Philips got to his feet and walked over to the window, to take a look out at the city.

"You know," Philips said thoughtfully as he looked down at the taxis and pedestrians on the avenue below, "I think I might want to supervise operations down there myself—just to make sure nothing gets out of hand. After all, it doesn't look as if the aliens are doing anything more here in New York. Maybe the attacks here were just meant to lure Schaefer to the jungle, so they could execute him on the same spot that Dutch killed the other one."

"Why would they want to do that?"

"A sense of what's fitting, son. Make the criminal return to the scene of the crime."

"But how could they know Schaefer would react this way?" Perkins asked.

"They think he's his brother," Philips answered impatiently. "They think he knows what they are, and they think he's smart enough to recognize what's been killing those people, and to go back to where he fought one before."

"But I still don't see . . . I mean, General, *I* wouldn't have expected Schaefer to do that, and these things aren't even human; how could they have guessed?"

"Who knows? Maybe they read minds, Perkins, and there's no question those bastards are smart, probably smarter than we are. Does it really matter?"

Again Perkins didn't answer.

"Get me a plane, son," Philips said, turning away from the window. "It'll take a while for Schaefer to get himself outfitted and find the right place—even if Dutch told him where it is, it's the ass end of nowhere."

"But if Schaefer's as good as dead, sir, what can you do for him . . . ?"

"I can pick up the body and make sure he gets a decent burial," Philips snapped. "It's the least I can do for Dutch's brother."

15

Rafe T. G. Mako strutted the empty streets feeling good. He was packing serious heat, he had a good buzz on from sampling the latest shipment, he had a hot new bitch waiting for him—all was right with the world.

He looked up, smiling.

The sky was still thick with smog and summer heat, but Rafe didn't really give a fuck about the weather, he felt too good to let that worry him.

The buildings seemed to dance against the dirty sky as he walked, a combination of his footsteps and something in the drugs playing with his mind, and he loved it. The whole damn city danced to his tune, all right. Word was out on the street that Lamb was dead and Carr had lost some of his best boys, and that meant there were opportunities to be had, room to move up, and Rafe intended to find himself some space at the top, somewhere he could rake in the big money, get himself a place to live that looked like a goddamn Hollywood movie set, take his women two at a time.

Something flickered overhead, leaping from one building to the next, and Rafe blinked. His steps slowed.

Wasn't anything up there, man, but he thought he'd seen something. . . .

Just a bit of hot air, he told himself, or a fart from some car's exhaust, playing tricks with his eyes in the heat. He strolled on, but just to reassure himself, just to scare off any fools might be on the roof planning something, he pulled out the Uzi he'd scored, pulled it out and checked to make sure it was loaded, and held it out pointed at the sky while he looked along the rooftops.

Heat shimmered along the sunlit parapets, in one spot in particular, and Rafe stared at it.

He could see through it, no question—he could see the chimney behind it.

So it wasn't really there. Unless the stuff he'd taken was giving him goddamn X-ray vision, that shape was nothin', just a trick of the light, a side effect of the drug.

But, hey, real or not, he didn't need to let it bother him. He fired a burst, three rounds, and sure enough, the shimmer was gone.

Rafe smiled.

Wasn't anything gonna mess with *him*, man!

Something thumped on the sidewalk behind him, and he turned, startled.

Wasn't anything *there*—but the air was shimmering, just a few feet away. He looked to see if there was a grating or vent or something where hot air might be coming up, but it was over solid sidewalk.

"Shit," he said.

This had to be the drug, messing with his head. This wasn't good, he didn't like this—they must've cut it with something weird, those bastards who sold him the stuff.

Then the shimmer moved, and something slashed across his chest, something he couldn't see, and he looked down at the twin red slits in his microfiber shirt, red on the blue fabric, and it sank in that that red was coming out of *him*, it was blood, something had *cut* him. The pain couldn't penetrate the haze of drugs, but he was *cut*, he could see it and feel it.

He swung the Uzi and sprayed the street with bullets but didn't hit anything, and he was scared now, there wasn't anything *there*, so what had cut him?

He turned, looking for his attacker, and a pair of blades plunged into his back, one on either side of his spine.

He flexed once, horribly, and the Uzi flew from his hand to land rattling on the sidewalk; then he slumped and hung limply from an invisible claw.

The blades slashed upward, cutting through ribs.

A few moments later a boy turned the corner and spotted the shape lying on the sidewalk in a puddle of something red.

A drunk lying in spilled wine?

Wine wasn't *that* red.

Paint, maybe?

He edged closer.

"Oh, shit," he said.

It wasn't a drunk.

Drunks have heads; this guy didn't. Something had ripped his head right off.

The boy inched away, then noticed something else lying nearby.

"Awesome!" he said as he snatched up the Uzi.

He looked both ways; no one had seen him, unless it was some nosy old woman looking out a window somewhere.

This was a fine weapon here—should be worth a hundred bucks or more!

He took the gun and ran.

Five minutes after that a woman found the body and ran screaming into the deli in the next block; the man behind the counter called the cops.

When the body had been loaded into the meat wagon, Officer Brownlow glanced at his partner.

"Think this is one for the feds?" he asked.

Ortiz looked up from his notepad. "What, the feds?" he said. "What for?"

"You know, that special bunch with the notices," Brownlow said. "They said they wanted to know about any really bizarre killings."

"They said bodies hung upside down, and people skinned, and like that," Ortiz said. "They said people with guns. You see any guns here?"

"Some shell casings back there."

"So someone dropped 'em—I don't see no guns. Nobody got skinned or nothin'."

"Got his head pulled off."

"You call that bizarre? Come on, they turn a guy inside out, maybe I'd call it bizarre. Those feds, man, they're too *busy* for us to bother 'em with every little detail. Too fuckin' *busy* with our own goddamn shootin' range they sealed off, too goddamn *busy* pokin' their noses into our business. *No*, man, I don't want to tell 'em about this one, any more than Lieutenant Thomas told 'em about the two last night!"

Brownlow nodded.

"Just making sure we understood each other," he said, tucking his own notebook away.

And at Kennedy International, General Philips told his aide, "It's just Schaefer they're after—otherwise there'd have been more killings by now."

And later that night, when Philips's plane was somewhere over the Gulf of Mexico, word reached Carr that someone had taken down Mako and kept his head for a souvenir.

"Shit," he said. It took an effort not to blow away the smirking son of a bitch who'd brought the news, but Carr resisted the temptation.

Besides, it wasn't as much fun with this wussy .38 he was carrying—he'd lost his .357 back on Beekman Street, and he was still royally pissed about that, too. He'd get another, but he hadn't got around to it yet, he'd been busy with more important shit.

Like these killings. T. G. Mako wasn't the first. He wasn't even the second.

Carr had been thinking Mako might take over Edgie's old post, and now Mako was just as dead as Edgie.

"Shit," Carr said again.

Someone was out there cutting down the baddest dudes around—except for Carr himself, of course, who'd been missed in that first big throwdown.

Word on the street said that whoever it was had hit a bunch of cops, too, so it wasn't the feds or the cops deciding to screw the rules and get serious—the self-proclaimed good guys wouldn't play *that* rough, not even if every cop who'd gone down turned out to be on the take.

But it might be some bunch of rogue cops out on their own. It might be that son of a bitch Schaefer and some of his buddies. *He* was crazy enough to try something like this, Carr thought.

He'd denied it, but that didn't mean shit.

After that first massacre Carr had figured it was a one-time thing, something meant to scare the crap out of him, put the fear of God out on the streets, and he'd gone back home and tried to get back to business as usual, tried to put together the leadership he needed to run the whole goddamn show now that that wimp Lamb was meat on a slab. He'd wanted to make sure none of the survivors in Lambikins's bunch got ideas about picking up where Lamb left off—they were *his* boys now, he didn't need fresh competition.

But then someone had iced Tony Blue, ripped his head off in a loft on St. Mark's.

And someone got Q.Q. at his woman's place on Avenue B, and his head was gone, too.

And there were people saying it was Carr's boys finishing off Lamb's gang, and others who said one of Lamb's punks was trying to show how tough he was.

That didn't explain the first massacre or the reports of dead cops, though.

Carr didn't know who the hell it was, or why, but he knew one thing.

He had to stop it.

He wasn't going to be able to do any normal business, wasn't going to get things straightened out, until it stopped.

So he stopped worrying about business. He started lining up muscle.

Sooner or later the killers were going to screw up, and Carr would find out who they were. When that happened, he intended to come down on them *hard*, take them all out in one big hit.

To do that, he needed the baddest men in the city—not just his own people, not a regular gang, but muscle he could call on once, for this one job. He needed to have them standing by, ready to move on a moment's notice. He started compiling a list of phone numbers—his own boys, the toughest of Lamb's survivors, uptown muscle who didn't mind a little freelance work, hard-core muscle from out on the Island, serious bad news from all five boroughs.

Maybe it was Schaefer, maybe it was the Colombians, maybe it was someone else; Carr didn't care.

When he found out who it was, he'd be ready.

16

The town, such as it was, was called Riosucio.

It had taken Schaefer some time to get there.

On the flight from New York to Panama City he had worked out a course of action, from what he remembered of what Dutch had said and his own knowledge of how the drug trade operated in Central America; he couldn't be sure there was any connection between Dutch and the drug-runners, but it was the way he was betting it, at least for the moment.

First stop had been an old friend from Special Forces who'd got himself a job in the DEA; Schaefer had stayed in touch, since it's always useful for a cop working narco to have contacts in the DEA. That was a good way to pick up information that he might miss otherwise.

It wasn't information Schaefer was after this time, though. It was weapons.

He'd seen that thing in the tenement; he'd felt its fist. He'd heard Dutch talk about how unstoppable his theoretical superhunter would be, and Schaefer didn't doubt that the killer he was up against was the same one.

He wasn't about to tackle it bare-handed. He wasn't even planning to take it on with ordinary armaments if he could help it. He wanted something with *real* stopping power, something that would take down anything he ran up against, including an eight-foot monster.

A Vulcan Gatling gun would have been about right, Schaefer thought, but Hanson, his friend at the DEA, couldn't get him one on short notice.

He did all right, though, and not just with weapons—Hanson was able to get Schaefer enough cash, both dollars and the local stuff, to cover whatever other expenses might come up.

Of course, he'd put it all on Schaefer's credit cards, but Schaefer had no complaints, about the money or the ordnance. He owed Hanson a *big* favor now.

Once he was armed, he had to figure out where to go and how to get there.

He was doing all this because he wanted to know more about what he was up against. Dutch had fought it somewhere and had gotten away alive. He'd lost all his men, and maybe the son of a bitch had caught him later, maybe Dutch had been skinned and hung upside down somewhere eventually, but he *had* gotten out alive once.

Maybe he'd left some clues about how he'd managed it. Maybe they were still there, even after eight years, and maybe Schaefer could learn enough from them to ensure that he'd survive, too—and maybe even take the bastard down once and for all.

First, though, Schaefer had to find where it had all gone down.

Dutch hadn't given him a map, but he'd talked about his rescue mission, and Schaefer could remember damn near every word. Dutch had talked about coptering in over the Pacific, then going up over a ridge and across a border, then heading northeast down a valley to make pickup.

Schaefer had put that together with whatever other information he could come up with, had bought himself a ride north out of Panama, and had followed his conclusions as far as he could, into the back country, to where the roads ended and there was only jungle—and that had eventually brought him to Riosucio, where his last ride had refused to go any further no matter what Schaefer paid.

Schaefer had shrugged and put out word of what he wanted through all the local channels. He'd settled in and made a table in the local saloon his headquarters.

It had all taken time, time when that thing might be killing innocent people back in New York, but Schaefer had to live with that—he didn't see any other way to get at the thing, and besides, it gave him time to heal up. He didn't much care to go into the rematch with his ribs still aching or his jaw still sore.

Riosucio was little more than a clearing in the

jungle where a dozen huts, built in the traditional palapa style, were gathered. The polite liberals back in the Big Apple could call the green hell a rain forest if they wanted, but as far as Schaefer was concerned, and as far as the locals were concerned, it was jungle, sweltering hot and thoroughly hostile, and it was all around.

The saloon where Schaefer made himself at home was the showplace of Riosucio; it had a floor of smooth black dirt with good drainage and nothing growing on it, and the roof was tin over planking, rather than thatch. It didn't leak enough to water the drinks, which Schaefer considered a plus, since the bartender watered them enough to begin with. The windows had shutters, but no glass—which didn't really matter, since the screen door had holes big enough to let in buzzards, and even the biggest of the mutant mosquitoes in the jungle outside could fit through if they tried.

There were no ceiling fans, no electric lights, and the idea of air-conditioning was the wildest of fantasies here; the air felt as hot and thick as soup, and the inside of the saloon was no different in that regard from the jungle outside. The lessened air circulation was roughly balanced by the greatly reduced sunlight.

Far more important than any of this, from Schaefer's point of view, was the fact that Riosucio was built at the foot of the ridge that marked the border between this particular stretch of malarial rain forest claiming to be a nation, and the next, equally backward chunk of jungle.

As the real-estate folks said, location, location, location. Riosucio might not have much, but as far as Schaefer was concerned, it had the right location.

Dutch had gone over that ridge, Schaefer was sure. Dutch had said that his rescue mission was hush-hush stuff because of the risk of starting a war, and at the time, this particular pair of banana republics had been closest to escalating their perpetual disagreements and border incidents into something bloodier and more formal.

They weren't anymore, and as Schaefer sat at his chosen table, he wondered whether Dutch had had anything to do with this inexplicable bout of reasonableness, or whether it had just been one small part of the general political shifts of the last decade.

"*¿Otra cerveza, señor?*" the bartender asked.

"*Sí,*" Schaefer replied, looking up. "And don't spit in it this time."

He had no idea whether the bartender understood the English; around here Spanish was usually a second or third language, after the local Indio dialect and maybe Maya, and English was a long shot at best.

He noticed a shadow on the screen and turned to face the door.

A man in green fatigues, tire-tread sandals, and a wide-brimmed green hat stepped in—tall, by local standards, and bearded. He stood for a moment, letting his eyes adjust, while the bartender delivered Schaefer's beer.

Schaefer paid for the bottle without ever letting his attention leave the newcomer, and left the beer sitting untouched on the table.

The man in fatigues had no visible weapons anywhere, but that looked somehow unnatural—he was plainly a man who *ought* to be armed.

He spotted Schaefer quickly enough; there weren't many men in the place, and of those few there was only one of Schaefer's size and with his blond hair. Even in the dimness Schaefer was very obviously a *norteamericano*.

The stranger crossed the room to Schaefer's table and looked down at him.

"I understand that you are looking for a guide," he said in clear but accented English.

"Word travels fast," Schaefer replied, finally picking up the beer and taking a swig. "Sit down."

The man sat.

"I'm told you're a policeman from New York," he said after a moment. "That you have many enemies among the La Costa, the Medellin, the Cali."

"You have a problem with that?" Schaefer asked.

"No," the guide said with a toothy smile. "It just means I charge more."

Schaefer shrugged. "It shouldn't matter anyway. I'm not interested in drugs this time; I'm looking for some *norteamericanos* who disappeared over the border eight years back."

"Eight years?" the guide asked.

Schaefer nodded. "That's right."

"Eight years is a long time *señor*."

Schaefer shrugged. "I've been busy. Didn't get around to it until now."

"These men—they were all men? No women?"

"The *norteamericanos*, *sí*, all men. Six of them." Dutch's squad had been six men.

And five of them had died somewhere in this goddamn steam bath.

"The way you say that," the guide asked, "were there others? You say you are looking for these six?"

"There may have been others, but that's who I'm looking for," Schaefer agreed. "Them, and something else, something that comes with the heat."

The guide considered him thoughtfully.

"And what would this be, that comes with the heat?" the guide asked. "A man?"

"I don't know," Schaefer said. "That's what I want to find out."

"Ah," the guide said, smiling. "I see. You're *mad*, Mr. New York policeman. Which means I charge even more."

Schaefer smiled back.

"I think we're gonna get along fine," he said.

17

It took another day in Riosucio to put everything together.

Schaefer had thought he had all the supplies he needed, but the guide had other ideas. He found two mules and stocked up on rope, blankets, camping gear, and arcane herbal remedies, as well as more mundane concerns such as food and fresh water and a few boxes he didn't bother to open for his unappreciative gringo employer.

No weapons were visible anywhere in the guide's acquisitions, though, not even a knife. Schaefer noticed that and asked about it.

The guide shrugged. "You have already done that, *señor*. I will trust you to have what we need."

Later, as they were climbing the ridge, the mules zigzagging back and forth up the slope, the guide told Schaefer that he used to do recon work for the

143

U.S. military. Schaefer didn't argue with that or ask for proof—but he didn't necessarily believe it, either.

The guide might trust Schaefer as far as the armaments went, but Schaefer didn't trust the guide, about weapons or previous recon work or anything else.

But, then, Schaefer didn't trust much of anyone, and nobody at all in that particular hellhole.

"What you're looking for, these six men who came here eight years ago," the guide had said, "I think for that, you want to head up to Mangabe."

Schaefer decided not to ask what gave him that idea. He just shrugged and followed.

They camped in the jungle, on the south side of the ridge, each night a little higher than the night before.

Early on the third day after leaving Riosucio the guide announced that they were crossing the border; Schaefer took his word for it. One stretch of hilly jungle looked like another, as far as he was concerned, and crossing the border didn't make the air any cooler, the humidity any less, the undergrowth any easier to get through.

The only difference Schaefer could see was that the ground was now mostly sloping downward, rather than up. They'd crossed the top of the ridge, as well.

Half a day later the two men and their pack mules arrived at a spot in the jungle where the guide stopped, smiling, and waited expectantly.

He didn't say anything, just waited, and it took Schaefer a moment to realize that he was supposed to be seeing something, that something here made this particular place different from the rest of the country.

He looked, but at first he saw only more of the damned jungle; then he made out the straight lines in the greenery ahead, the colors that weren't quite right, and put it all together.

This was what the guide wanted to show him, what the guide had been aiming for. Schaefer was looking at the remains of a camp of some kind.

He grunted, to let the guide know that he had eventually figured it out. Then he dismounted and walked cautiously forward.

It had been a good-sized encampment once. There had been several buildings, walls of bamboo or corrugated tin over wood frame, roofs of thatch—the traditional Central American palapa design.

Here some of the floors had been stone and concrete, though, and that was not anything any of the ordinary villagers around here would bother with.

Eight years of neglect and tropically enthusiastic plant growth had reduced the pavements to mere fragments, of course, as well as ruining just about everything else. Two buildings, off to one side, were still standing, overgrown with greenery; the others were mostly green mounds of wreckage, full of rustling birds and squeaking rodents and an occasional snake that fled when Schaefer came near.

As he poked around in the ruins, Schaefer found a rusted blackened metal object he eventually identified as the burned-out remains of a helicopter. Other, smaller objects might have been a flatbed truck and a generator, and elsewhere there were fragments of steel drums, pieces of ammo boxes, sections of stone flooring, some of it burned, all of it encrusted with moss and vines.

There were no bodies, but after eight years there wouldn't be.

The guide said something about guerrillas and rebels; Schaefer didn't bother to listen to that. It was clear enough, even now.

This had been a staging area of some sort, and someone had come calling with some heavy-duty shit. Brass shell casings, turned to green and black corruption by the jungle, were strewn everywhere; Schaefer could see blast patterns in the debris and rapid-fire trails in the burned-out and rusted remains of vehicles and machinery.

Schaefer had a pretty good idea who it was who'd dropped in. It smelled like one of his brother's operations—messy, but thorough.

He wondered why. Dutch had been in the rescue business, not search-and-destroy; had there been hostages here?

There could have been, certainly.

So if Dutch had gone in after hostages, had he gotten them out?

Did it matter?

How did this relate to the thing Schaefer had fought in New York, the thing that had slaughtered Lamb and his men and butchered everyone in the police firing range? Dutch wouldn't have lost all his men in an operation like this, an ordinary hostage recovery—that sort of stunt had been his bread and butter.

Had that monster been one of the camp's defenders? Or might it have been sent to retrieve the hostages after Dutch rescued them?

Schaefer frowned, then returned to his mule. There wasn't anything here that was going to help him; he could spend weeks digging through the rubbish, and he doubted he'd find a clue if he tried it.

"There are no winners in a place like this," the guide said sententiously. "Only the jungle."

"Shut up," Schaefer told him as he swung himself awkwardly into the saddle. He wasn't in the mood to hear bad movie dialogue. If the guide thought that sort of crap was going to impress anyone, he'd picked the wrong employer.

"Which way?" he asked when he had his mount under control again.

"How am I to say, *señor*?" the guide asked.

Schaefer turned in the saddle and glared at him. The guide's smile vanished.

"Ah . . . perhaps this way," he said, pointing.

Schaefer nodded and followed as the guide rode on.

A mile or two past the camp they headed northeast, down a narrow valley—it didn't look like the best route to Schaefer, but the guide led the way, and Schaefer didn't argue.

The jungle looked different here—thicker, and somehow almost alien. Schaefer could see it in the trees, the plants, everything.

And it was hotter than ever.

On the fourth day after leaving Riosucio they crossed a small river, then picked their way down the side of a cliff into a broader valley where a good-sized river flowed. Here the jungle was even stranger. Schaefer looked around warily, trying to

decide whether the strangeness had anything unnatural about it.

"Do you feel it?" the guide asked, noticing
Schaefer's discomfort. "You said you were looking
for a thing that comes in the heat?"

It was hot enough, certainly.

"This is where the natives say the sun appeared
at midnight once, on a very hot night eight years
ago," the guide said with a sweeping gesture.

Schaefer didn't answer; he was staring ahead.

There was a break in the jungle, a hole where
golden sunlight poured in.

There was more than that, Schaefer saw as his
mule emerged into the light.

There was a crater.

Most of it was green, of course—nothing could
hold the jungle back for long. At the bottom lay a
pool of mud and water, but ferns and creepers covered the bowl, the trees around the rim were already well over Schaefer's head.

It was still plain that sometime not all that very
long ago, something had cut a hole in the jungle a
quarter mile across, had blasted away everything.

Any normal explosion big enough to do that
should have taken truckloads of explosives, and
there should be visible wreckage, even now, and
there wasn't.

"My God," Schaefer said, staring, "what the hell
happened here?"

He sat and looked at the devastation for a moment longer, then demanded, "And what the hell
did that bastard do to my brother?"

He wondered whether he was looking at Dutch's
grave.

Probably not, since he knew Dutch had gotten out of here alive once, but had he come back? Had he died here?

If not Dutch, had his men died here? Billy, and Hawkins, and Blain, and the rest?

And he also wondered what a Geiger counter would register here. That crater looked big enough to have been made by a small nuke.

Who would be throwing that kind of ordnance around?

He spent the remainder of the afternoon criss-crossing that crater, looking for some sign of what had happened, something that might tell him what he was up against.

He didn't find it. There were no fragments, no scraps of wreckage, nothing he could find to indicate what had made that hole.

At last he slogged back up out of the mud and asked the guide, "Now what?"

The guide shrugged. "I do not know," he said. "The trail ends here."

Schaefer knew that for bullshit; the guide hadn't been following any trail. He had known where to go. Schaefer supposed the destroyed rebel base and this crater were famous; all the locals would have heard of them, would know they dated back to eight years ago. This would be the natural place to lead someone who came looking for men who had vanished eight years ago.

But that seemed to be all this man knew, or at least all he would admit to.

It looked as if it might be another dead end—but Schaefer wasn't in any hurry to give up.

"We camp here," he said.

The guide shrugged.

That night Schaefer sat up late by the fire, thinking—thinking, and remembering.

He remembered that Dutch had talked about the thing as a hunter.

He remembered how, as kids, he and Dutch would hunt in the woods behind their father's cabin. They hadn't looked on it as a *sport*, exactly—it was a *challenge*, being on their own, testing themselves against nature.

One year, on the opening day of deer season, the two of them had come across a bunch of local boys shooting up the woods. The lot of them had been drinking since daybreak, from the look of it, and they had this weird *look* in their eyes.

Schaefer had figured they were all trying to impress each other with how wild and tough they were.

Then Schaefer saw what they were shooting at. They'd cornered a buck and took turns pumping slugs into it, watching it bleed in the cool October air.

Schaefer'd been disgusted by it, by the unnecessary sloppy viciousness of it, the waste and the pain, but then he'd realized that those boys weren't really all that different from Dutch and himself. They were out there, pitting themselves against nature by killing deer.

The only difference was that those boys needed to be wired up, needed to drive themselves into a killing frenzy, needed to see the blood. They had to make it into a perverse sort of *fun*, or they couldn't do it at all.

Schaefer had thought that over carefully. He'd

thought it over, and he'd decided that there was a world of difference between killing because you have to, to do whatever it is you're out to do, and killing because it's *fun*.

Schaefer had decided he didn't want to kill for fun, and after that day he never had.

But that didn't mean he hadn't killed.

He was staring into the dying embers of the fire, thinking about that, when the thing in his neck suddenly jabbed at him—not digging into the artery, but doing *something*, something that *hurt*.

Even distracted by the pain, he knew what that had to mean. He hadn't felt anything like it before, but he'd have to be an idiot not to understand.

The thing that had marked him was getting his attention, letting him know it hadn't forgotten him.

And it wouldn't bother doing that if it was still back in New York; it must have followed him.

"Son of a *bitch*," he growled, clenching his fists in pain. "He's *here!*"

He looked around, scanning the jungle.

He didn't see it anywhere.

He knew it was out there, though. Maybe he wasn't going to find any clues to the thing's origins here, maybe the crater wouldn't tell him anything, but he'd have a chance to tackle it again.

And if he could kill it, who would care where it had come from?

18

The guide watched with interest as Schaefer unpacked and checked out some of the little presents he'd gotten from his pal in the DEA. He'd built the fire back up enough that both men could see what Schaefer was doing.

"That is a very big rifle," the guide remarked at one point as Schaefer assembled the contents of a steel suitcase.

Schaefer hefted the weapon in question. "This?" he said. "This isn't a rifle. It's a shotgun—full auto. Six rounds a second. You hear it popping, you get the hell out of here, *comprende*?"

"*Comprendo,*" the guide replied.

That shotgun was the centerpiece of Schaefer's armament, but he also had a more ordinary automatic rifle slung on his back, and grenades and knives on his belt. He wanted to be *ready* when he met that big ugly sucker.

The twanging sensation in his neck was getting stronger; Schaefer assumed that meant the thing was getting closer, and he tried to hurry. He didn't want to be standing there chatting with the guide when it came for him; he didn't want the mules to get caught in the cross fire.

He didn't want to screw up by rushing, either; he checked each weapon carefully but quickly. He had to work by firelight, which didn't help any.

There were flashlights and a lamp in the packs of supplies, but Schaefer had no intention of using them. That would make him a bit too visible.

When his preparations were complete, he told the guide, "Stay here." Then, with the auto shotgun held at ready, he charged off into the jungle, choosing his direction more or less at random, more concerned with getting away from the mules and finding someplace with cover so the bastard couldn't just pick him off from a distance like some stupid two-point buck hanging around a clearing, than with getting to any particular destination.

The throbbing lessened slightly as he moved into the blackness of the surrounding jungle, and Schaefer began to weave back and forth, moving slowly and as silently as he could in the tropical darkness, trying to figure out from the sensation just where his enemy was, and which way it was moving.

It wasn't hard to estimate; when he moved toward it, the gadget hurt more, and when he moved away, it hurt less. Simple enough. Before he'd covered half a mile, he thought he knew where the creature was.

It had caught him by surprise, back there in New York, but this time he was ready; this time he knew what he was up against—oh, maybe not what the thing *was*, or where it came from, or what it was doing here, but he knew roughly how big and how strong and how fast it was.

Bigger and stronger and faster than *he* was, Schaefer knew that, but somehow he didn't care; he was sure he could handle it anyway.

For one thing, the arrogant bastard was probably planning on some kind of one-on-one duel, a "test of wills," all that macho crap. Why else would it have warned him with the gadget on his neck? That was bluster, a challenge, an invitation to come out and fight like a man. It wanted to prove how tough it was in a fair fight.

Schaefer wasn't worried about proving his manhood; he just wanted the thing dead.

The best way to do that, he figured, would be to come up behind it and blow its head off. With that in mind he was circling around, trying to come at it in a contracting spiral; it would know he was getting closer, but with any luck it wouldn't know which direction he was in.

"You want a *mano a mano*, creep?" he muttered to himself. "That it? Hand to hand, may the best man win? Well, fuck that, you can just kiss my . . ."

Blue-white fire exploded from a tree behind him, turning the forest darkness to bleached-out chaos. The roar echoed through the darkness beyond.

"Wha . . ." Schaefer whirled. "Shit!" He dropped, diving behind the nearest available plant life.

The thing fired again; this time Schaefer saw the flash as he dived, saw the charge, whatever it was, coming in; the instant he touched dirt, he flung himself aside.

The blast tore through another tree; for a moment it hung, suspended by the tangle of vines and branches, then it sagged and toppled.

By the time the echoes of the initial explosion had faded, and well before the shattered tree thumped into the surrounding jungle, Schaefer had taken cover behind a low ridge of stone that thrust up through the undergrowth.

"So much for *mano a mano*," he muttered, annoyed at himself for making assumptions about what the thing wanted.

But on the other hand, that first shot hadn't been anywhere near him—a warning shot, he guessed. The bastard did want the hunt and the kill to be a challenge.

The second shot had been serious, though. The hunter wasn't going to be obsessive about making things hard on itself.

And that shot had been damn close, despite the darkness. Could the thing see in the dark? Was it using infrared or some other sort of high-tech stuff to aim?

Another shower of blue-white fireworks blossomed up from the other side of the rocks.

"Okay, that's two," Schaefer said. "My turn!"

He jumped up, shotgun ready, and cut loose, spraying slugs at the point those blasts had come from. He couldn't aim properly in the dark, not with the risk of incoming fire, but he'd gotten a pretty fair idea where that last fireball had come from.

The roar of the gun on full auto was deafening, and its flash lit the jungle a sick yellow-green.

Schaefer was aiming at the crotch of a tree, but he realized he couldn't see anything there but flying wood chips and leaf fragments as his slugs tore through the greenery.

He released the trigger and dived sideways, looking for cover.

His hearing was no use to him; his ears were ringing from the shotgun's thunderous report, and he cursed himself for not considering that when he chose his weapons. His eyes were slowly adjusting to the darkness again, now that no weapons were flashing; he crept forward through the underbrush.

He didn't hear any movement—but his ears weren't working. He couldn't see anything moving, either, but it was fucking *dark*. The monster might be right on top of him, and he wouldn't know it—or it might be back in its tree.

It wasn't shooting at him, though.

Had he hit the thing, knocked it right out of that tree? Killed it, or at least wounded it?

Or was it hiding somewhere? Had it dived for shelter in time?

Could it dive out of a tree that high without injury? Schaefer knew that *he* couldn't have.

But the creature was bigger and stronger and faster than he was.

He couldn't tell if he had hit it, so he decided to take the battle to it, to try to take the initiative. Shotgun in one hand, assault rifle in the other, he charged out of concealment toward the tree.

Bad move.

He didn't even see what hit him.

He didn't understand that; how could he not *see* something that big, even in the jungle dark, if it was close enough to hit him? His ears were still out, but his eyes were okay, weren't they?

But he *didn't* see it—just something slammed him across the chest and he went over backward, weapons flying.

He landed rolling, he had enough self-control for that, and he came up with a grenade in his hand.

Something shimmered faintly in the moonlight, and he pulled the pin, but then he held the grenade, trying to see his target before he threw.

It wasn't the creature he had fought in New York, with its yellowish skin; that would have shown up at this distance. Instead, there was something green and black and hard to see even though it was only a few yards away. . . .

Camouflage. That damned perfect camouflage. It *was* the same creature. The *size* was right.

He threw the grenade.

The thing dived aside in plenty of time—he couldn't really see it, but he could make out the faintest flicker of movement, like leaves in the wind; he'd forgotten how fast it was. Dodging grenades was easy for it, Schaefer thought as he flattened, covering his eyes against the grenade's flash to preserve his night vision.

What little hearing had returned was gone again, and the ringing in his ears was an entire carillon; shredded bark and leaves and dirt showered over him.

The instant the debris stopped falling, Schaefer

lifted his head, scanning the jungle quickly. The bastard had been moving *that* way. . . .

Blue sparks were crawling through the darkness, ten feet away; ribbons of electricity were twisting around a dark outline, and the whole thing flickered like a TV screen in a thunderstorm, sometimes the green-and-black section of jungle, sometimes something else.

It was moving closer.

And then it flashed once, and the flickering was gone, and the creature he had fought in New York was standing there over him, looking down at him.

It had replaced its mask, he saw—maybe it needed it to breathe.

It had maybe changed its clothes, too—Schaefer hadn't gotten a really good look at it in his few seconds in that dim fifth-floor room, and he wasn't exactly studying its qualifications for Mr. Blackwell's list now, either, but some of the details seemed a bit different.

For one thing, something was dripping from its arm, something greenish yellow that glowed like liquid neon; either the shotgun or a grenade fragment had hit something wet.

And the grenade must have taken out the camouflage—as he had guessed, it wasn't just face paint and fancy clothes, but some kind of electronic gadget, practically an invisibility screen.

If that worked as well with asphalt and concrete as it did with trees and vines . . . Schaefer understood now how the thing had been able to move through New York so easily without ever being spotted.

And if that glowing stuff was the creature's

blood, and not just the equivalent of hydraulic fluid for its gadgets, Schaefer thought, it was hurt. If it could bleed, it could die.

He came up fast, as fast as he could, combat knife in his hand, and the blade punched through the thing's mesh and into its grayish flesh.

"This is for Dutch!" Schaefer shouted.

The sound was muffled; his hearing was still shot.

The creature roared in pain, and that, too, was dull, almost inaudible. Before Schaefer could even think about dodging, its foot came up and kicked him away, hard. The knife stayed in its side.

Schaefer guessed that the bastard hadn't expected anything like that.

He had it figured; this thing chased and killed people for the sport, like a big-game hunter. It didn't expect to get hurt. The game was supposed to struggle, but it wasn't supposed to fight back; to the creature, people were *prey*, not competition.

So he'd surprised it.

But the surprise was all done now. When he landed, he scrambled up and headed away from the thing; he couldn't fight it on even terms, not even with a knife in its side. He'd lost both his guns; the monster hadn't, it still had that weird little cannon on its shoulder, the one that had blown holes through the walls back in New York and had chopped down trees here in the jungle.

Schaefer thought it wouldn't want to *use* the cannon, not at close range—that wouldn't be sporting. But if he came at it again, while it was wounded, it might decide to play it safe and blow him away.

So he ran and hoped that the thing would be too busy with the knife wound to come after him right away.

He figured that while it was distracted, he could get back to the mules and put together enough firepower to handle the son of a bitch—even with the auto shotgun gone, there was plenty more in that case from Hanson at the DEA.

Then his foot slipped, and he caught himself at the last second.

He'd lost track of where he was, which way he was going, and had just come within inches of charging right off a cliff into the river.

"Oh, *shit!*" he said, and he still couldn't hear his own voice.

And before he could step back, the thing's claw closed on his head from behind, its fingers over his eyes, the long black talons digging into his cheeks.

He hadn't heard a thing, hadn't known it was there. Even without its invisibility gadget, it was better at concealment than it had any right to be.

It picked him up, lifted him up by that grip on his head, and for a moment Schaefer dangled as helplessly as a puppy; then it flung him against the nearest tree.

He landed hard and sat, stunned and unable to move, as the thing marched up to him.

He looked up at it and spat, still defiant despite his helplessness.

"You ought to tell your hairdresser," he wheezed as he saw the black, banded tendrils dangling down either side of the creature's head swaying and catching the moonlight, "that Rasta shit's been out of style for years."

He didn't know whether he had actually spoken aloud or not; his ears were still out.

Then the thing reached down for him, and Schaefer flung his hand up, grabbing the bottom of its mask.

After all, it had almost worked in New York.

This time, though, the mask didn't come free. It twisted, and the thing stepped back to straighten it, stepped away from Schaefer, and he had the second or two he needed to recover his wits.

Schaefer rolled and grabbed up a fallen branch as thick as his own leg. He came up swinging and caught the creature solidly on the side of the head with the limb, twisting the mask back out of line.

The blow would have killed a man, but this bastard didn't even stagger. It just flung up an arm to ward Schaefer off and turned away, using its other hand to straighten the crooked helmet.

It was standing on the edge of the cliff, facing away from him, partially blinded and thoroughly distracted, its camouflage still not working, and Schaefer knew this had to be the best shot he would ever have, maybe his *last* shot; he lowered his makeshift club into a spear and charged.

The wood splintered with the impact, and Schaefer was knocked backward; the creature tottered, swayed, and then fell over the brink.

Schaefer's hearing was beginning to return, finally—enough that he heard the sound of the impact.

At first he thought his ears were still fucked up somehow, because it wasn't a thud, like a body hitting the ground; it was a crunch.

He waited, dazed, for the creature to climb back up.

When it didn't, he crept forward and peered over the edge, half expecting a blue-white fireball to take his head off at any minute, or a claw to grab his face.

Nothing hit him; nothing moved.

The creature was lying there motionless, sprawled across the trunk of a fallen tree, with a big smear of that yellow-green goop across its chest, glowing in the darkness and lighting the scene.

And thrusting up from the center of that luminous smear was a pointed, broken-off tree branch that had punched right through the bastard.

That didn't necessarily mean the fight was over, Schaefer tried to tell himself. Maybe that wasn't where the creature's heart was. Maybe it was not just bigger and stronger than anything human, but tougher in ways Schaefer couldn't even imagine. Maybe there were still some surprises in it.

But maybe not.

To Schaefer, the thing looked deader than hell.

19

The guide was sitting on a tree root beside the fire, waiting.

He wasn't really sure just what he was waiting for—dawn, perhaps?

Not for Schaefer, certainly; Schaefer wouldn't be coming back.

He supposed he might hear a scream.

He hoped not, though. This whole assignment was bad enough without that.

He looked around the campsite once again, his hands nervously checking his pockets and belt to make sure he had no weapons, nothing that could be mistaken for a weapon. If he stayed unarmed, he should be all right.

The thing that had killed all those men eight years ago had let the woman with them go, because she wasn't armed. And they'd told him that the one that had slaughtered all those cops in New York had left that one cop, Salvati, alive, because he wasn't armed.

The guide did not want to be armed.

He didn't have so much as a pocketknife, which had made it a little tricky to keep the fire going, but he had managed it—and he had been careful never to pick up anything that was burning, as a brand could be a weapon.

He suspected there were more weapons in Schaefer's baggage, which was one reason he never touched it, never even considered searching it or pilfering anything.

If a jaguar or a snake attacked him, he'd have to rely on his bare hands—but it was worth the risk.

Leaves rustled, and he looked up warily.

Something was approaching, something that walked upright, a dark shadow against the moonlight; he froze.

It stepped out into the circle of firelight, and he recognized Schaefer.

Detective Schaefer, alive and with all his limbs intact.

The guide's jaw dropped.

"Shit, you're *alive!*" he said. He saw the gun Schaefer was carrying, and that was another shock—Schaefer was alive, and *armed*. "But what about the . . . I mean . . ."

The only possible explanation sank in.

"*Oh, my God!*" he said.

He sprang up as Schaefer dropped the gun and settled heavily against a tree.

"Ummm . . . ," Schaefer said wearily, "is it my

imagination, or is your English suddenly improving?"

"Laugh it up, Schaefer," the guide said as he threw open the leather flap on one of his saddlebags and pulled up a telescoping antenna. "Christ, I don't *believe* this."

Schaefer sprawled comfortably and watched, amused, as the guide worked controls.

A crackle of white noise came from the saddlebag, and then an electronic voice said, "This is Capa-Alpha, over."

The guide picked up a microphone and said, "Capa-Alpha, this is Decoy-Niner. Get me the CO—*now*."

He waited, staring at Schaefer.

"You really did it, didn't you?" he asked quietly. "You killed it."

Schaefer smiled and nodded.

Maybe, Schaefer thought, he could get some answers now. Maybe he could get an explanation as to what the hell was going on, what that thing was he'd killed, what had happened to Dutch, all of it.

Or maybe not, but what the hell, he'd *got* it, he'd beat it, and it wasn't going to leave any more flayed corpses hanging from the rafters in New York, not in *Schaefer's* city.

Somewhere off the coast a radioman told General Philips, "Sir, I'm getting a signal from Decoy-Niner—says he wants to talk to you."

Philips nodded unhappily; he'd been expecting this call, but not looking forward to it. He crossed the room and picked up the mike.

"This is Philips, Niner," he said wearily. "Prepare

whatever's left of Schaefer's body for transport back to the States, and . . ."

The speaker crackled, interrupting him.

"Sir, you don't *understand*," Decoy-Niner's voice said. "Schaefer's *alive*. He *killed* it. Repeat, Schaefer's *still alive!*"

In the jungle, in the little ring of firelight, Schaefer smiled and threw his guide a sardonic salute.

The guide stood by the placid mule, staring at Schaefer, the microphone in his hand.

"Oh, my God," Philips whispered. He went pale.

Another one of the creatures had died. Last time that had meant a miniature nuke took out a chunk of jungle, but this time it wasn't just one lone hunter—the things were all over New York.

Anything might happen now.

"Stand by, Niner," he said. He turned. "Perkins," he shouted, "radio Washington, scramble everything—we're going on full combat alert. And get me the President—the shit's about to hit the fan!"

Perkins hurried, and Philips tried to think.

One of the things was dead—but there hadn't been any blast. Dutch had described how the one he had killed had done something with the device it wore on its left wrist, and that that had caused the explosion—perhaps this one hadn't had time to set the device before it died?

But, then, it was still lying out there in the jungle somewhere, with all that alien technology, just waiting to be found. . . .

"General," someone called, "we have a report from the radar analysts—they're picking up activity of some kind."

"Shit," Philips said. He looked down at his hand and realized he was still holding the butt of a cigar; he stubbed it out and tossed it away in disgust.

Was it starting already? Did the things know about the death? Were they already preparing their retaliation?

What would happen if Philips could get his men to the corpse before the aliens could collect their fallen comrade?

Was it worth the risk?

"The President, sir," Perkins said.

"Damn," Philips said. "Get me those radar men—I'll want to talk to them as soon as the President hangs up." He picked up the microphone.

"Sir," he said, "I'm afraid I have bad news."

He explained the situation quickly; the President had been briefed before, of course, and he followed the explanation readily.

"You know the situation better than I do, General," he said. "I'll trust your judgment on this—but you know my position. We can't afford to fight; we can't afford to come out in the open. I don't like appeasement any more than you do, but in this case I don't think we can afford anything else—so give them what they need to keep them happy."

"And the dead one . . ."

"I don't have the information I need to make the call on that, General. Do whatever you think best—but let's keep the risks to a minimum. We're playing for stakes we can't afford to lose."

"Yes, sir."

The connection broke.

And that left Philips holding the bag.

The radar report was next.

Something had left New York—and not at any measly six hundred miles per hour this time; it was moving so fast that the radar had lost it almost immediately.

It had been heading south, though.

"Was it all of them?" Philips asked.

"No," came the reply—surprisingly unequivocal, for once. "No, most of 'em are still in New York."

Holding the city hostage, Philips thought.

Maybe two could play at that game. Maybe he could find something to trade, something to give them in exchange for New York.

The aliens had never wanted to communicate, and there'd never been any way to force the issue, but maybe, just maybe, that had changed. There might be something out there in the jungle those bastards wanted enough that they'd talk in order to get it.

And if he could get them to talk, maybe he could get them to lay off New York, stay out of American cities. Maybe he could barter for some of their gadgets.

This might be a disaster, they might just torch everything in retaliation—or it might be the greatest opportunity humanity had ever had.

"Get a squad ready," he barked. "Choppers loaded. We've got a pickup to make." He smiled grimly and reached for another cigar.

"Maybe two," he added as he lit the cigar.

Then he reached for the microphone to give Decoy-Niner his new instructions.

20

After a day back in the city, doing nothing but worrying about Shari and the boys, Rasche decided he couldn't stand to stay home any longer.

There weren't any calls on the answering machine at the house; a call to the department told him he hadn't had any calls there, either.

So there was no word from Schaefer.

He did call Shari's mother—from a pay phone, just in case—and she reported that everything was fine, Shari and the boys were there in Elmira, safe and well.

Rasche talked to his wife, and the sound of her voice was a relief. He reassured her that he was fine, too.

But he couldn't talk to her forever—his supply of

change wouldn't holdout, and he didn't want to use a calling card, since that would leave a record.

He went home, and after a day he couldn't stand it anymore; he phoned in to say he'd cut his vacation short and would be in the next day.

McComb grumbled; it was obvious he'd just as soon never see Rasche again, but he could hardly argue.

Then Rasche went down to Police Plaza and picked up a portable police radio and spent the evening installing it in the rental van, just in case.

That first morning back at work was dismal—the paperwork had piled up during his absence, but he couldn't concentrate on it. He kept thinking about Shari, out there in Elmira, hours away, and he kept remembering those swaying flayed corpses on the fifth floor on Beekman Street and in the basement on Twentieth, and he kept having nightmare visions of Shari hanging upside down with her skin peeled off, dripping blood in slow circles on the floor of her mother's front hall.

He couldn't even imagine where Schaefer might be, or what might have happened to him.

Some kind of hunter, Schaefer's brother had said—but what did that mean? How was that different from any ordinary hit man? Why did this hunter skin his victims?

Did he *always* skin his victims?

And how many had there actually been? Did Rasche know about all of them, or were there some the feds had managed to keep quiet?

It was on the way back from lunch that Officer Brownlow caught him in the hallway.

"'Scuse me, sir," he said as he brushed Rasche's sleeve. "You're Detective Rasche?"

Rasche admitted it. He'd been taking a cup of coffee back to his desk, and he sipped it, then asked, "And who're you, the Easter Bunny?"

Brownlow introduced himself.

"I understand you're Detective Schaefer's partner? The one who got thrown out at Twentieth Street?"

"It was the scene at Beekman where he got *thrown* out," Rasche corrected. "At Twentieth Street they just politely asked us to go away."

Brownlow nodded. "Right," he said. "Well, I thought you might be interested in a couple of recent cases, sir. Nothing special, you understand, nothing that would interest the feds, but I thought you might want to take a look."

Rasche stared at him over the rim of the coffee cup.

"Oh? What sort of cases?"

"It'd be easier to show you the files, sir." He held up a thick sheaf of manila folders.

Rasche figured he wasn't going to get anything more important done anyway; he nodded, and the two men returned to Rasche's office.

Brownlow wouldn't tell him anything more; he left the folders on the desk and departed.

Rasche sighed and opened the first folder.

He spent the afternoon going over the cases that Officer Brownlow and others like him in the NYPD had decided wouldn't interest the feds.

Brownlow was right, though; the cases definitely interested Rasche. And they answered the question he'd wondered about earlier.

No, Rasche saw, it seemed that the hunter–hit man didn't always skin his victims—not if that was really who was responsible for these killings.

But when he didn't skin them, he took their heads and spines—he didn't just detach them, he *took* them. None of the heads had been found anywhere.

And, Rasche realized, they'd never found any of the skin from the other victims. It was just gone.

Heads . . . that wasn't unheard of. Killers had done that often enough. From ancient conquerors to sex killers, lots of people had cut off heads and taken them as trophies.

But spines?

Or skins?

This guy—if it *was* just one guy, which Rasche was beginning to doubt, despite what Schaefer thought—was very weird indeed. He remembered what Schaefer had said about the fight on Beekman—that his opponent hadn't been human.

Maybe Schaefer was right.

Hours after his shift ended, Rasche was still at his desk, but he was no longer even pretending to work. He just couldn't bring himself to leave the office.

After all, where would he go? Home, to an empty house? Shari and the kids were upstate; going home would just be depressing. It was too early to go to bed; the sun hadn't even set yet; it was one of those long summer afternoon that seems to go on forever.

And there wasn't anything to do at home but sleep—assuming he *could* sleep, knowing that that killer was out there somewhere roaming the city, ripping people apart and taking pieces as souvenirs.

And if Schaefer called, he'd probably call the office—at least Rasche thought so, but he could never be sure. Even after six years he didn't understand how Schaefer's mind worked. Sometimes Schaefer was smart and sharp and right on top of everything, and sometimes he'd be off in the twilight zone somewhere.

And right now he was off in Central America or Colombia or some goddamned place, and he hadn't bothered to call in.

Unless he'd tried calling the house while Rasche was here at the office.

But if he couldn't reach Rasche there, he'd have tried the office.

So he hadn't tried. He was still playing it solo. Rasche hated that; he was supposed to be Schaef's partner.

Not that he was about to fly off to Central America; he was too old and out of shape to go slogging through the jungle with Schaefer looking for monsters.

And Dutch had been Schaefer's brother, not his; Rasche had never met him. He wouldn't know what he was looking for, following Dutch's trail.

And Schaefer was the one who'd been Special Forces; Rasche's military career had consisted of a couple of years at Fort Bragg picking up cigarette butts. If it came down to some kind of pitched battle, Rasche wouldn't be much help.

But Schaefer still should have called.

So Rasche sat in his office, ignoring the stack of unfinished reports and the case files on three dozen unsolved murders, and stared at the screen of his battered old portable TV.

The TV was supposed to be there in case there was some breaking news story that concerned police, but mostly it was there so Rasche could watch WWOR when he didn't feel like pushing any more papers and there wasn't anything for him to do on the streets and he didn't want to think any more about the killings he was supposed to be investigating—or, in the present case, killings he was supposed to be ignoring.

And right now WWOR wasn't coming in, no matter how much Rasche fooled with the rabbit ears.

Reception had been lousy for the last two weeks even by New York standards, bad enough that the local stations had done news reports in which scientists from Columbia and NYU made wild-ass guesses about sunspots and radioactive pollutants trapped by the temperature inversion, but today the interference was worse than ever.

Rasche slapped the set in frustration, and Mr. Ed vanished in a blur of snow.

"Shit," he said. He got up and stared around the tiny room in frustration.

Maybe there was something in one of the desk drawers that he could distract himself with for a little while; he pulled one open at random.

He gaze fell on a bundle stuffed into the drawer—his jacket, wrapped around that helmet-mask thing that Schaefer had given him for safe-keeping, the thing Schaefer had pulled off the killer's face just before being thrown out of the fifth floor of that empty building.

He had forgotten it was there; he had been too

busy with other matters, like getting Schaefer to the hospital, and then to the airport, and then getting Shari out of town. He'd dumped it in there that morning when he and Schaefer had come in and McComb had called Schaefer in his office, the morning Schaefer had left for Central America.

Neither of them had ever really looked at the thing.

Maybe it was time somebody did.

Rasche didn't expect much; it was probably just a fancy hard hat, nothing but a chunk of inert metal, but it wouldn't hurt to look.

He unwrapped it.

The thing looked as if it was meant to cover a face and the top of a head, but the shapes and proportions were wrong—nobody had a face angled like that, and it was bigger than it needed to be.

It was smooth gray metal, with a dull finish but with no scratches or scars that Rasche could see. The eyeholes weren't just holes—they were lenses, dark glass, maybe red, Rasche couldn't really be sure.

He turned the mask over.

The inside was lined with something he couldn't identify, something slightly spongy, slightly leathery. There were metal insets that looked as if they might be decoration, or might be something electronic. There were little tubes on either side that looked as if they were meant to connect up to something, but they weren't quite right for any of the standard plugs or connectors Rasche had ever seen.

And something was glowing faintly beside the left eyepiece, a small yellow shape he couldn't identify.

Rasche frowned.

This wasn't just a mask, it was a gadget of some kind. But what did it *do*?

He held it up to the light from the window and peered through those eyeholes.

Then he blinked. He lowered the mask.

He saw the street, the sky awash in the orange fire of a spectacular sunset, the windows gleaming golden, the towers above the rooftops across the street shadow-black to the east, midday bright to the south and west.

And that was all he saw.

He turned back to his office—the desk, the TV, the bookshelves. He raised the mask and saw them all, eerily changed, but still recognizable—the desk, the TV, the bookshelves, masses of strange color that almost seemed to vibrate.

The mask changed what he saw, somehow—like those night-vision scopes the military used. Infrared, was it?

Whatever it was, he was still seeing what was really there, it wasn't some sort of computer simulation. He held the mask up to his face—he couldn't put it on, his head wasn't big enough, wasn't the right shape, but he could hold it so that he saw out the eyeholes.

Desk, TV, bookshelves, chair, door, lamp, the TV antenna like blue lines of light, the TV itself hot pink; he could even read his own name backward on the glass of the door, purple-blue on green-blue.

Then he turned and looked out the window again.

And he saw the ships, cruising over the city—

gigantic and alien, huge red-gold shapes against a deep-red sky.

Rasche wasn't stupid. He could recognize the incredible when his nose was rubbed in it.

Spaceships. Invisible spaceships that he could see only through this alien helmet.

Schaefer had been right all along. The killer wasn't human at all.

No, not "the killer." "Killers," plural. He could see three ships just from this one window.

And he could guess now why TV reception sucked.

"Sunspots, my ass," he said softly.

21

When dawn broke, the guide wanted to see the thing, to be sure it was really dead. He insisted on leading the mules to the edge of the cliff, and then climbing down for a good close look at the monster's remains.

Schaefer had no problem with that; he wasn't much for bragging, but he didn't mind showing off his handiwork if the other guy *asked*.

Just for the hell of it, he climbed down the cliff to look at the body, too.

The creature was still lying there, still dead; the pool of yellow-green blood on its chest, the smear on the branch that had impaled it, and the trickle that had spilled down one side had all faded to a greener, less luminescent hue.

Schaefer was interested to note that none of the local wildlife had made any visible attempt to feast on this particular gift; there were no flies, no ants, no beetles crawling on the corpse.

He was no scientist, but he could guess what that meant—this thing wasn't anything that had ever lived on Earth, and its chemistry was sufficiently different that the local fauna didn't recognize it as food.

Maybe it *wasn't* food; its flesh might well be as toxic as its attitude.

For the first time Schaefer was able to get a really good look at it, at the black mesh covering, the cannon thing, the metal-bound braids—if they were braids; now that he saw them, he wasn't sure. They looked almost solid, as if they weren't hairs plaited together, but some sort of thick tendrils.

That might have just been some sort of oily covering, though. He wasn't curious enough to remove the metal bands and see what happened.

The metal mask, the leathery guards at wrist and ankle with their intricate gadgetry, looked very high tech, but barbaric at the same time. The string of skulls it wore slung over one shoulder—mostly animal skulls, but with a human one at the end of the string—was just barbaric, without any tech. Schaefer noticed that there were a lot of blades and sharp edges involved in its various equipment.

This character had obviously considered itself a real badass.

Schaefer had run into people a few times before who thought that way. Most of them were wrong. *This* son of a bitch had at least had some justification for considering itself serious bad news.

"My God," the guide said, staring at it. "You really killed it."

Schaefer glanced at him. "You say that as if it were a bad thing," he remarked.

"You weren't supposed to kill it," the guide told him. "You weren't . . . We didn't think you *could* kill it. You and your damned brother. Do you have any idea what this means?" He knelt by the body, carefully not touching it, as if he were afraid it would burn him, or pollute him somehow.

Maybe it would, Schaefer thought. Maybe he'd caught some weird alien disease by fighting the thing.

Or maybe the guide was just a wuss.

"Yeah, sure I know what it means," Schaefer said. He grinned. "It means it's Miller time."

"Oh, laugh it up," the guide said bitterly. He pulled something from his pocket, a gadget of some kind that Schaefer didn't recognize, and set it down by the dead creature. "Jesus, Schaefer, this isn't professional wrestling—these guys play for keeps!"

"So do I," Schaefer said, his smile fading. "You think I'm going to apologize for not dying? Get real." He turned away, disgusted, and started climbing back up the cliff, using the vines as ropes.

"This whole business was a setup from the minute I left New York, wasn't it?" Schaefer asked as he hauled himself up. "The reports I got that took me to Riosucio, you showing up, the way you led me right here—it was all an act. 'Native guide,' huh? That's cute—what are you really? CIA? DEA?"

"Neither," the guide said, gasping slightly with the effort of climbing as he followed Schaefer up the cliff. "You never heard of us."

"Don't be too sure of that."

"Oh, we're sure," the guide said. "I don't suppose it matters anymore, so I might as well tell you— we're new, formed after your brother met one of those things. He killed his, too—but he lost his entire squad doing it, and it died more slowly, slowly enough to use a self-destruct that made that crater you saw."

"Lost his squad?" Schaefer turned as he reached the top and looked back down at the guide. Here was confirmation of what he had suspected. "That thing killed all of them? Blain, Hawkins, all of them?"

"All of them," the guide confirmed.

"And Dutch? Did it get him?"

Schaefer knew Dutch had survived the first encounter—had killed it, the guide said.

But that meant that there was more than one, that the one Schaefer had just killed was *not* the one that took out Dutch's men.

So had it gotten Dutch? Had it been after revenge for its dead buddy?

"Dutch got out alive," the guide said, "but that's all I can tell you."

That wasn't necessarily so, Schaefer realized; it just meant that the guide's people didn't *know* whether the second one had got Dutch.

Either that, or they knew but weren't saying.

"And it's all secret as hell, right?" he asked.

"Yeah," the guide agreed.

"So when I started poking around, you people decided to feed me to that bastard? Give it what it wanted?"

"Dammit, Schaefer," the guide said as he

stepped up onto solid ground, "*you're* the one who decided to come down here and play tourist! We didn't set *that* up! You practically *volunteered* for a suicide mission."

"Yeah?" Schaefer sneered. "And what about Dutch? Was he another of your volunteers?"

"We didn't *know* back then!"

"But you do now, so you sent me to play patty-cake with that thing."

"Look, we don't like this any more than you do," the guide said, "but it's here, it's real, and we're forced to deal with it."

"And just what is it you think you're dealing with?" Schaefer demanded. He paused and looked back down at the dead thing as the guide pushed past him.

"We don't *know*," the guide said. "We can only guess. But what we *guess* is that these things come to Earth every so often to have a good time, play the great white hunter, collect a few trophies—and then they go home again and leave us alone for years at a stretch."

"Come to Earth," Schaefer said as he took a final look down at the creature. "From outer space, you mean? Like in the movies?"

"Something like that," the guide said. He reached the waiting mules and pulled out Schaefer's gun.

Schaefer turned away from the cliff at the sound of the safety being released and found the guide pointing the weapon at him.

"Come on," the guide said. "The general wants us out of here, away from that thing—he doesn't want you fucking up anything else. We've got six hours to make the rendezvous down at the end of the valley. You just keep your hands off the packs, don't touch any weapons, and we'll be fine. Maybe we can still salvage something out of this mess."

Schaefer stared at him silently for a moment.

"You know, chief," he said at last, "you're really beginning to get on my nerves. That thing's *dead*. It's *over*."

"Jesus, you don't have a clue, do you?" the guide said, amazed. "You think that was the *only one*? Come on, move!" He waved the gun.

Schaefer sighed and began marching.

Yeah, he'd thought that was the only one—but so what if it wasn't?

He'd be glad to take on however many might be out there.

22

"You really think those things are going to fucking *invade*, just because I killed one of them in self-defense?" Schaefer asked as he pushed aside yet another overhanging giant fern.

The two men had been slogging through the jungle for hours, arguing off and on; Schaefer's suggestion that they at least try riding the mules had been vetoed as making an escape attempt too easy.

They had heard a copter overhead at one point but had been unable to see it through the canopy, and the sound had faded away again. Schaefer had looked at the guide, who had just shrugged and kept walking; apparently that hadn't been their intended pickup.

"We don't know what they're going to do," the

guide said, "but we don't expect them to just ignore it."

"So why didn't they blow us all away when Dutch waxed one eight years ago?"

"Because it blew itself up," the guide said. "They must have thought your brother bought it in the explosion. He damn near did."

"Or maybe they figured their buddy knew the risks," Schaefer suggested.

"Come on, Schaefer," the guide said, "these things are from another *planet*, they've got starships and shit, they're maybe a million years ahead of us—you think they're going to let a bunch of apes like us blow away tourists?"

"Why not?" Schaefer asked. "You seem to think *we* should let them blow away *our* people—wasn't that what was happening in New York? Let the boys have some fun, and so what if they kill a few of the natives."

"Better they take out a few than the whole lot of us," the guide said.

"Better they not take out *any*," Schaefer replied. "A point I was trying to make when I came down here looking for that son of a bitch."

"Oh, right. Did you really think you could waltz down here and end it as easy as that?"

Schaefer didn't reply, and the guide went on, "You're not in Kansas anymore, pal. You can't roust these guys like your standard-issue gang-bangers or drug push—"

The sound of a rifle shot interrupted the guide in midword, and Schaefer turned, startled, to see blood spurt from the man's shoulder.

"Pushers," the guide said, swaying unsteadily,

trying to bring the auto shotgun around, trying to locate the source of the shot.

Schaefer didn't wait for any more surprises; he dived for cover, throwing himself as far from the guide and the mules as he could.

As he hit the ground, the jungle erupted in gunfire.

The guide tottered and went down.

Schaefer listened, looked at the shots he could see hitting, and counted at least four shooters concealed in the jungle, all within thirty yards.

One of the mules went down—a stupid waste, in Schaefer's opinion, but he wasn't about to try to do anything about it. He lay still, half-hidden in ferns, and waited for the shooting to stop.

At least whoever was shooting was using ordinary guns, and not that high-intensity alien shit—this wasn't the revenge of the invaders from space that the phony guide had been so worried about.

Small consolation, Schaefer thought; the poor son of a bitch was just as dead as if he'd caught the alien's fireworks in the chest.

He shifted, very slowly, very carefully, turning to see what was happening.

The firing trailed off and stopped.

The guide didn't so much as twitch; he was pretty clearly dead. The downed mule was still kicking, though, and a man in green fatigues stepped out of the bush, put a gun to the animal's head, and snapped off a single, final shot.

The other mule had skittered off into the jungle; Schaefer couldn't see it as he watched the men appearing out of the forest.

Four of them, all right—two with MAC-10's, two with Chinese AK-47's.

The choice of hardware and something about their attitude convinced Schaefer these guys were Colombian drug-cartel men—but what the hell were they doing *here*? This place wasn't on the regular smuggling routes, so far as Schaefer knew.

Maybe they'd shifted the routes again, though; the DEA and the local *policía* might've done that much.

One of the gunmen lifted the guide's head and looked at the bloody, mud-smeared face.

"*Éste marrano está muerto,*" he said.

Another, just behind the first, gave a sharp bark of disgusted laughter. "*Eschevera lo quiere vivo.*"

Eschevera?

Schaefer knew a Colombian named Eschevera.

Eschevera had tried to be a big man back in New York, acted like one of those suave *Miami Vice* types, but as far as Schaefer was concerned, underneath the spit shine Eschevera was just another two-bit drug-dealing prick.

Back when he and Rasche had still been working narcotics, Schaefer had heard about Eschevera from a couple of underlings. Schaefer and Rasche had put in some legwork trying to get something on him, something that would stick, and word must have got around; a couple of Eschevera's boys had shown up with an invitation.

Schaefer had gone along, just for laughs.

Schaefer and Rasche had met with Eschevera in the rooftop garden of a fancy Manhattan brownstone, surrounded by tropical plants that were dying of the New York cold. It had been just the three of them; the bodyguards had stayed out of sight, as a sign of trust and respect.

Rasche had let Schaefer do the talking.

There'd been some preliminaries, each man demonstrating how tough he thought he was, and then Eschevera had spilled a million dollars in small bills across the bark dust and told Schaefer that he and Rasche could have it, that very day, if they'd just back off and leave him alone.

And he'd had a switchblade in the other hand as a warning of what might happen if they didn't take the money.

A million dollars, he'd said, and Schaefer had believed him—the pile of bills hadn't been small.

Schaefer had thought it over for a couple of seconds, just to be fair to Rasche. Half a million could have kept Shari and the boys comfortable for a long time; Rasche wouldn't have had to worry about his pension.

But Schaefer had seen the look on Rasche's face, and he knew that Shari would just have to put up with New York a few years more. He'd expected that.

That settled, Schaefer had grabbed Eschevera and thrown the son of a bitch off the roof.

Only three stories. Eschevera lived.

And Schaefer'd walked out untouched while the bodyguards were running in circles.

Schaefer'd reported it as an accident, said Eschevera tripped. There weren't any other witnesses. Eschevera hadn't pressed charges, he'd packed up and gone home to Colombia to lick his wounds.

Schaefer had figured he'd bump into Eschevera

again sooner or later, though; the people of the Cali cartel were known to carry grudges.

This wasn't quite how or where he'd expected the encounter, though.

Had Eschevera's men been after *him*?

He couldn't see why they'd want the guide in particular, or what drug dealers would have to do with aliens, so, yeah, they'd probably been after him, and nailed the guide just because he was there.

So how'd they known he was anywhere in the vicinity?

He wondered if Hanson had sold him out, told Eschevera where to look for him; it was possible, though he'd always thought Hanson was still straight.

Maybe one of Philips's men had leaked.

Or it might have just been a coincidence, a stroke of bad luck—but if so, it was one *hell* of a coincidence.

"*Yo voy a mirar aquí,*" someone said, reminding Schaefer where he was.

The gunmen were looking around now; whether they were after Schaefer specifically or not, they apparently knew the guide hadn't been alone. Not that it was hard to figure that out, when there were two mules, and they both had saddles.

They weren't being too bright about the search, though; they'd spread out and weren't watching each other.

Schaefer moved slowly into a crouch, ready to spring. One of the men was approaching.

Then he was right on top of Schaefer, and the detective burst up through the ferns, planting a solid right on the man's jaw; the Colombian went down, and Schaefer snatched up his MAC-10.

By the time he'd untangled the shoulder strap from the dazed man's shoulder, though, the other three had turned and opened fire; Schaefer dived for cover again.

He checked the gun quickly, found the magazine still half-full, and returned fire.

The thing wasn't very accurate; it was meant for spraying fire across an area, not for hitting targets. Schaefer didn't really expect to hit anything, but it would make the Colombians keep their heads down.

Now that he'd been spotted, there was no point in staying quiet or trying to hide; he worried about cover, but not concealment, and he kept moving, cutting from one tree to the next in short dashes, spraying bullets each time.

The Colombians fired back but usually only succeeded in putting a dozen rounds through the space between trees after Schaefer had already reached cover. That didn't mean they were stupid, just human—reaction times weren't fast enough. They didn't know when he'd move, or which way.

If they'd had the firepower, they could have kept up a steady fire and pinned him down while one circled around behind—but they didn't. There were just the three weapons, and they'd probably shot off half their ammo taking down the guide and the mule.

The *one* mule, the guide's mule. The other one, the one Schaefer had ridden originally, was still alive and unhurt, and Schaefer figured his best chance—his *only* chance, really—was to get to the animal, and to the rest of the arsenal he'd brought up from Riosucio. The Colombians hadn't touched it yet. With that stuff he could lay down enough fire to maybe take out one or two of his enemies, despite the thick jungle, and if that didn't scare the others off, it would at least keep them down long enough that he could mount up and make a run for it.

He wished the damn mule would hold still, preferably behind some sort of cover; it was wandering slowly through the jungle, staying well clear of the larger trees.

It didn't seem to be bothered by the gunfire, and Schaefer wondered just where the guide had got it, and how much experience the animal had had with this sort of thing.

He worked his way closer to the animal, and when he thought he had a chance, he made a run for it.

The mule started and shied away at his approach—gunfire hadn't scared it, but Schaefer apparently did.

"C'mere, damn you!" he shouted, grabbing for the bridle. He got a hand on one leather strap, and the mule pulled away, rearing slightly.

"*Down*, dammit!"

Holding the bridle with one hand, he reached for the gun box with the other, turning the mule to keep it between himself and the Colombians as he pulled out his reserve shotgun. Hanson had been generous, and Schaefer appreciated it.

"All right," he said, "my turn." He lifted the

weapon—and froze as hard steel touched the back of his head.

"Drop it, *marrano*," a cold voice said in his ear, "or I fear that Señor Eschevera will be deprived of his evening's entertainment."

Maybe they hadn't been able to pin him down, but one of them had circled around anyway, and Schaefer hadn't heard or seen a thing.

His grip tightened on the shotgun as he considered his next move—and then a gun butt hit his head with a sharp crack, and Schaefer, no longer considering anything, went down.

23

"**T**he transponder signal's coming in fine," Doheny said as he swung the radio locator in a narrow arc. "Now let's hope Niner put it in the right place."

Behind him the other three men of the pickup squad were unloading the metal mesh basket that was supposed to hold the dead alien.

The copter had set down in the crater—it was the closest thing to clear terrain anywhere in the area.

"Over that way," Doheny said, pointing.

"Come on, then," Johnson barked.

Together, the four men pushed their way through the jungle, hauling the basket between them; the chopper waited, engine idling.

The general had said to keep the engine running, to be ready to run at any moment—the aliens might be coming to make the pickup themselves.

No one knew if they cared about their dead the same way people did, but judging by the bomb the first one had used, there was *something* they didn't want to leave lying around—bodies, equipment, something.

Doheny knew all that. He'd been working with Philips's group for years, and he knew the aliens were supposed to be very real and very deadly—but somehow, deep down, he didn't quite believe it. Intellectually, sure, the aliens were real, but emotionally the idea just hadn't sunk in.

He swung his machete—the briefings had said they'd be safer unarmed, but he'd insisted they needed to be able to clear the way to get the basket through. And there might be more mundane menaces than the killer aliens around here; besides the machete Doheny had his sidearm, as did the others.

Philips had advised against it—but Philips wasn't out here in the jungle with the snakes and vines.

When the four men reached the cliff edge, Romano, holding one of the front corners, almost went over before he caught himself. Johnson swore at him.

Doheny looked over the edge and spotted the creature almost immediately, lying at the bottom thirty yards off to the right, draped across a fallen tree with a five-foot limb stuck through its chest.

"Shit," he said quietly.

It *was* real.

And it was going to be a royal bitch to get it off that chunk of wood and into the basket.

And there was no way in hell they were going to haul it up the cliff by hand, through all that brush; they'd have to rig a harness, get the chopper over with a line and hook, and hoist it up.

At least with the river right there they'd be able to get a hook down without snagging in the canopy.

"Come on," he said, starting the climb down the precipice, "let's get on with it."

Reluctantly, the others followed, tipping the basket up and sliding it carefully over the edge in a controlled fall.

Doheny was halfway down when he glanced over at where the dead alien lay, and froze. He blinked, hoping it was some sort of illusion, maybe some kind of refraction caused by spray from the river, something that would disappear.

It didn't disappear.

"Shit," he said again.

Johnson, Romano, and Sturgill glanced at him, saw where he was staring, and turned their own gaze.

All four men froze, staring.

There were four of the things—five, counting the dead one. The four of them were standing in a circle around their fallen comrade.

Then one of them looked over at the men, hanging there halfway down the cliff.

Johnson let go his hold on the basket and began climbing upward. "Go!" he called. "Get out of here! Back to the chopper!"

Sturgill, caught by surprise by the sudden increase in weight when Johnson released his share, slid several feet farther down before he was able to free himself of the basket. The basket crashed downward past him, tearing through leaves, flipping end for end every time it hit an obstruction, until finally it landed with a splash, half on the bank, half in the river.

Sturgill hung for a moment, making sure his hold was solid; then he turned to find that Johnson and Romano had already scrambled halfway back up.

Doheny was waiting for him, though.

"You okay?" Doheny called.

Sturgill nodded. He glanced over at the enemy, then blinked.

"They're gone," he said.

Doheny looked, startled.

Sturgill was right—the four live aliens had vanished.

Had they imagined it, then? Had the creatures been an illusion of some kind?

No, that was nonsense—all four men had seen them there. Johnson and Romano wouldn't be fleeing in panic otherwise. They'd seen *something*.

So where had the four creatures gone? Doheny hadn't heard anything, hadn't seen any movement, just suddenly they were gone; could they be that fast, that silent?

He remembered the briefings.

Yes, they *were* that fast, that silent. Doheny had discounted it when he'd heard the story, had figured that lone survivor from eight years ago had dressed up his account to make himself look good, but now, very suddenly, Doheny believed it all.

They were fast, strong, silent. They could move through the jungle as well as anything on earth.

And they had their invisibility screens, too.

And they killed people just for fun.

"Oh, God," Doheny whispered as he scrambled upward.

He'd dropped his machete—he was glad of that now. He wondered if it was too late to ditch his pistol and decided not to worry about it.

If he could reach the chopper, he'd be safe; they couldn't catch *that*, no matter how fast or strong they were. They didn't have wings, they couldn't fly.

At the top he turned to see if he could lend Sturgill a hand—Johnson and Romano were already running through the jungle, smashing through the undergrowth, making enough noise to wake the dead, sending birds and insects flying in all directions as they ran for the crater and their ride out.

Sturgill wasn't there.

Doheny had thought Sturgill was right behind him; he leaned over and peered down.

Sturgill was almost at the bottom, he saw, down by the abandoned basket—he must have slipped again. He wasn't moving—was he hurt?

Panicky, Doheny threw a glance at the dead alien. There was no sign of the live ones.

He looked back down at Sturgill and realized that that red he saw down there all around the fallen man wasn't part of the jungle, it wasn't flowers or insects or butterflies.

That was Sturgill's blood.

Sturgill was already dead.

The things had gotten him.

"Oh, shit," Doheny said as he turned and ran for the copter.

About halfway to the crater he almost tripped

over Romano—or what was left of him. Doheny recognized him by his size and his gear, not by his features; Romano's head was gone.

"Oh, Jesus," Doheny cried, stumbling on.

Johnson had made it as far as the edge of the crater; he lay on his back, his chest ripped open.

Doheny hardly glanced at him—the chopper was there, waiting, hovering a few feet off the ground. The pilot must have seen Johnson die and he'd gotten moving, gotten off the ground, but he was staying low, staying in reach, waiting for the others—a brave man, Doheny thought gratefully.

And there was the copilot, Jim Wyatt, leaning out the door shouting something—Doheny couldn't make it out.

He ran down the slope, stumbling on vines, and when he was closer, he heard Wyatt call, "Where the fuck are the others? They coming?"

"Dead!" Doheny shouted back. "They're all dead! Back there!"

"Come on, then!" Wyatt called, holding out a hand, and Doheny ran, getting ready to jump, to grab Wyatt's arm and be pulled aboard.

And that was when the blades slashed through his side.

He couldn't run anymore, he wasn't dead but the pain in his side was too much, he could feel hot blood spilling down his leg and his side was suddenly icy cold despite the jungle heat, he couldn't make his legs work; he folded up and fell.

He saw Wyatt hesitating, saw him inch forward, he was obviously thinking about jumping down to help, but he wasn't sure he should, and just then the pilot's nerve finally broke, before Wyatt could move any farther.

The chopper began to rise, to pull away from the earth, and Doheny knew they were leaving him behind, leaving him to die, to become another grisly trophy for the aliens, and he began to cry, his eyes filling with tears, his breath coming in gasps.

He was bleeding to death, he knew he was bleeding to death, and they were abandoning him to save their own worthless lives, and he hated them with a sudden intensity he hadn't known possible.

For an instant he was almost glad when the blue-white fireball hit the copter's fuel tank and the craft blossomed into an orange inferno before plummeting back to earth. He could hear Wyatt's scream, saw Wyatt try to dive free of the wreckage, his uniform already burning.

And then something grabbed him by the hair and lifted him up, and a jagged blade flashed, and Doheny was dead.

Miles away a radioman reported, "General, we've lost the chopper."

"Damn." Philips glared. "What happened?"

"I don't know, sir. The pilot didn't have time to say much. The transponder's out, though; it's gone."

"Find out . . . no, forget that. I know what happened."

The aliens, of course. The monsters from outer space had been displeased that humans had been poking around their dead comrade.

Any chance of giving them the body as a goodwill

gesture was gone. Any chance of getting a look at the technology on that body was gone.

And six good men were gone, too.

"Should I send a rescue mission to look for survivors, sir?" Perkins asked.

Philips turned, startled.

"Hell, no," he said. "There aren't any survivors."

"According to the radio reports, the pickup crew wasn't onboard when the chopper went down, sir. . . ."

"They were probably already dead," Philips said.

"But . . ."

"All right, look," Philips said, "if they're on the ground, they'll be okay for a while—we'll go in and look after those things have had time to finish up and leave. But I'm not sending more men in to be slaughtered."

"Yes, sir," Perkins reluctantly agreed.

The general saw his face, knew that Perkins thought they should at least *try* to rescue the pickup crew.

Philips knew better. Maybe Schaefer had managed to kill one of the aliens, maybe Dutch had managed to kill one, but the men of the pickup crew had been ordinary mortals. And they'd been armed. Philips wished he had ordered them to go in unarmed, maybe then the aliens would have let them go—but maybe they wouldn't have. This wasn't a hunt, this was defending the dead; the rules might be different.

And besides, he'd wanted volunteers, and if he'd insisted on no weapons, he might not have got any.

That might have been better all around, of course. Because despite what Perkins might think, Philips knew those men were dead.

Well, there was still Schaefer and his "guide," and Philips intended at least to get to *him* before the aliens could.

24

It seemed to Rasche that he'd been staring out the window for over an hour.

Maybe he *had* been, and he still couldn't believe it.

Those ships cruising over New York, visible only through the helmet-mask . . .

They showed up golden-red; Rasche wondered what color they were really. The mask twisted colors, changed them, and the resolution was weak, shapes became soft-edged and indistinct; details vanished—or appeared, set in sharp relief by the shifted colors.

For a long time Rasche couldn't really accept what he was seeing. He knew it had to be true, nothing else made sense, but this stuff happened on *My Favorite Martian*, not in the real world.

Not on *My Favorite Martian*, either, he corrected

himself. They never had the budget. Maybe *Star Trek* or one of those other sci-fi shows—he never watched them. Or the blockbuster movies with Schwarzenegger.

It all fit together, though. Schaefer had said the killer wasn't human, and Schaefer had been right.

The killer had been a goddamn Martian.

And the feds must have known all along. That explained everything. They *knew* that those things were out there—Rasche didn't know how, but they knew.

Schaefer's brother—Dutch must have found out about the Martians.

Had the aliens killed him?

Or worse, had the *feds* killed him, to keep those things secret?

Or was he still out there somewhere? Was he helping the feds?

That was one thing Rasche couldn't figure out, but it didn't matter—he saw the rest of it. Those ships out there had brought some kind of superhunter to earth, something that hunted human beings just for fun. The feds knew about it, but they were keeping it hushed up.

Why?

That one wasn't too difficult to figure—all those UFO nuts, who maybe weren't quite so nutty after all, had an answer for that. Hell, they had half a dozen answers. The feds didn't want anyone to panic. Maybe they wanted to capture the alien technology for themselves. Maybe they were dealing with the aliens. Maybe they'd all sold out to invaders from another galaxy. Maybe they *were* aliens, Martian shape-shifters who'd replaced the real humans.

Rasche had always thought that was all a bunch of crazy paranoid fantasy—but those ships were out there.

Ships, plural. Schaefer had thought there was just *one* killer, *one* of these hunters from outer space—but Rasche could see four ships just from this one window, and they looked *big*, not like anything that would carry a single passenger.

Jesus, Rasche thought, if *one* of them took out Dutch's squad, if *one* of them slaughtered the gang-bangers at Beekman and Water . . .

He put the mask down, and the ships vanished; picked it up and looked through it, and they were back.

At last he put it down and went for a cup of the sludge that served as coffee.

"Man, you look awful," a voice said as Rasche tried to pour without spilling; his hands were shaking enough to make it very tricky. He looked up.

"I've seen mimes with a better tan, Rasche," the other detective said. "You all right?"

"Beat it, Richie," Rasche answered, picking up his cup—it wasn't full, but it was good enough.

Richie shrugged. "Just trying to help," he said.

"You can't," Rasche answered, shuffling back toward his office, walking as if he were afraid the floor might tip and throw him off at any moment, holding the coffee as if it might explode at any second.

And how did he know it wouldn't? The whole world had gone mad on him. He picked up the mask.

Maybe it wasn't the world that was mad; maybe it was him. Maybe he was losing his mind.

He needed to talk to someone.

Shari was still in Elmira, and besides, how could he talk to her about this? She already worried about him so much—she'd think he'd finally cracked. Something like this on top of his behavior at Niagara Falls—she'd assume he'd gone nuts, become a complete paranoid loon.

He didn't *think* he'd gone nuts—the mask was solid enough. And those men *had* been looking for him at the motel.

They couldn't have been the killers, though, not if the killers were alien monsters. They must have been feds, after him for some reason.

Or maybe the aliens really *were* shape-shifters.

He had to talk to *someone* about it. And not by phone; he needed someone who could see the mask, touch it, know that it was real.

The feds?

But they already knew. They would just take the mask away and go on hushing it all up, and that wasn't enough.

He tucked the mask under one arm, the coffee in his other hand, and headed downstairs to see McComb. He smiled uncomfortably—he *must* be losing his mind, he thought, if he was going to talk to *McComb* about something like this.

McComb didn't answer the first knock, but Rasche knew he was still in there, that he hadn't gone home. He kept pounding, and eventually the captain opened the door.

"What the hell is it?" he demanded.

"Captain, I need to talk to you," Rasche said. "Now. Inside."

McComb stared at him for a moment, then said, "All right, you have one minute. And lose the coffee—I don't want any oil spills on the new carpet."

Rasche tossed the cup in a nearby trash can—he didn't really want to drink it, anyway. He stepped into McComb's office with the alien mask held out before him in both hands, like an offering.

"If you've come to apologize on behalf of your partner, Rasche, you can save it," McComb said as he closed the door. "You're days too late. I filed for disciplinary action against Schaefer and requested dismissal just as soon as he walked out of here— and where the hell did he go, anyway? Will you look what he did to my phone?" He gestured, but Rasche didn't bother to look. "Don't touch it, it's evidence against that son of a bitch. . . ."

"I know we've had our problems, Captain," Rasche said, "but this is *big.*"

McComb stopped talking and glared at Rasche.

"There . . . there's something *out* there," Rasche stammered. He couldn't quite bring himself to say right out that there were spaceships—if *he* thought he might be going crazy, what would McComb think? McComb *already* suspected Rasche was nuts, just for putting up with Schaefer.

He held out the mask. "Schaefer snagged this from the thing he met at the scene of the first massacre, on Beekman," he said. "We . . . "

"Hold it!" McComb held up a hand. "Are you saying you've been withholding evidence?"

Rasche stared at McComb for a moment, then

lost it. He was talking about entire worlds, and McComb was worrying about legal details?

He slammed the mask down on the captain's desk. "Would you *listen* to me?" he shouted. "There are dozens, maybe *hundreds*, of those things out there, just *waiting*—all you have to do is *look*—"

"I'm not looking at anything," McComb bellowed, "except *your ass* in a holding cell pending a full departmental review! Goddammit, you're going down for this, Rasche, same as Schaefer did! Trespassing on a sealed crime scene, withholding evidence, lying in your signed statement . . ."

"Fine!" Rasche shouted back, snatching up the helmet. "Fine, I'll have my little chat with the chief!"

He stormed out of McComb's office.

"Hey, Rasche, you're not going *anywhere*," McComb called after him.

Rasche paid no attention—except to change his intended route, taking the back stairs to avoid any attempts to interfere. He was going to take this to the chief, to the mayor, to anyone who would listen. It was obvious that McComb had all the good sense of a possum crossing an interstate—New York was under siege by alien monsters, and McComb was worrying about stains on his carpet.

"Jesus, Schaefer," Rasche muttered to himself as he trudged down the concrete steps, "where are you when I need you? Central fucking America, for Christ's sake!"

His only chance of getting anything done without Schaefer there to make things happen was taking his case to McComb's superiors—but as the steel fire door at the bottom of the stairs slammed open with a crash like thunder, Rasche realized that Philips and his people would know that.

And McComb would call them. He still had the phone Schaefer had broken on his desk, but he had a replacement, too.

The three men in suits and sunglasses who had burst in at the foot of the stairs had the jump on him; Rasche didn't reach for his pistol.

"Federal agents," the one with the 9mm automatic announced. "That's far enough, Detective Rasche." He flipped open a credentials case in his left hand, but Rasche was too far away to read the badge.

One of the others lifted a walkie-talkie and told it, "It's okay—we've got him."

The third man had a pistol and an outstretched empty hand; the first waved at him and said, "Hand my friend the helmet, Rasche."

Rasche grimaced and hauled back to fling the helmet.

Three pistols pointed at his gut.

"Easy, easy," the first fed told him. "Just hand it over easy, you won't be needing it."

Reluctantly, Rasche lowered his hand and handed the mask over.

"Good," the fed said. "Come on, then; you're coming with us."

"Where?" Rasche asked. "Can I call my wife first, or at least tell someone upstairs?"

The agent shook his head. "Uh-uh, Rasche. No calls, no one sees you leave. Car's waiting."

Rasche frowned. "That's not standard procedure. That's more like kidnapping."

He also realized that even if McComb had phoned the instant the door closed behind him, these bozos couldn't have gotten here and set up so fast.

They must have been waiting for him all along.

"Never mind what you call it," the fed said. "Just come on."

One of the others took Rasche by the arm and gave him a shove in the right direction.

Rasche came, but as they left the building, he protested, "You have to be shitting me—you can't kidnap a police officer from the middle of Police Plaza!"

"The hell we can't," one of the feds muttered.

"You're not regular feds," Rasche said. "Even those pricks from the FBI wouldn't pull this. Who the hell *are* you?"

"You don't need to know," the spokesman told him as he shoved Rasche roughly into the backseat of an unmarked black sedan.

25

A pan of dirty water flung in his face brought Schaefer around; as the cool wetness shocked him back to consciousness, he heard a voice saying, "Time to wake up, puppy dog."

Schaefer blinked and looked around.

He was sitting in a low wooden chair, feet on the floor and his knees sticking up, his wrists tied behind him with something stiff—it felt like coathanger wire.

Whatever it was holding his hands, it was strong and tied tight; he couldn't even come close to snapping it, couldn't slip it off. Eschevera, if that was who was responsible, wasn't taking any chances.

His arms were bound to the chair's back with plain rope.

The chair stood near the center of a fair-sized,

dimly lit room, one with plank walls and a plank floor; it wasn't anyplace Schaefer recognized. Daylight was coming in under the eaves; there were no windows or lamps.

He guessed he'd been out for hours, maybe days—long enough for Eschevera's men to drag him back to whatever they were using for a base, anyway. Whoever had clouted him had known what he was doing; Schaefer had a headache, but his thoughts were clear enough, he didn't think there was any concussion.

He wondered where the hell he actually was—and how hard it would be to get out. If they'd hauled him all the way down the full length of Panama and this was the Cali camp just across the Colombian border, and if the DEA reports were right, the place was a goddamn fortress, and his chances of escape were right up there with the odds of St. Peter giving Hitler the benefit of the doubt. If this was just some little cabin somewhere along the smuggling routes, though, he might be okay.

He'd beaten a monster from outer space; he had no interest in dying at the hands of a bunch of drug-dealing punks who claimed to be members of his own species.

The man who had splashed him tossed the empty pan at Schaefer's feet with a clatter; then he checked the wire on Schaefer's wrist, gave it a twist to tighten it further, and said, *"Bueno."*

Schaefer felt the metal biting painfully into his flesh, felt blood start to ooze from beneath. He growled in anger and pain.

"Perhaps the wire is too tight?" the man said in good English. "Not to worry—we're only just beginning. In a little time you won't even notice so minor a pain." He turned, leaned out the room's one and only door, and signaled to someone Schaefer couldn't see.

A moment later a taller man in military fatigues stepped into the room; he nodded a greeting to the man who had splashed Schaefer.

The first man saluted and left the room; the new arrival crossed slowly to a spot beside the chair, where he stood and smiled down at Schaefer.

Schaefer knew the face; he'd seen it before, back in the Big Apple. Seen it, hell, he'd been tempted to punch it in. This was Eschevera.

Schaefer took a certain pleasure in seeing that Eschevera limped as he walked.

"Detective Schaefer," Eschevera said. "I'm hurt—you came all this long way to Central America, you passed so close to my home, and you didn't stop by to pay your dear old friend a visit?"

Schaefer grunted.

"Perhaps you sought me but were misled?" Eschevera suggested. "You made a wrong turn somewhere, someone gave you faulty directions? After all, what else could have brought you to this corner of the world but a desire to renew our acquaintance?"

"Somehow I managed to avoid that particular desire," Schaefer said.

Eschevera grinned. "The last time we met, I made you a very generous offer. Perhaps now you're sorry you responded as you did?"

"I'm only sorry we didn't meet on a taller building," Schaefer snarled.

The grin vanished. "That's very funny, Detective

Schaefer," Eschevera said. "You've always had a good sense of humor, haven't you? I regret I won't be able to appreciate it for very much longer."

Eschevera turned as the other man reentered; he was holding something in one hand, something black and bright orange. In his other hand was a coil of black cable; he was paying it out as he entered.

He held up the black-and-orange object.

"Black and Decker," he said. "Very sharp."

It was a power saw, circular blade, one-half horsepower motor; the safety shield had been removed.

Schaefer didn't like that; for one thing, it meant this place had electricity, which meant it was more than just some stopover on the trail.

Eschevera smiled again. "I'll be back in a bit, after Paolo's had a few minutes with you alone. Perhaps you can entertain him with more of your amusing stories." He saluted sardonically, then turned and limped out.

The sadist with the power saw grinned. He revved it a few times, just to test, and light glinted from the spinning blade. "So little time, so much to do," he said.

He circled around behind Schaefer, put a hand on his head, and pressed, tipping Schaefer's head down and exposing the back of his neck, like a barber preparing to trim the hairs there.

Paolo revved the saw again, then clicked the switch into the lock-on position; the blade and motor settled into a steady hum.

"Yeah, I know the feeling," Schaefer said, and he

leaned farther forward, pulling away from Paolo's hand.

Then he pressed his feet against the floor and stood up, chair and all. One of the back legs caught Paolo in the kneecap, hard.

"Wha . . . ?" The Colombian torturer staggered back, limping and startled.

Schaefer squatted and then threw himself backward, smashing Paolo against the wooden wall. He drove his wired fists into Paolo's belly; Paolo made a strangled noise, barely audible over the power saw's hum, and doubled over.

Schaefer dragged the sharp ends of the wire across Paolo's stomach and felt blood dripping; then he leaned forward and let Paolo fall.

The saw was still running; Schaefer twisted around and pressed the chair back against the spinning blade.

The motor howled and sawdust sprayed as the saw cut into the wooden chair, and in seconds Schaefer was able to break free and stand upright.

Paolo was stirring, struggling to get up; Schaefer kicked him in the gut, and when he'd curled into a ball, Schaefer kicked him in the head.

Blood sprayed from Paolo's nose across the scattered sawdust.

"Fun's fun, Paolo," Schaefer said, "but I don't have time for this bullshit."

He put his hands on the floor and stepped back through his arms to get his hands in front of him, then began picking with his teeth at the wire on his wrists. After a moment he managed to get one end loose; after that it was easy.

His mouth was bleeding in four separate places

where the wire had cut him, and his wrists were bloody as well, but he didn't worry about any of that.

He moved the saw around, then kicked Paolo a couple of times to make sure he was out, and to provide sound effects for whoever was guarding the door. There was no reason to think Paolo and Eschevera had been alone; after all, there were the four men who had brought him in. They were probably still around, and there might be others.

Then he took a flying leap, booted foot first, at the closed door, hoping it wasn't any stronger than it looked.

It wasn't; the latch and upper hinge gave, and he tumbled through to find himself sprawled on top of a startled guard.

The guard was holding a Kalashnikov. Schaefer punched the guard in the jaw and tore the gun out of his hands, then looked around.

He was in an empty corridor with a door at each end and three doors on either side; he'd just emerged from the center of one long side.

That was bad; it meant a bigger building than he had hoped. This place was definitely more than a mere way station.

Schaefer figured that his only chance to get out of this alive was to disappear into the jungle and make his way back to somewhere civilized, somewhere he could get a plane back to the States.

That would probably take weeks.

And the bigger this place was, the harder it would be to slip away unseen in the first place.

Well, it wasn't as if he had a choice.

The guard on the floor was moaning; Schaefer

brought the butt of the Kalashnikov down on his head, and the moaning stopped.

He didn't risk shooting, though; that would draw too much attention.

He looked at the seven closed doors, saw daylight under the one at the left end of the corridor, and headed for it.

The narrow strip of daylight wasn't broken by the shadows of feet; if there was a guard, he was standing to one side, not directly in front of the door.

Schaefer put an ear to the wood and heard voices, but he couldn't make out words, couldn't tell who they were, how many, or how far away.

Cautiously, he lifted the latch with one hand, weapon held ready in the other.

Nothing happened.

He swung the door inward, as quickly and silently as he could, and stepped through.

And froze.

A dozen men were waiting for him, rifles trained on him; he was facing a broad, open courtyard, with no shelter, nowhere to hide, nowhere to run. The courtyard was surrounded by solid tile-roofed buildings of stucco or adobe, separated by narrow alleys. Watchtowers stood at the corners, watchtowers equipped with searchlights and heavy machine guns.

This was obviously Eschevera's home camp, the one the DEA intelligence reports had said was staffed by over a hundred men, with equipment capable of repelling a full-scale military assault.

"It's not going to be that easy, Mr. Schaefer," Eschevera said from behind two of the riflemen. He smiled. "Paolo was careless, as I thought he might be—I know you're a resourceful man, but Paolo . . . well, Paolo was not impressed. Perhaps now he will be, if you have left him alive."

Schaefer stared at Eschevera, thinking. They obviously expected him to drop the Kalashnikov and put his hands up, and that would probably be the smart thing to do, but if they were going to kill him anyway, why not try a dash for the gate? He wouldn't make it without a miracle, but miracles could happen, and whether he got a miracle or not, he might manage to take out Eschevera on the way.

He hesitated, though. Something felt wrong.

It was a feeling he'd had before, both in the jungle and back in New York.

Schaefer looked up at the nearest watchtower, where a man in a bush hat had a machine gun trained on him. That wasn't what was bothering him—a machine gun was worth some thought, but that wasn't what felt wrong. There was something in that general direction, though. Schaefer blinked and stared at the machine-gunner.

The man's chest exploded in blue-white fire.

Half the riflemen turned, startled, at the sound of the explosion; the other half were sufficiently well trained to keep their eyes and weapons on Schaefer.

Eschevera was one of those who turned to look, and then turned again as a second white fireball blew the head off the rifleman on his right.

"Son of a bitch!" he said, staggering on his bad leg, trying to see what was happening.

Then a real barrage began, and the riflemen scattered.

Other men began pouring from the buildings. The watchmen in the towers had swung their guns around and now began spraying machine-gun fire into the surrounding jungle, but Schaefer, remembering the dead monster's camouflage device, doubted that any of the gunners had a clear idea what they were shooting at, or where it was.

He noticed that the fireworks came from more than one direction. So the guide had been right, after all—the dead one must have had friends, and now they'd come to play.

Eschevera was shouting orders at a group of men doing something to a small outbuilding near one of the far corners of the courtyard; as Schaefer watched, the walls of the building fell outward, revealing an antiaircraft battery.

Eschevera really *had* been ready to fight off just about anything, up to and including a full-scale military assault—but how could he have prepared for what he was up against?

The heavy guns began firing, throwing shells randomly into the bush. "*¿Dónde demonios esté el?*" one of the gun crew shouted.

Eschevera's men couldn't see the enemy, and it was spooking them.

And in the excitement and confusion, they'd forgotten all about Schaefer.

Still, Schaefer hesitated for a moment longer. Even if Eschevera's men were drug-dealing slime, those outer-space things had no right to treat them as playthings, animals to be killed for sport.

Then a line of white fire stitched across the courtyard, walking up to the antiaircraft emplacement, cutting men down, and Schaefer realized this wasn't sport. They weren't playing around any-more.

They were *pissed*.

The guide had been right. Those things didn't like losing tourists.

But on the other hand . . . they were still doing this up close and personal, they weren't just sitting back and nuking the camp from orbit, and some-how Schaefer didn't think that was because they *couldn't*.

It might not be sport, but it wasn't war, either, and he remembered those drunken hunters back home, long ago, pumping shells into that deer.

The heavy guns exploded then, distracting him from his thoughts; the shrapnel took down a dozen men. Eschevera had been hobbling about, trying to organize resistance, but now he fell headlong on the dirt.

After the battery went, the concerted alien fire focused on the watchtowers, and within seconds two of the four were flaming ruins.

"Jesus," Schaefer said.

It was definitely time to get the hell out of there—especially since those things had probably come looking for *him*, and they'd remember it sooner or later, and he still had the tracking device embedded in his neck, and they'd remember that eventually, too. And Eschevera's men weren't about to waste time on stopping him when they were under this sort of attack; they were too busy staying alive.

He turned to the right and ran for one of the al-leys between buildings, hoping it led to a way out.

Behind him Eschevera looked up, dazed. He saw

Schaefer running and called out, "Schaefer! His people must have followed him here, it must be them! Schaefer's doing!" He raised a hand, pointing after the fleeing *norteamericano*.

A bolt of blue-white plasma took his hand off at the wrist; Eschevera screamed and rolled onto his back.

One of his men, gun in hand, ran up.

"Get him!" Eschevera shouted, waving the cauterized stump. "I want him dead! *He* did this!"

The gunman hesitated, looked around, then charged down the alley after Schaefer.

"He's mine," he called back.

As he vanished down the alley, back in the courtyard Eschevera looked up as something crackled and electric sparks danced.

A monster appeared out of thin air, a monster that walked upright on two legs but had a face of blank metal and mottled skin a color no human being had ever had, a monster taller than any man. Something perched on its shoulder, like a parrot on a pirate captain, and swiveled about.

And there were at least three other monsters, visible now, walking calmly through the fire and smoke that blanketed the courtyard, carrying things like blades and spears; they moved with power and assurance, alert but not troubled.

"Mother of God," Eschevera gasped.

Three red dots appeared on Eschevera's forehead, weaving about for a moment before settling into a precise little triangle. The black thing on the monster's shoulder pivoted and pointed directly at Eschevera's face, and Eschevera's very last thought was to recognize it as not a pet, but a weapon, a gun of some kind.

Then it fired.

The creature looked up from the smoking corpse, and in a perfect reproduction of the dead man's voice shouted to the world, "Mother of God!"

26

In a way, Schaefer thought as he ran down the alley past the compound's latrines and out into the jungle, Eschevera was right—he *had* been followed to the camp.

Just not by *his* people.

He no longer heard as many explosions, and the gunfire seemed to have stopped completely, to be replaced by the sound of men screaming.

From the screams Schaefer figured that those things were taking the time to enjoy themselves with Eschevera's surviving men. That would keep them busy for a little while, but it wouldn't be long before they remembered why they were there and turned their attention to him.

And when they did, the thing on his neck would lead them right to him.

"Goddamn dog collar!" he growled.

He ran on, trying to think.

He still had the Kalashnikov, but somehow he didn't think it was going to do him a whole hell of a lot of good against those things—not when they could take on Eschevera's whole private army.

He was alone in the jungle, didn't know where the hell he was—not even what *country* he was in, really—with no supplies except a stolen Kalashnikov; he still wasn't completely over the injuries from his fight back in New York, let alone the batterings he'd gotten here. His wrists and mouth were bleeding. For all he knew the goddamn gun wasn't even loaded, he hadn't had time to check. Half the drug dealers in Colombia might be after him by now, the fucking alien monsters were after him, and Philips and his goddamn secret agents probably wanted Schaefer dead as well. . . .

He paused to catch his breath and decide which way he should go.

He looked around at the jungle and saw nothing but green in every direction except the one he'd just come from. He could still hear men screaming, but the shots and explosions had stopped completely now.

Oh, he was in *great* shape, he was. What was the old saying? "It's always darkest before the storm," was that it?

New Age shit, Schaefer thought, as he was knocked to the ground by a flying tackle.

The Kalashnikov went flying.

Schaefer rolled over and looked up.

He was royally pissed at himself; he hadn't heard

the guy coming, hadn't seen a thing. He never *used* to let the bastards sneak up on him like that.

At least it wasn't one of the monsters. It was one of Eschevera's men, in a leather vest, brown Levi's, and a T-shirt. He was standing over Schaefer, straddling Schaefer's legs and grinning, pointing an AK-47 at Schaefer's head.

"What the hell do *you* want?" Schaefer demanded. "You planning to drag me back there? Think that's gonna do Eschevera any good?"

"Eschevera's dead," the man said.

At least he spoke English—but, then, most of Eschevera's men seemed to.

"You don't sound real upset," Schaefer said.

"I'm not," the man said. "It means there's room for advancement. The Cali cartel will be seeking a new liaison for the Mangabe district—that's what Eschevera did after you drove him out of New York. And if I'm the one who brings them your head, Detective Schaefer, the choice will be obvious."

"What about those things shooting up your camp?" Schaefer asked. "If we don't get the hell away from here, you aren't going to have a chance to take my head anywhere."

"Your friends? Why should they bother about us? They have the camp, the drugs—they might look for you, but come after us into the jungle?"

"They aren't my friends," Schaefer said. "Didn't you see what you were up against?"

"Ah, the pretty fireworks," the man said. "Yes, the authorities have brought more firepower than usual, but who else could it be? It's obvious."

"You like that word, 'obvious.' "

The man shrugged.

"Speaking of the obvious," Schaefer said, "lemme show you something." He brought his boot up in a sudden kick that would have done a Rockette proud, and caught the Colombian in the crotch.

The man doubled over, and Schaefer swarmed up and landed a fist on his jaw, knocking him sprawling.

Schaefer grabbed the AK-47 and tossed it away, then grabbed the Colombian up by his leather vest.

"You seem a little unclear on the concept here, pal," Schaefer said. "Those things playing laser tag with your buddies don't give a shit about your stinking cocaine. They're *not human, comprende*?"

"Go to hell, you lying . . ." The man was still clutching at his crotch.

"Goddamn it," Schaefer said, shaking him, "I'm telling the *truth*!" He dropped the man and stood over him—to the side, though, not where the Colombian could use Schaefer's own tactic against him. "Look, you son of a bitch, I'm tired, I'm sore, and I haven't had a decent cheeseburger since I left New York. So just don't *push* me, dig?" He turned away and picked up the Kalashnikov.

Even before the other man spoke, Schaefer knew he'd done something stupid. He didn't know why he'd done it, exactly—usually he had more sense than to turn his back on an enemy, no matter how beaten the enemy looked. Maybe, he thought, he just wasn't thinking straight—or maybe he was just so blown out he didn't *care* anymore.

Whatever the reason, he'd turned his back on

Eschevera's boy, and the Colombian had immediately rolled over and grabbed the AK-47.

"Hey, *pig*," he said, grinning, as he got to his feet and aimed the gun.

Schaefer turned, knowing he'd done something stupid, knowing he was probably about to be shot, knowing he'd be lucky just to get off a few rounds himself before he folded . . .

He heard a burst of automatic fire, like a gigantic steel zipper, and he didn't even have time to tense . . .

And he saw the blood blossom from the Colombian's chest and realized that it hadn't been the AK-47 that had fired.

The man who had wanted Eschevera's job wasn't going to get it; he folded up and fell to the ground, the AK-47 beneath him, blood soaking the smooth metal.

Standing behind him was General Philips, a smoking gun in his hands.

"Whatta ya know," Schaefer said, marveling. "The goddamn cavalry."

Philips frowned. He was in no mood for attempts at wit. This had been too damn close—he needed Schaefer alive if he was going to trade him to the aliens.

He should have just picked him up at the crater, instead of getting fancy with the separate rendezvous and pickup—*both* parts had gone bad on him.

At least it hadn't been the aliens who took out Decoy-Niner and got Schaefer.

Philips didn't know just who it *was*, and he didn't much care—the important thing was that he'd been able to track Schaefer down, and Schaefer was still alive.

But the aliens were back there at that camp, looking for Schaefer, and they could be along any minute.

Hell, they could be all around right now, with their damned invisibility screens. There was no time to waste on idle chitchat.

"You want to live?" he shouted at Schaefer. "Then shut up and follow me!" He turned and started dogtrotting through the jungle, not bothering to look back to see if Schaefer was following.

Schaefer *was* following—he wasn't stupid enough, or exhausted enough, to pass up a miracle like this.

A moment later, as bladelike leaves whipped against him, Schaefer caught a flash from the corner of his eye; he turned his head and saw flames and white fire erupting somewhere in the direction of Eschevera's fortress.

The roar came a second later.

"Hear that racket back there?" he shouted to Philips. "Your foreign friends are taking down Eschevera's drug empire piece by piece!"

Philips glanced back at Schaefer, then at the mounting column of smoke. "Drugs?" he said.

That made sense—who else would have a base like that out here in the middle of nowhere?

Schaefer nodded. "Hell, I'd put them all up for departmental citations if I could figure out where to pin the medals."

"They don't give a damn about drugs," Philips said. "They don't give a damn about this Eschevera, whoever the hell he is. They don't give a damn about *anything*. . . ." The two men burst through a final wall of brush into a clearing, where a helicopter waited, rotor turning slowly. Philips slowed to a walk and turned to Schaefer.

"Except *you*," he finished, raising the gun.

27

Rasche got up from his seat on the fold-out bed—he couldn't keep still.

This had been a recurring problem for some time; he just got so fucking *bored*, sitting here in this midtown apartment with these goddamn G-men. He'd been held prisoner here for days, without so much as a change of clothing—they'd given him a white terry-cloth bathrobe to wear when he wanted his clothes washed, and every couple of days one of the three made a run to the laundromat. Meals were all take-out—the kitchen was dark and empty. Which of the three went to pick it up varied, but it was always just *one* who went out, whatever the errand; there were always two of them there guarding Rasche.

They'd given their names as Smith, Jones, and Miller. They hadn't even smiled when they said it.

At least Rasche didn't have to share the bedroom with them; they slept out here on the folded-out couch, never more than two at a time, taking turns sitting up on watch.

There was a phone, but they didn't let Rasche use it, and when he sneaked out of the bedroom one night at two A.M., when the on-watch agent was in the can, and tried it, he couldn't get a dial tone; watching the feds the next day, he saw that they were punching in a four-digit code before dialing, and that the code changed with every call.

Rasche wasn't a cryptographer, and they didn't like him watching when they dialed; he couldn't crack the code.

There was a TV, but the reception was so bad even Rasche wasn't desperate enough to watch it— especially because it was a constant reminder of *why* the reception was bad.

Those goddamn ships were still out there, cruising over the city.

The helmet, or mask, or whatever it was, sat on the same desk as the trick phone; that was another reminder. Rasche didn't know for sure why they hadn't turned it over to their scientists, but so far they hadn't; they kept it right there, which seemed stupid.

He'd asked bout it, but for days they wouldn't give him an answer. Finally one of them said, "It stays with you until Philips gets back; you had it when we found you, so it's part of the package."

That was just stupid enough that Rasche figured it was probably true, but it opened up a slew of other questions—like where the hell was Philips, and when would he be back?

Naturally, they wouldn't tell him that. They wouldn't answer any of the important questions. If he asked how long they were going to keep him, they just said, "Until we're told to let you go."

And that was one of the more responsive answers.

Still, it was pretty clear what was going on here. They wanted to make damn sure that Rasche didn't tell anyone about the ships.

Which means they *knew* about the ships, had known all along, just as he had thought.

And Schaefer was tangled up in it all, though Rasche didn't know how. It was more than just that he'd gone after the killer and come away with the mask, Rasche was sure.

And the whole thing might be more complicated than he had thought. Those spaceships out there—that didn't look like any mere hunting party, but if it was an invasion fleet, why weren't they taking out whole neighborhoods, instead of slaughtering individuals or small groups and then leaving?

Was that thing Schaefer had fought an escaped criminal the aliens were hunting, perhaps?

Or did the ships belong to some other species entirely, a different one from the hunter? If so, who was on which side? Were the ships friend or foe?

And what was the government's relationship with those aliens? With the killer?

What the hell had happened to Schaefer? Was he still off in Central America somewhere, or had he come home? Was *he* sitting in some apartment somewhere with a bunch of federal agents, eating bad Chinese take-out because these dweebs were too lazy to hike down to Mott Street for the good stuff?

Rasche doubted a mere *three* agents would be enough to hold Schaefer. They probably had a dozen guarding him.

Rasche frowned at that. He wasn't as young as Schaefer, and he'd *never* been as big as Schaefer; he'd never had Schaefer's insane ability to handle violence. But he wasn't a wimp. He'd taken on tough guys in the past.

"This sucks," he said.

Miller was out getting lunch; Smith was leaning by the door, while Jones had a batch of papers spread on the desk.

"This *really* sucks," Rasche said. "How long do you think you can keep me here?"

"As long as we have to," Smith replied without moving.

Jones didn't even look up; as far as Rasche could tell, he was so involved in his paperwork, whatever it was, that he hadn't heard.

And the chain lock and dead bolt weren't locked, since they didn't want to make things hard for Miller; maybe, after all these long, boring days, these guys were getting sloppy.

"Hey, Smith," Rasche said, "your shoe's untied."

"Get serious, Rasche," Smith replied. He didn't look down, didn't unfold his arms. "We're trained professionals. That ruse only works on Cub Scouts."

Rasche glared at him, then turned away in disgust. He marched over to the desk and glowered over Jones's shoulder at the papers.

"What the hell is this, anyway?" he asked. "Doing your homework?"

"Doing my taxes," Jones replied without looking up.

"In August?"

"I missed the deadline and got an extension, okay, Rasche?" Jones put down his pencil and glared up at the detective.

"Oh, great," Rasche growled. "I'm stuck here with a fucking accountant!"

"Hey," Jones said angrily, pushing his chair back, "I don't *like* this, you know. I don't like this assignment, I don't like *you*, and I don't like doing my goddamn tax returns, but I can't *afford* a fancy accountant, I was busy on a *real* case in April, and I've got some investments, so I can't use the short form, okay? You got a problem with any of that, Rasche?"

"Well, jeepers, you're a regular Eliot Ness . . . ," Rasche began.

"Lay off, Rasche," Smith said, standing up straight.

The phone rang.

Rasche started at the sound; this was the first time it had rung since he had been brought there.

Jones snatched up the receiver and listened; Rasche tried to listen, too, but Smith wasn't having it.

"You just watch that mouth of yours, Detective Rasche," Smith said. "We've been trying to make this easy, but we can give you a hard time if we have to. You give us any grief, maybe when this is over, you'll find the IRS taking a look at *your* taxes—they'll audit you and have you hunting receipts and check stubs back to your goddamn *paper route....*"

"Suburban boy, aren't you?" Rasche growled. "I never *had* a fucking paper route."

Jones hung up the phone and announced, "That was Peterson. Schaefer's due in six hours. They'll chopper him straight to the MetLife building and make delivery there—"

"Wait a minute," Rasche demanded, interrupting. "What do you mean, 'delivery'?"

Jones didn't answer.

Neither did Smith.

They both just stared silently at Rasche.

And Rasche put it together.

That gadget on Schaefer's neck, the invisible spaceships cruising over the streets, General Philips telling them to just stay out of the whole thing, Schaefer's brother disappearing eight years ago . . .

He didn't understand all of it, there were pieces that didn't fit yet, but that delivery . . .

"Jesus," he said, "you're going to give Schaefer to those aliens, aren't you?"

Smith and Jones didn't deny it, and Rasche's temper snapped. "You lousy *bastards* . . . ," he began.

Smith pulled his pistol and shoved it under Rasche's nose. "Back off!" he bellowed. "One more move and I'll cuff you to the damn toilet!"

Rasche backed off; he backed over to the sofa bed and sat down.

"Yeah, yeah," he said, trying to sound harmless. He could feel his heart hammering with fury, but he kept his voice down. "Look, I'm sorry. I'm just a little *tense*, after all that's happened, waiting here and everything. You have to understand, Schaefer's a *friend* of mine. . . ."

Smith stared at him for a moment, then relaxed and holstered his automatic.

"Sure," he said. "No problem. Six more hours and it'll be over, and you can go home to the wife and kids."

"Yeah," Rasche said. "Thanks."

He wondered whether the wife and kids had come home yet. Were they still up in Elmira? Or had they come back and found him gone? Shari must be panicking, not hearing from him for so long—had anyone thought to tell her what was going on?

Or at least tell her a comforting lie of some kind?

The bastards probably hadn't bothered.

That pumped his anger up further, but he refused to let it show.

He sat for a long moment, letting the tension clear from the air, letting Smith and Jones relax, letting them think *he* had relaxed; then he stood up again, as restless as ever. He wandered to the window and looked out.

He knew where he was, of course; if he could see the street, he could tell where he was, just about anywhere in Manhattan, and this one was easy. The Lexington Avenue subway was only a block away. If he could once get out of the apartment and the building . . .

He wandered away again back toward the desk.

Smith was back by the door, not moving, his pistol tucked away.

Jones was back at his tax forms.

Miller was still gone, taking his own sweet time at the deli.

Rasche leaned over Jones's shoulder, feigning friendly curiosity.

"Hey," he said, "isn't two plus five *seven*, instead of eight?"

"Wha . . . ?" Jones looked where Rasche pointed, startled—and Rasche's other hand grabbed the back of Jones's head and slammed his face down onto the desk, hard.

Rasche heard the distinctive crunch of a nose breaking.

Taking a page from his partner's book, Rasche snatched up the alien mask from the desk and smashed it down on the phone, shattering plastic and circuitry; that would slow these two down when they tried to call in. Then he flung the mask sidearm at Smith.

Smith instinctively warded it off, costing himself a second or so in his attempt to reach for his automatic.

Then Rasche launched himself at Smith, slamming the G-man up against the wall.

Charged with adrenaline, Rasche picked Smith up completely and rammed him headfirst through the door. Wood splintered and a hole opened, giving Rasche a view of the hall's wallpaper; Smith went limp.

"That's what you get for insulting the Cub Scouts, you son of a bitch," he said, dropping the G-man. "My younger son's a Wolf."

He snatched up the mask with one hand, yanked out Smith's pistol with the other, then smashed his way through the broken remnants of the door.

"Shoddy modern construction," he said. "If you'd picked the Dakota for your hideaway, I couldn't have done that."

Then he ran for the stairs.

"MetLife building, six o'clock," he said as he heard Smith moaning and Jones cursing behind him. He took a final look back in time to see Jones step into the hallway, clutching his nose as blood streamed down his face, his 9mm in his other hand.

Jones got one shot off before Rasche was safely through the fire door and down the stairs, but it wasn't even close—it chipped plaster from the ceiling.

Rasche knew he might not have a chance; those two could call in the whole federal government. If he'd taken the time to tie them up or something . . . but Miller could be back at any time. That was why Rasche had taken the stairs instead of the elevator.

His only chance was that they might not expect him to do anything other than run and hide, and might not bother coming after him. Searching for a rogue cop in New York would be hard to keep quiet, and these guys desperately wanted to keep whatever they were doing a secret. They might just let him go.

After all, they needed only another six hours, and it would all be over.

28

The feds hadn't moved the rental van—Rasche found it still sitting just around the corner from Police Plaza. He supposed they hadn't thought it was important, or maybe they hadn't realized it was his. It had been sitting there untended for days, but miraculously it still had all its tires, no engine parts were missing, and the only graffiti was WASH ME! written in the greasy dirt on the back door.

He'd obviously picked the right neighborhood—one with plenty of cops coming and going at all hours.

Rasche had never planned to keep the rental this long. The bill when he turned it in was going to be a real killer.

He needed it a little longer, though.

He drove the streets for a while, planning, trying

to figure out just how he could keep the feds from turning Schaefer over to those monsters from outer space.

He didn't know enough. He didn't know whom he could trust, didn't know what it would take to stop those things.

Well, he'd just have to go up there ready for anything—and he thought he had an idea how to do that.

He left the van double-parked while he ran into the police academy building on Twentieth.

The firing range was still closed, but Salvati was back on duty upstairs, despite the fading bruises that made one side of his face look like an oil slick. He looked up at the sound of the door.

"Jesus, Rasche," he said, "where the hell have you been? People have been trying to reach you for days, Brownlow and those guys . . . "

"I was doing my taxes," Rasche said. "Look, Sal, I need a favor."

"I dunno, Rasche," Salvati said nervously. "I don't need McComb after *my* ass."

"I'm after those bastards who trashed the range," Rasche said.

Salvati's expression changed abruptly.

"What do you need?" he said through clenched teeth.

"Firepower," Rasche replied. "Whatever you can get me. And no paper trail—this has to be off the record."

"The feds?" Salvati asked. "Are those bastards trying to cover up?"

"Something like that, yeah."

"I *knew* it! Goddamn it, Rasche . . ."

"So what have you got?"

Salvati thought for a moment, then said, "Anything you want from the cases downstairs that didn't disappear, plus the stuff we took from those Jamaicans—you were in on that, remember? It's all still in the lab, the boys got pretty backlogged with all that shit from the Beekman massacre and the mess downstairs. There's all kinds of heavy stuff there—the Somalis got a bit carried away on the deal."

"I remember," Rasche said, smiling grimly.

This was better than he had expected. Chances were half the stuff wouldn't work, since most criminals were too stupid to take proper care of their equipment, but Rasche remembered how extensive that arsenal was. You could lose half of it and still have enough to take out damn near anything. Not just machine guns, but grenades, rocket launchers, everything.

That ought to be enough to get Schaefer away from the feds, or from whatever was flying those ships.

"Give me a hand with it, will you, Sal?"

Salvati nodded. "I'll get a cart."

People looked up and watched curiously as Rasche and Salvati hauled the weapons out to the sidewalk and loaded the van, but no one said anything, no one interfered. After all, Rasche thought, who would be crazy enough to walk out with that stuff in broad daylight if they weren't supposed to?

Rasche smiled to himself. He might not be as crazy as Schaefer, but he was getting there.

For his part, Schaefer had been choppered out of the jungle, flown to Newark aboard some sort of fancied-up army jet that looked as if it was meant for VIPs, then marched straight across the tarmac to a waiting copter.

He was being treated as a very important person, and that made him very nervous.

"All right," he said to Philips as they boarded the chopper, "we're back. Now I want some answers."

Philips looked at him but didn't answer. He did wave off the two guards; they looked surprised. Schaefer guessed they had thought they were coming along.

Maybe that meant that once they were in the air without any unwanted ears listening in, Philips would be willing to talk. Schaefer climbed aboard and strapped in without saying anything more.

Once they were aloft, though, Schaefer demanded, "What the hell are we dealing with? What *was* that thing I killed? Who were those things that took out Eschevera's camp?"

Philips shook his head. "You want a name?" he said. "We haven't got one. You want a place? Not earth. And that's damn near all we know."

Schaefer glanced at him, obviously disbelieving.

"You want theories, though, we've got a dozen, a hundred," Philips told him. "We've got legends and guesswork up the wazoo. The people back there in the jungle tell us they've been coming here for centuries—always in the heat, when it's hot even for the goddamn tropics; they don't like cold, don't like anything we'd consider decent weather, but when it's a fucking steam bath . . ."

"Like this year," Schaefer said.

Philips nodded.

"Yeah," he said. "Anyway, they hunt. They like

the chase. We've got people who think it was these things that wiped out the dinosaurs—hunted 'em to extinction. For all I know, it's true—all that *Enquirer* crap about aliens and ancient astronauts, for all we can really tell about these things, it could be true. There's one guy we've got who says these things may have bred us, helped our technology, started our wars, to build us up into more interesting targets, more challenging prey—and for all we know, the son of a bitch could be right." He shrugged. "Or he could be full of shit. Maybe they've only been coming since we started shooting each other, maybe the smell of gunpowder brought 'em. We don't *know*. We don't know shit about them. And everything we thought we *did* know . . . Well, we never thought we'd have to deal with them this far north."

Schaefer said, "Not our problem if they don't mess with us, huh?"

"Something like that," Philips admitted. "Up until now, going by the stories we've heard, by the radar traces we've mapped, they've only hit the equatorial countries—South America, maybe Africa, possibly Asia." He grimaced. "Goddamn greenhouse effect."

"Or maybe they just got bored with the jungles," Schaefer suggested. "Hell, if Earth's Disneyland, New York's gotta be an E ticket."

"Could be that," Philips agreed. He hesitated. "Or it could be something else."

Schaefer looked at him, waiting.

"You think it's a coincidence, that thing tagging the brother of the one man we know has beaten them? Not one man in a million ever sees one of these things, and the two of you do, thousands of miles apart? These things seem to *like* you Schaefer boys. Maybe they can track the genetic patterns somehow, maybe they just *smelled* you, we don't know, but maybe they came to New York looking for *you*."

Schaefer stared at him silently for a moment, considering that. "Good," he said at last. "They'll like me even more after I blow their ugly asses straight to hell."

Philips shook his head and drew his trusty old .45. "I'm sorry, son," he said, "I'm afraid we've got something else in mind." He leaned away from Schaefer and pointed the pistol at him.

Schaefer stared again, then said, "I should have guessed. You're giving me to them, aren't you?"

"I'm afraid so," Philips said. "You killed one of them, Schaefer—if we don't turn you over, there's no telling what they'll do."

"It was trying to kill *me*."

"That doesn't matter. They came after you, Schaefer—you saw that, in that camp. They don't care about this Eschevera, they wanted *you*."

Schaefer nodded. "I'd figured that much for myself," he said. "So why'd you pick me up? Why didn't you let them have me?"

"Because we need to make a goodwill gesture," Philips replied. "We need to let them know we're trying to help them, trying to communicate with them."

"They don't seem real interested in *talking*, General."

"We have to *try*."

"Because you're too goddamn chicken to fight them?"

Philips exploded. "Dammit, Schaefer, be realistic! We're talking about hundreds of thousands of lives here—maybe millions, maybe the whole damn planet! We *need* to show them we aren't hostile, so they'll go away and leave us alone! They don't consider us worth talking to, or they wouldn't hunt us, and we can't let ourselves be too dangerous, or they'll wipe us out, so we're trying to find a middle ground, show 'em we're smart but friendly."

"Why? Why not fight back, if you want the bastards to respect you?"

"Fight?" Philips shook his head. "Schaefer, you saw that blast site in the jungle, that crater—Dutch told us that was done by a gadget the one he fought carried on its wrist! Even if they don't bring in their heavy artillery, imagine the devastation if something like that exploded in New York—the city would be *destroyed*!"

Schaefer glared at him. "You say that as if it were a bad thing."

"Christ, Schaefer . . ."

"So you're going to give me to them—what do you think that'll do? You think they'll say, 'Oh, thank you, sir, sorry we bothered you,' and go away and never come back?"

"I think it'll get them the hell out of New York. They'll have got what they came for."

"Wasn't me they butchered, Philips. They came for *fun*, not for me."

"You were the one they *marked*, though, with that thing on your neck!"

"And maybe they want the fun of finding me for

themselves. Maybe you're going to be the guy who gives away the ending of the movie, handing me over. Maybe they'll be more pissed than ever. Ever think of that?"

"Dammit, Schaefer, we can't let them chase you through the streets—innocent people will get hurt! And everyone will see them, it'll start a panic! We've been keeping this hushed up for years. . . . "

"Maybe you shouldn't have," Schaefer interrupted. "Maybe you should let people know what's out there, let 'em stand up for themselves."

"You *can't* stand up to these things!"

"I did. Dutch did."

"All right, but nobody else—most people just *die* when they come up against one of these hunters. Look, Schaefer, this may be our chance to talk to them, to convince them we're intelligent, to make real contact . . ."

"They know how intelligent we are," Schaefer said, "which isn't very, in most cases. Thing is, they don't *care*."

"Yeah, well, maybe if we *show* them that we can help them, they'll care. They want you, Schaefer, and we're going to give you to them."

"I've got a better idea, General." Schaefer's hands flew out without warning and grabbed Philips's wrist, shoving upward; the .45 fired, and the slug punched a hole through the copter's roof.

"Sorry about this," Schaefer said as he snatched the pistol away with one hand and knocked Philips aside with the other. The general struggled, tried to hold on to the gun, but he'd been caught by surprise and was no match for Schaefer in any case.

His head hit a steel rib, and the old man folded into an unconscious heap on the floor.

Schaefer checked the general's pulse—Philips was still alive, just out.

Then he took the .45, pulled aside the drape separating the passenger compartment from the cockpit, and put the pistol's barrel to the pilot's head.

"Hi," he said. "Where are we headed?"

The pilot started, looked up, saw the pistol, gulped, and said, "The MetLife building. The heliport on the roof there. The brass are trying to arrange some kind of special meeting, I heard."

"What kind?"

"They didn't say—just told me not to be surprised by anything I saw there."

"Right," Schaefer said. "You just keep on, then—you're doing fine."

"Yessir."

Trying to arrange a meeting, he had said—so Philips wasn't really in communication with the aliens. He'd probably been planning just to stake Schaefer out on the rooftop there, like a goat as bait for a tiger.

It probably wouldn't even have worked; those things had their own ideas. If Philips had *really* wanted to keep them happy, he should have just left Schaefer loose in the jungle and let them track him down there.

Schaefer watched the familiar skyline sliding past; as they approached the midtown heliport, he counted six military types on the roof.

He didn't see any of the creatures—but, then, even if they were there, he wouldn't see them. Not with that invisibility gadget they used.

Six men didn't seem like very many; he supposed the feds were trying to keep the operation low-key.

Wishful thinking.

Maybe that was their problem, Schaefer thought. You don't *wish* this kind of trouble away—you've got to face it. It was time to quit pretending there was some easy solution, time to show those ugly mothers who was the boss around this particular planet.

They'd had their way long enough.

"Set it down nice and easy," he told the pilot. "Then just sit quiet and be a good boy."

"Yessir."

The landing came off without a hitch; then Schaefer just waited. He didn't open the door; instead he stood beside it, waiting, with the pistol still pointed at the pilot.

Sure enough, the men who had been waiting on the roof got impatient; one of them slid the door open.

Schaefer's fist took him in the face, and in an instant Schaefer was out of the copter and snatching up the M-16 the man had been carrying.

He stood and faced the others on the rooftop with a weapon ready in each hand and shouted, "Drop 'em!"

The other five hesitated, then, one by one, they dropped their weapons.

Schaefer smiled. He was back in control. The aliens weren't here, but they were going to come after him sooner or later, he was sure.

And when they did, he'd be ready for them—not staked out and helpless, but able to give them the fight they probably wanted.

Maybe he could convince them not to mess with the Schaefer boys.

He might die doing it, of course, but that was nothing new. He could die anytime.

"Put on some music and open the bar, boys," he said. "It's party time!"

29

Rasche looked up from the Park Avenue sidewalk in angry frustration as the helicopter descended toward the MetLife building; the damn thing was early! It was only five forty-five, and the copter was landing!

He'd been trying to get there in time, he'd been caught in traffic, he'd gone through hell getting the van parked, he'd finally made it with ten minutes to spare, and the goddamn copter was early!

He didn't have time for subtlety. He'd been thinking about trying to sneak up there with a hidden weapon, maybe take a hostage or something, but there was no time to try anything that complicated.

Instead, he went for the direct approach—he pulled an automatic rifle out of the collection in the back of the van, slung an ammo belt on his shoulder, and headed for the MetLife building.

He charged in from the north, the side away from Grand Central, with the rifle ready in his hands. Terrified late commuters scattered as he ran through the lobby.

When an elevator door opened he pointed the weapon into the car.

"Police," he shouted, "everybody out! This is an emergency!"

The frightened businessmen hurried to obey, and a moment later Rasche had the elevator all to himself and was headed upward.

Five minutes later he burst out onto the rooftop, shouting, "All right, *drop . . .*"

Then he saw Schaefer standing there, M-16 in hand, guarding half a dozen unarmed men with their hands on their heads.

". . . 'em," he finished weakly.

"Jesus, Rasche," Schaefer said, "where the hell have you *been*?"

Rasche stared angrily, then smiled.

"Got held up in traffic, Schaef," he said.

"Well, you're here now—let's get the hell out of here and get on with business!"

They left Philips and his men sitting on the roof of the MetLife building, their wrists tied behind them, and headed for Rasche's rented van.

Schaefer smiled at the sight of the arsenal in the back, but he didn't say anything about it; instead he climbed into the passenger side, laid his appropriated M-16 across his lap, and told Rasche, "Head downtown."

Rasche shrugged and started the engine. "You

want to tell me what the hell happened in Central America, and how you wound up at the MetLife heliport holding that popgun on a U.S. Army general?"

"Nope."

Rasche backed out of his parking spot. "Okay, it can wait," he said. "Care to tell me what we're going to do now?"

Schaefer nodded at the weapons. "We're going to use this stuff to blow those alien shits to hell."

Rasche considered that as he maneuvered the van out into traffic and got it headed south on Park Avenue.

He considered it very carefully.

Schaefer obviously knew they were up against aliens—Rasche didn't know how he knew, but he knew. Maybe Philips had told him.

But how much did he know about them, really?

Talking about blowing them to hell—Rasche didn't think Schaefer appreciated just what he was saying.

As he waited for the light at Twenty-third Street, he remarked, "You know, Schaef, you've been out of town, maybe you're not up on everything. I've been giving this some thought, and it seems to me we're outgunned."

"Why's that?" Schaefer asked, shifting the M-16 and glancing at the darkly gleaming weapons in the back.

"C'mon, Schaef, you have to ask?" Rasche said. "They're invisible, they've got spaceships, they probably have ray guns the way they shot up those guys . . ."

"They do," Schaefer agreed. "I've seen 'em."

"You haven't seen their ships, have you?"

"Nope."

"I have," Rasche told him. "Big ones, cruising over the city. You can see 'em through that mask you took off the one on Beekman. I don't know how many ships, or how many of those things are on each ship—more than one, though. I've seen at least four."

"So?"

"So I'll go through doors with you any day, Schaef, but we can't take those fuckers on alone. It's suicide."

"So who said anything about taking them down *alone*?"

The light changed and Rasche stepped on the gas, trying to figure out what Schaefer was talking about.

The feds weren't going to help—the whole damn government seemed to be on the side of the aliens, going by the plan to hand Schaefer over to them. And Philips would make sure that the rest of the NYPD was out of the picture, too—McComb and company weren't about to argue with him.

Salvati and Brownlow and a few others might have helped—except Salvati hadn't been out on the streets in years, he'd been running a desk, and right now he was still banged up enough Rasche wasn't sure he could handle *that*. And Rasche didn't know where Brownlow was, or how far he'd be willing to go—he and Ortiz and the rest still thought this was some kind of terrorist deal the feds were hushing up.

Besides, Schaefer didn't know about Salvati or Brownlow—he hadn't asked where Rasche had gotten all the guns. Schaefer had never exactly had a lot of close friends on the force. So he wasn't talking about recruiting more cops.

So who did he think was going to help?

"Take Fourth Avenue," Schaefer said as Union Square came into sight. He turned around in his seat and began looking through the array of weapons in back.

"You mind telling me where the hell we're going?" Rasche asked.

"Carr's place." Schaefer put the M-16 down and reached back.

"Carr?" Rasche's foot hit the brake without conscious direction.

"Keep rolling," Schaefer said. "Yeah, Carr. Who else's got a personal grudge against those things, besides you, me, and the rest of the department?"

"Carr's a complete psycho!"

"I know," Schaefer said, coming up with a pump-action shotgun. He began loading shells. "Seems to me that's what we need for this."

"How the hell do you know where Carr is now? You've been gone for more'n a week!"

"I don't know for sure," Schaefer replied, "but I have a pretty good idea."

"How?" Rasche demanded. "Why should Carr be anywhere you know?"

"Because Lamb's dead," Schaefer explained. "Carr's going to try to take over the whole schmear, and that means he's gotta be where Lamb's people can find him, so they can sign up—and that includes all the junkies who are down to their last few brain cells. So Carr's gonna be where Carr always is when he's not hiding."

"And you know where that is?"

Schaefer didn't bother to answer that. "Turn left," he said.

Rasche decided not to argue anymore; he drove, following Schaefer's directions.

A few moments later they pulled up across the street from a decaying tenement with DEATH ZONE painted across the door.

"That's it?" Rasche asked.

Schaefer nodded.

"He might be out to dinner or something."

"He might be, but he isn't," Schaefer said. "I can feel it."

"You and your goddamn feelings," Rasche muttered. "What if he isn't in there, Schaef?"

"Then we'll look somewhere else until we find him," Schaefer said as he got out of the van. He looked over the building, then leaned back in the window of the van and said, "You wait here. If I'm not back in ten minutes, come inside and kill anything that moves."

Rasche glanced back at the arsenal, thinking about the possibilities, and smiled grimly.

"My pleasure," he said.

He watched as Schaefer crossed the street.

Schaefer seemed to know what he was doing, but Rasche had doubts. Yeah, they needed manpower, but recruiting off the streets like this . . .

Well, Schaefer had always had a knack for bringing out the best in people, one way or another. Sometimes it was their best effort to kill the big son of a bitch, but hey, it was their best.

The door was open a few inches; Schaefer

pushed it open farther with his foot and stepped cautiously inside, shotgun ready.

The front-hall light was out, but lights were on somewhere upstairs, and the glow from the stairwell was more than enough to see by. The floor was strewn with debris, the walls were painted with obscene graffiti that failed to hide the stains, and the whole place stank of human waste. A chunk of ceiling had fallen away, exposing badly corroded pipes; one pipe was dripping slowly.

"Hey, Carr!" Schaefer bellowed. He marched forward to the foot of the stairs and shouted upward, "Carr! It's Schaefer! I know you're here, you son of a bitch—come on out! I want to talk!"

Schaefer heard the crunch of plaster underfoot a fraction of a second before he heard the shotgun blast; he had started to turn around when the gun boomed, and plaster dust, sawdust, and water showered down on him.

Carr had been in one of the darkened front rooms that Schaefer had passed without checking and had fired a warning shot into the ceiling. The corroded pipes overhead had been punctured a dozen places by the pellets, and only the low water pressure kept the spray from blinding Schaefer.

By the time he had turned around to face Carr, he had heard the distinctive ratchet of a fresh shell being pumped into the chamber.

Carr was standing there, grinning. "Okay, Oprah," Carr announced, "if you want to sing in the shower, I'm game. Lose the scattergun, and we can talk." He shoved the shortened barrel of his shotgun up close to Schaefer's ear.

Schaefer dropped his own weapon, safety on,

tossing it far enough that it landed clear of the spray.

"I gotta admit, you've got balls coming here," Carr said conversationally. "I've been picturing your brains on a wall since the night Lamb and the rest bought it. You got a reason I shouldn't get to see that?"

"Come on, Carr," Schaefer said. "My men didn't kill your punks. Get real."

"Oh?" Carr grinned. "Then whose men *did*?"

Schaefer could see Carr's finger tightening on the trigger. Carr, arrogant bastard that he was, might be crazy enough to blow him away without waiting to hear what he had to say.

"Wasn't men at all," he said. "It was something *worse* than men."

"Good trick," Carr said, and he closed one eye, sighting down the barrel.

Schaefer ducked, dropping below the gun's muzzle, and came up fist first into Carr's face.

Carr stumbled back, and Schaefer was on top of him, too close in for the gun to be any use except perhaps as a club; the two men fell to the floor, splashing dirty water in all directions.

After a moment's struggle Schaefer had Carr in a headlock and shouted at him, "Goddamn it, listen to me! I need your *help*, you son of a bitch!" He slammed Carr's head against a baseboard. "I didn't come here to fight you!"

Carr didn't bother to answer as he struggled to free himself.

Schaefer began to loosen his grip slightly, hoping Carr would listen to reason—and suddenly agony cut through his neck and up the side of his head, like a hot knife under the skin, a pressure on his throat almost choking him.

He released his hold on Carr and stumbled back.

"Aggh," he said, "it's here! Son of a bitch, it's around here somewhere!"

30

C arr watched as Schaefer staggered down he hallway toward the stairwell, looking around wildly.

"It's here!" Schaefer shouted again. "Come on out where we can see you, you bastard!"

There wasn't anything there, so far as Carr could see; Schaefer was yelling and clutching at his throat, but there wasn't anything there.

It had to be some kind of stupid cop trick, Carr decided after an instant of confusion, and he wasn't going to fall for it. He jumped to his feet and raised his shotgun.

"Yeah, sure it is, Schaefer," he said as he marched through the spray of water to get a clear shot at his opponent. "It's here, there, and everywhere. Talk show's over, pig—say bye-bye!"

Schaefer looked up at the barrel of the gun, at

Carr's finger tightening on the trigger, at Carr's grinning, maniacal face—and at the waterfall behind him, the spray from the ruined pipes, where blue sparks were crackling and crawling across a familiar silhouette. He tried to shout a warning to Carr, but it felt as if something were caught in his throat.

And, besides, the bastard was about to blow his brains out—why warn him?

And then any warning would have been superfluous, as the alien creature appeared out of thin air, its invisibility screen down for the moment, one taloned hand closing around Carr's neck from behind.

"The water . . . ," Schaefer said, his throat clear again. "Jesus, the water shorted something out."

The creature picked up the gang boss easily, and Schaefer ducked again as Carr fired; the shotgun blast went safely over his head, just as the warning shot had before.

"What in the hell . . . ?" Carr managed to say. He twisted in the thing's grip, trying to get a look at it, trying to see what was holding him up by the throat as if he weighed no more than a kitten.

"That's" what killed your boys, Carr," Schaefer shouted. "Those goddamn things've been tracking me ever since. It didn't give a damn who you were, Carr—your men were all just trophies to it!"

"Oh, yeah? Trophy this, piss-face!" Carr shouted back, as he struggled. He spat, managing to hit a corner of the thing's metal mask.

"Say bye-bye," the creature replied in a close approximation of Carr's own voice of a few moments before. It reached up and placed its other hand atop Carr's head, preparing to twist.

Schaefer, looking around, spotted his own dropped gun; he dived for it, calling, "Not yet, pal!"

He came up with the gun held like a club; he swung it by the barrel and caught the monster on the side of the head.

Startled, but clearly uninjured, the thing threw Carr aside and looked at Schaefer.

The gadget on its shoulder popped up and began to swivel, and Schaefer dived sideways as a blue-white fireball blew a two-foot hole in the wall.

He rolled and brought the shotgun up, and realized the barrel was bent, the action twisted into uselessness—he'd hit the alien harder than he had realized.

A blow that would bend a shotgun would have killed a man instantly.

Well, as he'd told Carr, this thing was worse than a man—and a hell of a lot tougher.

He didn't dare fire the gun; it would probably blow up in his face. He flung it aside and looked up at the hunter from outer space.

Its expression was hidden behind its mask; he couldn't tell if it was angry, frightened, amused, or just bored—and even if he'd seen its face, how could he read those inhuman features, that mouth with the layers of fangs?

The snakelike braids, or whatever they were, trailed down across its shoulders; the ray gun, or laser cannon, or whatever the hell it was on its shoulder, was pointed straight at Schaefer's face.

It didn't fire.

Instead, the creature raised one hand, and the

pair of jagged blades mounted to the back of its wrist suddenly snapped out into an extended position, projecting well past its clenched fist.

Schaefer had seen blades like that before, on the arm of the monster he had killed in the jungle, and on the monsters that attacked Eschevera's camp.

One swipe of those could tear out a man's throat, or lay open his chest.

This one wasn't shooting at him because it wanted to take him on hand to hand—more macho *mano a mano* shit.

And this time Schaefer didn't have any way to run or dodge, he didn't have any surprise weapons; he'd have to fight on the creature's own terms.

Which meant dying.

Well, hell, he'd known he'd have to die sometime.

"Come on, then," Schaefer said, crouching, bracing himself. "This is what you've been *waiting* for, isn't it? Your chance to get the one that killed your buddy? Your shot at one of the *tough* ones? Go ahead, then—finish it!"

"Let's not and say we did," called a voice from the shadows by the building's front door, a good thirty feet away.

The creature started to turn.

"You're under arrest . . . ," Rasche began as he raised and sighted-in the Soviet-built shoulder-mount antitank gun he had hauled in from the van. God only knew what the Jamaicans had thought they wanted with something like that.

Then he got a good look at the creature and said, "Aw, screw it."

He pulled the trigger, and the rocket tore

through the intervening distance in a fraction of a second.

Still, Schaefer thought the alien might have been able to dodge; it was fast enough, he'd seen that—but it didn't dodge. Maybe it was too surprised.

The thing's body shielded Schaefer from the worst of the blast, but the entire building shook, and the walls on either side of the hallway buckled outward; plaster and shattered wood showered down. The flow of water was abruptly transformed from a scattered spray into a steady spill down one broken wall as the remains of the pipes above the passage vanished completely in the explosion.

When the dust had mostly cleared, Schaefer climbed to his feet, took one look at the condition of the building, and ran for the door.

He almost tripped over the dead alien, but he didn't stop to gloat; he could hear wood creaking ominously.

Rasche was waiting on the stoop; he'd been farther away from the blast but unshielded, and his forehead was bleeding where a bit of shrapnel had nicked him; plaster dust had powdered his hair and clothes.

Together, the two detectives ran into the street, back toward Rasche's van; they were about halfway across when Carr stumbled from the wreckage, a yard or so ahead of a great crash of masonry as a wall fell in.

All three men turned at the sound and stood staring.

"Anyone else in there?" Rasche called.

Carr shook his head. "None of mine. We were

moving out—I was just back here checking. Schaefer here got lucky with his timing."

His voice didn't have its usual sardonic edge; he sounded shaken.

"You saw that thing, right?" Schaefer asked.

Carr nodded, backing down the stoop as Schaefer came up beside him.

Rasche was back at the van, rummaging for something.

"Any of this sinking in, then?" Schaefer asked. "Or are you twice as stupid as you look?"

"Oh, I get the picture," Carr said. "And okay, maybe your cops didn't trash my men and take out Lambikins, but that thing's pieces, right? So it's over."

Schaefer shook his head. "That was what *I* thought the first time."

Rasche, emerging from the van with the alien mask in his hand, called out, "It's not over, Carr—like the song says, we've only just begun."

He held up the mask, scanned the streets with it, then turned his attention to the dark skies above. He growled, then handed the mask to Schaefer. "Over there," he said, pointing. "Coming this way."

Schaefer looked, tracking the approaching ship's movement, and nodded. "They're not going to be very happy when they find what's left of their buddy," he said. "That's two down and counting." He handed the mask back to Rasche.

"What are you two *looking* at?" Carr demanded. "There's nothing out there!"

Rasche ignored him; he was watching the red-gold shape coming in over the rooftops, coming toward them.

It was coming in low, and descending even farther.

"Not very happy at *all*," Rasche said. "Shut up and run, Carr!"

He took his own advice and sprinted for the van.

This ship wasn't just cruising over the city—*this* ship was diving for them in what looked for all the world like a strafing run.

"Get down!" Schaefer shouted as something flashed.

The three men dived to the pavement as the building behind them erupted into white fire and flying brick.

Rasche rolled over and looked through the mask.

The ship had veered off and was looping back for another pass; the building's facade had a ten-foot hole in it where the door had been a moment before, a hole full of dust, firelight, and clattering brick fragments.

"Come on," he called, leading the way toward an alley that he hoped would provide some shelter.

The ship came back for its second run, and it was immediately obvious that the first had been a sighting shot—this time the thing laid down a deafening barrage of blue-white fire that cut the entire building to bits.

The three men stared, dumbfounded.

"Jesus," Rasche muttered as the ship ceased its fire—it was past the building now, no longer had a clear shot. "So much for urban renewal," he said. "No yuppie's ever gonna gentrify *that* place!"

"And no one's going to salvage anything of that dead one," Schaefer said grimly. "They're making sure no one makes a trophy out of one of their own!"

"What the hell?" Carr shrieked. "What did that? What are we up against? I still don't fuckin' *see* anything!"

"Here, have a peek," Rasche said, thrusting the mask in front of Carr's face and directing his gaze.

Carr stared up at the departing spaceship.

"Wild, huh?" Rasche asked, glancing at Carr. "Just like *War of the Worlds*."

Schaefer snorted. "They all died of a cold in that one, Rasche, but I didn't notice that thing reaching for a tissue, did you?"

Carr grunted, and Rasche took the mask back.

"The feds are scared of them," Schaefer said, "so it's going to be up to us to bring them down, let them know they aren't welcome here." He looked around. "We have to get off the streets, find some place to make a stand."

Rasche nodded. He scanned the sky quickly. "I don't see it right now," he said. "Let's get in the van and move, talk while we drive."

"They can track me," Schaefer said, gesturing toward his neck.

"I know that," Rasche said, "but maybe not that fast. Come on."

Schaefer nodded, and the three men ran for the van.

Rasche took the driver's seat, Schaefer took shotgun, and Carr climbed back between the seats—and saw the weapons.

"Jesus," he said. "You've got more stuff back here than *I* have in the whole goddamn city!"

"That's the point," Schaefer said. "When those things have swept up what's left of their pal, all hell's going to break loose, and we're gonna need all the manpower we can put on the streets if we want to still be standing when they're done. That's what I came after you for in the first place, Carr—we want you and your boys to help us."

Carr stared at him for a moment."

"Why us?" he asked. "I mean, we aren't exactly your buddies, Schaefer—I always figured you'd like to see me dead. Hell, I know I'd like to see *you* dead."

"Yeah, well, I need manpower, and your people may be scum, but at least they've got some guts," Schaefer said. "So I'm offering a truce, just till these alien geeks are gone—after that it's back to business as usual."

"I'd have figured for something like this you'd call out the goddamn army, not come looking for me."

"The army's scared," Schaefer said. "They figure to let the aliens do what they want, and when they're done, they'll go home. Rasche and I don't think that way—if those things are having fun, why would they leave?"

"So here you are, talking to me."

"Here we are. With the guns back there."

"And you'll let us use all this hardware?"

Schaefer nodded. "That's the deal—just for the duration. I don't know if we can take out their whole damn fleet, I don't know how many of them are out there, but maybe we can make it a little less fun. So what do you say, punk? Feel like a little rock and roll?"

Carr grinned. "You got it, Schaefer. Cops, aliens, I don't care *who* it is—nobody offs my men without some serious payback. You supply the guns, and let *me* handle the rest!"

31

Traffic was light as Rasche headed uptown. He wasn't sure just where he was going, but there was more of the island uptown than down, so he'd turned north.

Behind them they could hear the alien spaceship making a third pass at Carr's building, but Rasche figured by now they were just making the rubble dance—there wasn't anything still standing.

He pulled onto FDR Drive at Houston Street, looking to make better time, and for a few moments the breeze through the van's windows cut the stifling heat.

The air was heavy with humidity; Rasche felt as if he could almost touch the moisture, and off to the west, between the towers of the city, he could see dark clouds on the horizon and distant flickers of heat lightning.

The damp air seemed cooler, and the clouds had the look of an approaching storm—he thought the heat wave might finally be about to break.

The lightning reminded him of distant artillery, though, and he remembered the spaceships—he couldn't use the mask while he was driving, but they could be up there, anywhere, watching, scanning for the thing on Schaefer's neck, and the van was exposed up here on the elevated highway, an easy target.

And besides, where the hell was he going that he needed to make time?

He got off onto Twenty-third Street and headed west, then turned north again on Third Avenue.

The police radio Rasche had installed in the van was chattering—Carr's building was gravel by the time anyone got there, gravel that was still churning.

McComb came on and said that was settling, but McComb wasn't there—the officers at the scene said it looked like something was shoving debris around, searching for something.

They stayed the hell away—settling or searchers, it didn't look safe.

Rasche thought that was a good idea. The movement would be the invisible aliens, on the ground now, recovering the body of their fallen comrade. Anyone who got in their way would be hamburger.

At Schaefer's direction Rasche got off the avenue and found a place to park on a cross street somewhere in the thirties.

"Carr," he said, "how many men can you get us? You lost Edgie and Hatcheck . . ."

"I lost more than that," Carr interrupted. "Those

bastards have been taking my people down one by one for weeks. Most of my boys who aren't dead are lying low."

Schaefer stared at him.

"You said you could help us," he said accusingly.

"That's right," Carr said. "I was figuring something big was gonna come down. Whoever was picking my people off wasn't going to keep it up forever, just getting 'em one or two at a time."

Rasche glanced at him but didn't say anything.

"Sooner or later whoever it was had to come out in the open, and I figured on being ready for 'em."

"And?" Schaefer asked.

"And I lined up some muscle—not my people, loaners and freelancers." He grinned. "Just what we need to use those toys of yours."

Schaefer nodded. "So what do you figure you'll need to get us the men we need, a week?"

Carr laughed.

"You're not listening, Schaefer—I said I wanted to be *ready*. Couple of hours should do it."

Schaefer looked at him silently for a moment. "No shit," he said at last.

"No shit," Carr agreed. "Gotta make some calls, but we can get this over with tonight."

"Go ahead," Schaefer said, pointing at a pay phone, "make your calls."

It was busted, of course, but they found a working one two blocks up.

"Yo," Carr said, holding the receiver, "gimme some change—I left my wallet at home." He grinned again.

"Rasche?" Schaefer asked. He was freshly back

from his little vacation in Central America and hadn't had time to worry about things like money.

"How many calls you making?" Rasche asked, digging for quarters.

"A lot," Carr answered.

"Just give him your card, Rasche," Schaefer said impatiently.

Rasche frowned, then dug out his MCI card and handed it over.

Carr took it, still grinning, and began punching numbers. "Why don't you boys go somewhere else for a few minutes?" he said. "I got stuff to say that maybe you might not want to hear."

"You don't . . . ," Rasche began.

"Come on, Rasche," Schaefer said. "We'll get a bite to eat." He jerked his head toward the hole-in-the-wall diner down the block.

Reluctantly, Rasche followed.

"Goddammit, Schaef," he said as they stepped through the door, "he's gonna run up God knows how much of a bill, and I'll *never* get reimbursed—you know what an asshole McComb is about unauthorized expenses. That son of a bitch could be calling his mother in Hong Kong for all I know."

"Yeah," Schaefer said, "but more likely he's calling every cheap hood, dope dealer, and gangbanger on the Lower East Side, and next month you'll have an itemized bill right there in your mailbox with every one of their private numbers on it—ever think of that?" He smiled thinly. "Carr's just as stupid as he is cheap."

Rasche shut up, reluctant to admit that no, he hadn't thought of it.

They sat at the counter and ordered sandwiches

and coffee, and while they ate, they brought each other up-to-date on what had happened while Schaefer was out of town. Rasche was mildly pleased to hear that Eschevera was dead; Schaefer was less pleased, but very interested, to learn about what Rasche had seen through the mask—he'd seen one ship for himself half an hour earlier but hadn't really had time to think about it.

They were just finishing when Carr came in and announced, "Let's go."

"Where?" Rasche asked.

"You just drive," Carr said. "I'll tell you."

They got the van rolling, and Rasche followed Carr's directions, arriving a few minutes later at the entrance ramp to the lower levels of a parking garage a few blocks farther up Third.

Somehow Rasche found it appropriate to be meeting Carr's friends below street level.

"Stop here," Carr said as Rasche pulled onto the ramp.

Rasche stopped. "What," he said, "we need the password or something?"

"No," Carr said. "You two wait here. I'll drive down alone; then we'll see. My people were expecting a blow-off, yeah, but against cops, not a bunch of little green men. Some of them aren't always easy to convince; you gotta give me some time to sell this."

"You've gotta be kidding!" Rasche protested. "We're carrying enough ordnance in here to start a small war—I'm not going to let you pass it out to your scumbag pals like party favors!"

Carr grinned, and Rasche wished he had the strength—and the nerve—to knock those teeth out.

"Let him go," Schaefer said as he picked up the mask and his appropriated M-16 and opened his door. "Do it his way for now, and if there're any problems, we'll kill *him* first."

He got out of the van.

"Wow, ultimatums," Carr said. "My little heart's palpitating in fear. Maybe when this is over, Schaefer, we can get together and see who's *really* king of the hill."

Schaefer grinned back at him, and Rasche reluctantly climbed out of the van.

Carr slid into the driver's seat and started the van down the ramp; Rasche and Schaefer watched him go.

"I'd like that, Carr," Schaefer said quietly. "I'd like it a lot."

Rasche sat down on the narrow curb at one side of the tunnel. He glanced down after the van but could see nothing—the entrance ramp curved. He sighed. He glanced at his watch and saw that it was half-past midnight—Carr's calls had taken well over an hour.

So here he was in the middle of the night, sitting in a parking garage, hoping to make a deal with an insane gang boss to join forces in a hopeless battle against monsters from outer space.

How the hell had it come to this?

These things from the spaceships were like something out of one of those paranoid sci-fi movies from the 1950's, killing just for the sake of killing. . . .

No, he corrected himself, they weren't; those monsters had had reasons. They wanted to conquer the world, or they killed people for food—they didn't kill just for fun.

These things did.

In the more recent movies the aliens were usually the good guys, come to save humanity from itself, or just paying a friendly visit.

These things obviously weren't doing that, either.

It didn't seem *right*, somehow.

"It's funny," he said.

Schaefer was still standing in the roadway, staring down the ramp after Carr; he didn't respond.

"It's funny," Rasche repeated. "Those things are *way* past us, technologically—their ships make the space shuttle look like a Matchbox toy, they've got ray guns and invisibility and God knows what else—and yet they still get off on hunting and killing things, they take trophies, they seem to love blood and pain. I wonder why. I mean, shouldn't they be more advanced than us socially, as well as technologically? Wouldn't they have outgrown all that?"

Schaefer glanced at him, then went back to staring down the tunnel.

"You think that's something you outgrow, Rasche?" he asked a moment later.

"Isn't it?"

"Maybe." Schaefer paused for a moment, then said, "Maybe they're just like us. Technology removes us from our true selves, lets us pretend we don't have to kill to eat, lets us forget we're all a bunch of killer apes. It takes us away from the beast inside. People talk about getting back to nature, and they just mean going out in the woods somewhere and treating it like a fucking garden, a bunch of birds and bunnies and flowers, and they forget that Mother Nature's a bitch, that claws and fangs and blood are natural, and gardens aren't. Nature's a jungle, not a garden."

"Well . . . ," Rasche began.

Schaefer cut him off. "Maybe those things up there don't forget what nature's like. Maybe the hunt is their way of getting back to nature, their way of keeping the beast alive, keeping that competitive edge that lets them develop their spaceships and ray guns. Maybe they *need* an edge—maybe they're worried about natural selection selecting them out, if they get soft. Maybe the whole goddamn galaxy's a fucking war zone, a big bloody free-for-all, the law of the jungle on a cosmic scale, and those bastards need to stay tough to survive." He shrugged.

"Or maybe," he added after a second's pause, "they're just naturally sadistic sons of bitches."

Rasche stared up at his partner. That was about the longest speech he'd ever heard from Schaefer.

"You really think we can beat them?" he asked.

Schaefer didn't answer.

They sat, and thought, and waited, but Rasche didn't ask what Schaefer was thinking or offer to share any more of his own thoughts.

He thought about Shari and the kids and hoped they were safe, up there in Elmira or back home in Queens, wherever they were. He hoped they weren't too worried about him.

He thought about those files Brownlow had shown him, about the string of hideous murders that *might* have been committed by the aliens—or might have just been an unusually vicious serial killer.

Carr thought that was the aliens.

Rasche *hoped* it was the aliens.

It bothered him that he couldn't be *sure* it was the aliens. What kind of a species did he belong to, that he couldn't be sure people wouldn't do that to each other?

And what kind of species did the aliens belong to that they apparently not only committed such atrocities against other intelligent species, but saw nothing wrong with it? Those ships weren't just a couple of desperate criminals or crazed degenerates running loose; those ships were an organized party of some kind, a *big* one, and that meant that whatever they were doing, it was just fine with the folks back home.

Or maybe it wasn't; maybe when those monsters got home, they'd find themselves facing the alien equivalent of a picket line, placards reading SAVE THE HUMANS, angry demonstrators throwing blood or paint at the hunters the way demonstrators attacked women in fur coats. . . .

People didn't have fur, but those things sometimes skinned their victims—what did they *do* with those skins? *Did* they wear them? Was Lamb's face going to wind up on another planet, stained with extraterrestrial paint?

Rasche was tired and hungry, and this chain of thought was making him feel slightly sick to his stomach—he was in *great* shape to save the world from the Martians, he was.

Or even just to tackle Carr and his buddies if they'd decided not to help, after all.

And besides everything else, his ass was sore from sitting on the hard concrete; he shifted uncomfortably and scraped a shoe across the pavement.

Schaefer raised a hand for silence.

Rasche listened.

Footsteps were approaching, coming up the ramp.

Rasche turned and watched as Carr came into view, an assault rifle slung on his shoulder, a machine pistol on his belt. At least a dozen other young men were beside and behind him, all of them armed to the teeth with the contents of Rasche's van, with the weapons Salvati had given him, everything the Somalis had sold the Jamaicans, all of it loaded and ready to go. Ammunition belts were draped across tattooed chests, automatic weapons were tucked under muscular arms, shotguns were clutched in sweaty hands.

"Hey, *Schaefer*!" Carr called. "We put it to a vote, and it was unanimous. Humans one, alien shits *zero*!"

Schaefer smiled, a humorless baring of teeth that Rasche didn't like at all.

"Good," he said. "So listen up while I tell you what you're up against."

A couple of Carr's buddies glanced at one another; someone said derisively, "Oooh, tell us, Mr. Policeman!"

"The things we're fighting are invisible, except through one of these." He held up the alien mask. "They all wear them—I figure they're invisible to each other without them, same as they are to us."

"You got those for all of us?" a black kid with a shaved head and an AK-47 called.

"Nope. Just the one. But you take one of 'em down, you want to get its mask."

"How we take 'em down if we can't see 'em?"

"You'll see a weird shimmer in the air when they're near," Schaefer explained. "Aim for it with all you've got. And don't wait—these things are bigger and stronger and faster than you are, and I don't care *how* big and strong and fast you think you are, they're more."

"Faster and stronger and we can't see 'em?" someone mumbled. "Shit."

"That's why you've got the guns," Carr said.

"If they're invisible, how do we know they aren't watching us right now?"

"We don't, not for sure," Schaefer said. "Except if they were, they'd probably have already started killing us."

"Hell," another man said, hefting a tripod-mounted, belt-fed machine gun, "I didn't come here to hear no fairy stories about invisible bogey-men. Why don't we flash this pig and test-fire our new toys over in the diamond district?" He turned and looked around at the others for support.

Schaefer stared at the man for a second, then lashed out without warning—a single blow of the fist.

The man went down and lay gasping on the asphalt.

"Any *more* questions?" Schaefer demanded as he picked up the mask again.

"Yeah," Rasche said. "How are you planning to *find* them? How are we going to lure them in where we can get at them? Showgirls and dancing bears? A big sign, 'Today only, everything half price to killer aliens'?"

"I had an idea on that," Schaefer said. "A couple of ideas, actually. First off, you said you saw them cruising over the city, right?"

"Right," Rasche said, not sure where Schaefer was going with this.

"So they aren't hiding. They don't realize we can actually see them through this thing—they've got no *reason* to hide. They're probably still up there, cruising around—all we have to do is watch. Second thing, they're still tracking me." He touched the device on his neck. "I figure they're probably cruising over this place every few minutes, keeping an eye on me."

"So they're cruising overhead," Carr said. "You didn't bring us a goddamn F-16, Schaefer—how the hell do we get them down here? Or did you want us all to help you *watch* the pretty ships go by?"

"I think the arrogant bastards are getting cocky," Schaefer said. "Sure, we took out two of them so far, but they've trashed a lot more of us, and most of the time we've been running from them, not fighting. I figure if we get their attention, they'll come down here after us—that'd be the sporting way to get us. Shooting us from their ships would be like hunting deer with a bazooka—it'd work, but it wouldn't be any fun."

"Yeah, yeah—but just how do you figure to get their attention?" Carr asked.

Schaefer pointed to the Soviet antitank gun

that Rasche had used to kill the one at Carr's place.

"With that," he said. "I don't know if it'll punch through whatever armor they've got on their ships, but ten to one they'll *notice* it."

32

It hadn't taken long for one of the soldiers to get free and untie the others, and Schaefer and Rasche hadn't tied the knots all that tight to begin with, but Philips kept rubbing at his wrists as he sat in the copter.

He'd gotten the reports over the radio, heard how Detective Rasche had smashed his way out of captivity, how he'd made off with a cache of heavy weapons, and he didn't need to be a genius to figure out what that meant.

Schaefer and Rasche were planning to fight the aliens, even if it meant a goddamn war.

Philips couldn't figure out how the hell Schaefer and Rasche had worked it out, how they'd communicated when they were both being held in protective custody, but somehow or other they must have planned it all. He still remembered Schaefer standing there on the rooftop saying, "Jesus, Rasche, where the hell have you been?"

Schaefer had expected Rasche, had known what was happening, and he, Philips, the supposed intelligence big shot, hadn't had a clue.

And then there was the mask—the agents who'd picked Rasche up and held him while Philips was off in Latin America said that Rasche had had one of the aliens' face masks.

And they hadn't done anything with it.

A piece of the alien technology had been right in their hands, and they *hadn't done anything with it*.

And when Rasche broke out, when an out-of-shape New York cop took two highly trained federal agents by surprise and beat the crap out of them, he took the mask with him—the thing was *gone* again.

Philips didn't even know why Rasche wanted it, where he'd gotten it, he didn't know *anything*.

And those goddamn shit agents didn't know, either—they'd never bothered to ask Rasche about it, never asked him a damn thing.

Christ, Philips thought, what a bunch of fuckups.

This whole thing was going bad—no, it had started out bad; it was getting worse. It was, in fact, going straight down the tubes. They didn't have a damn thing to give the aliens—and they never had, not really. The aliens took what they wanted. They'd taken back their dead companion, and when they wanted Schaefer, they'd take him, too.

And they hadn't even shown up for the rendezvous. Philips's men had been transmitting every kind of signal they could think of as bait, to get the monsters interested—and as far as Philips could see, the aliens hadn't paid any attention.

They must have known what was going on. They could have had someone at the heliport if they'd wanted to.

So they didn't want to. They didn't want Schaefer as a gift. If they wanted him at all, they wanted him on their own terms.

Maybe they didn't want him, maybe the one who'd tagged him was the one he'd killed, and the others didn't give a shit. . . .

Too goddamn many "maybes"!

The truth, Philips finally admitted to himself, was that he and his experts didn't know a damn thing about how the aliens thought.

The Schaefer boys had both seemed to have something of a handle on it, though. For all the good that did.

And Schaefer had wanted to fight back. He'd thought that just waiting for the bastards to leave was a mistake. He'd thought trying to propitiate them, as if they were a bunch of little gods, was a mistake.

Maybe Schaefer was right.

The President had said they couldn't afford to fight—but what did he know? He'd also said he trusted Philips's judgment, and right now Philips judged that Schaefer was right—they couldn't afford *not* to fight.

For one thing, Schaefer and Rasche were out there somewhere with a vanload of heavy weapons, and *they* were going to fight. A fight was going to happen, it couldn't be stopped.

And as far as Philips was concerned, if he couldn't stop the fight from happening, then his job was to do everything he could to help the right side win.

He didn't really think he could pull if off; how could he fight a bunch of invisible spaceships, fight monsters with shoulder-mounted energy cannon?

But he had to try.

Schaefer and Rasche were trying—they were out there fighting back, somehow. And Schaefer, who seemed to understand how the aliens thought better than anyone except maybe Dutch, didn't think it was suicide. He didn't think they were going to lose New York.

Or maybe he *did* expect to die, *did* expect to lose New York—and didn't *care*. Schaefer was a crazy bastard. Dutch had been stubborn, but Schaefer was just plain nuts.

Maybe that was why he could understand the aliens; maybe they were crazy the same way he was. Maybe he was more like them than he was like an ordinary man.

Maybe *that* was why they'd tagged him.

Philips shook his head.

It didn't matter now why they'd tagged Schaefer. It didn't matter why they'd come to New York, instead of staying in the tropics. All that mattered was that the final showdown was coming, and Philips's job was to get whatever force he could out there to help.

He couldn't get the entire army in on this, there

wasn't time, but he could at least put together enough to let those damn monsters know they'd been in a fight.

"Turn on the damn radio," he told the pilot. "Get me Washington."

33

The sky was turning pale in the east, and before he slid the alien mask into place, Rasche could see the top of the Chrysler building, a few blocks uptown, beginning to glitter in the light of dawn. Half of Carr's men had dozed off, sprawled here and there along the garage entrance walls, surrounded by their weapons.

Schaefer knelt on the sidewalk, the Soviet anti-tank gun ready beside him, while Rasche took a turn watching the skies above Third Avenue.

"Come on, Schaefer," Carr growled. "Take your goddamn shot, for Christ's sake. You've let half a dozen of the bastards go by—if this was baseball, you'd have struck out watching 'em hours ago!"

"If this were baseball I'd have walked, not struck out," Schaefer replied calmly. "I want something I can hit—if I miss, a rocket-propelled grenade is going to make a pretty big hole in somebody's store-front."

"So who gives a shit?"

"I do."

"The insurance will cover it. Take a shot, for Christ's sake!"

"Here it comes again," Rasche called. "Lower and slower this time." He handed the mask to Schaefer.

Schaefer took the mask, held it up, and grinned. He raised the antitank gun.

"Got it this time, Carr," Schaefer exulted as he hefted the weapon and sighted. Rasche held the mask for him, so that Schaefer would have both hands free to work the gun.

"He's cruising right up the middle of the avenue, just where I want him," Schaefer reported. "I can put this baby just where I want it, right . . ."

He pulled the trigger, and the rocket spat out of the tube.

". . . there!"

A fraction of a second later the boom of the RPG echoed from the buildings on either side, and shrapnel rained down across Third Avenue, rattling off asphalt and taxicabs.

The sound woke the dozing hoods; hands grabbed for weapons, heads whirled.

For a moment after the flash everyone in the garage entryway glimpsed the outline of the ship, flickering above the streets in a shower of blue sparks and burning rocket fragments; then it vanished again, to everyone but Schaefer.

"Didn't do much more than scratch the paint," he said, "but I didn't expect any better. At least that should get their attention!" He took off the mask and waved to the others. "Come on, let's move out! Get ready for 'em! They'll be coming to see who took a shot at them!"

"Move yer asses!" Carr shouted, and the motley collection of New York's worst stirred, rose, and moved.

The little squad of New York's defenders trotted out into the street and found a thin scatter of people on both sidewalks—early risers and diehards from the night before who had been going about their business and had been drawn out by the explosion, curious about what new peculiarity the city had come up with.

"Clear the streets!" Schaefer bellowed. "Now!" He gestured to Carr's recruits. "Half of you on one side of the street, the other half come with me—get the civilians out of here before the aliens arrive!"

"You heard the man!" Carr shouted. He fired a burst in the air, half a dozen rounds. "Get the fuck outta here!"

Rasche charged out with the rest, but a bit less enthusiastically. This sort of action might be his partner's cup of tea, but Christ, he was just a cop, he'd never even worked Emergency Services. He watched Carr's men hounding citizens into doorways and down alleys, and wondered what the hell he was doing here—armed assaults on bug-eyed invisible saucermen were never part of his job description.

He realized suddenly that somehow, out of all that hardware that had been handed out, he'd wound up with nothing but his own familiar pistol.

He held it ready in one hand, but somehow he doubted it was going to do much good.

He paused in the doorway of a camera shop, between signs reading ONE DAY ONLY and OUR BIGGEST SALE EVER! and scanned the sky—pointlessly; the goddamn spaceships were invisible, he *knew* that.

A security guard emerged from the shop behind him. "Hey, Mac," the rent-a-cop called, "what's going on? Who the hell are you?"

"Police," Rasche said, fishing his ID from his pocket and flashing the badge. "We're being attacked by monsters from outer space."

"Right," the guard said after a pause. "Big green ones, I suppose?"

Rasche turned. "Look, bozo, you *asked*," he said. "This is for real, okay? You're in a fucking war zone."

The guard stared at him.

"Just get out of sight, will you?" Rasche said. "Believe me or not, but this whole neighborhood's going to be full of flying lead in a few minutes, and you don't want to be here."

"Jesus," the guard said. "You're serious? And on the big sale day?"

He turned and ran back inside, locking the door behind him—the *glass* door.

Lot of protection *that* was going to be when the shooting started, Rasche thought.

Still, it was probably better than being out here in the open, the way he was.

This wasn't anything he'd ever wanted. Schaefer had his own reasons for being on the force, maybe he'd always been looking for some kind of big apocalyptic shoot-out, but Rasche had just wanted a steady job where he felt he could do some good. He looked at one of Carr's gang waving some kind of machine gun around and felt a chill that wasn't just the breeze from the west.

It was fear.

He had a wife and children. He wanted to make pension, find a place upstate somewhere, settle down and watch his kids grow up, hear them laugh . . .

He didn't want to die, and it looked very much as if he was about to. He'd taken out one of these space predators down at Carr's place, but that one had been alone and he'd caught it by surprise, not to mention he'd been armed a bit more heavily; somehow he doubted he was going to be anywhere near as lucky against whatever came out of that ship Schaefer had just taken a shot at.

Hell, if they wanted to, the aliens could probably take out all of midtown without even warming up their heavy stuff. If this turned into a real fight, it would be because the aliens *wanted* to fight.

Rasche was beginning to think seriously about why he was still there, why he hadn't turned and run for his life, when he heard sirens.

"Oh, shit," he said.

Someone must have called in about the explosion and the lunatics running around with guns. Maybe a prowl car had seen something. Whatever the reason, the cops were coming.

And somehow Rasche didn't think they were coming to join the war against the monsters.

The familiar blue cars were charging up Third Avenue in an unbroken phalanx, lights flashing and sirens at full blast—and Rasche was in deep shit with the department, he knew that. McComb was in with the feds on this, siding with the monsters in hopes they'd go home happy—and even if no one cared about that, Rasche had walked off with about half a ton of illegal heavy weapons from the police lab, and he'd passed them out to a bunch of the worst hoods in the city.

McComb was going to *love* that.

Rasche faded back into the shelter of the doorway.

All along the block Carr and his men were doing the same—only Schaefer was still standing out there in plain sight on the east sidewalk, watching, as the cop cars pulled up.

And sure enough, just as Rasche had expected, it was Captain McComb, wearing a flak jacket and carrying a bullhorn, who climbed out of the lead unit.

"This is Captain McComb of the New York Police Department!" he announced. "We have the area sealed off—you're surrounded. You have ten seconds to throw down your weapons and give yourselves up, and then we're coming in after you!"

Schaefer stepped off the curb, M-16 in one hand, the alien mask in the other.

"You don't know what you're doing, McComb!" he called. "Those things have to be stopped!"

"What in hell . . . ?" McComb asked. He snatched a shotgun from the car and pointed it at Schaefer. "Schaefer? *You're* running this?"

"Someone has to!"

"You've lost it this time, Schaefer!" McComb shouted. "I'll probably make assistant chief for taking you out—and I'm going to *enjoy* it!" He raised the shotgun. "Last chance, Schaefer—drop the . . ."

Then, as Rasche watched from the camera-shop doorway, several things happened simultaneously.

Schaefer suddenly jerked his head sideways and clutched at his neck, at the device embedded there.

McComb stopped in midsentence and stared, openmouthed, up the avenue.

A shadow appeared from nowhere, instantly covering the full width of the avenue, blocking out the pink light of dawn.

Schaefer twisted to look behind himself, up at the immense spaceship that rested heavily on the pavement of Third Avenue, its central landing rib gouging into the asphalt, its curving surfaces shading the street and almost touching the buildings on either side. An oily black stain on the white hull, back near the tail, marked where Schaefer's RPG had hit it.

"Well, what do you know," Schaefer said. "Company!"

34

For a few seconds everyone on the street or huddled in the doorways stared silently up at the ship. It had not landed; it had simply appeared. Rasche realized it must have landed while still invisible, and once it was down, the aliens had turned their gadget off.

He felt a sudden renewed chill. If the creatures were giving up an advantage like that . . .

Then the first blast struck—one of the police cruisers exploded in blue-white fire and, an instant later, exploded again in yellow flame as the gas tank detonated. Cops ducked and dived in all directions, looking for cover.

That had apparently been a test shot; before the echoes had died, away the actual barrage began. Blue-white flared up on all sides as vehicles were scattered like toys and building facades crumbled.

Schaefer ran, dodged, and dived for cover, landing beside Rasche in the sheltered doorway of the camera shop.

"Jesus," he said as he sprawled on the sidewalk, "I think they're upset."

"This isn't just for fun, Schaefer!" Rasche shouted. "They're going to bring down half the city!"

Schaefer looked at him, then rolled over and looked up at the ship and the ongoing pyrotechnics. He saw that the buildings on both sides were still standing; the aliens were shooting at the vehicles in the street, and at the entrances, but they weren't really doing anywhere near as much damage as they might have.

Schaefer had seen what a group on foot could do when they'd taken out Eschevera's camp; he'd seen a ship reduce Carr's building to rubble in a matter of minutes. Somehow he suspected that the ship out there could have done a lot more damage if that was what the bastards really wanted.

"You know," he said thoughtfully, "maybe I was wrong—maybe they aren't upset. I think they're just clearing the area so we won't ambush 'em as they emerge. Hell, if they chase enough people away, maybe I'll finally be able to afford a decent apartment!"

Rasche was too shocked to react to Schaefer's attempt at humor.

Out in the street Captain McComb crouched by one of the cars that was still intact and shouted into the radio, "Sweet Jesus, we need *help* up here! I've never seen anything like it—that son of a bitch Philips . . ."

Then, abruptly, the barrage stopped; echoes rolled away down the avenue and up the streets on either side.

In the sudden silence the survivors on the ground peered cautiously from whatever shelter they had found.

"Now what?" Rasche asked.

"Now they come out after us," Schaefer replied. "That was just to drive us back. Look."

Rasche looked and saw an opening appear in the side of the ship. Something shimmered in the shadow there; then the shimmer dropped to the street below.

A second shimmer followed, and a third . . .

Rasche ducked back out of sight.

McComb didn't notice the shimmerings; he didn't know what to look for. He saw the door open, but he didn't see anything emerge.

"What do you want?" he shouted. "You want someone to come in there and parley? Is that it?"

"Is that it?" his own voice called back.

And then, suddenly, one of the creatures was standing over him, looking down, its face hidden behind a metal mask.

"What . . . what are you?" McComb gasped.

The monster didn't answer. The black thing on its shoulder swiveled, aimed, and fired, blowing a hole through Captain McComb's chest.

"There's one of 'em!" one of Carr's men shouted. "Over there!" He lifted his Uzi and sprayed bullets at the creature standing over the dead cop.

It flickered and vanished.

The hood stopped firing, lowered the gun, and stared. "Jesus," he said, "he disapp—"

Then the blue-white bolt from the shoulder cannon tore through his side, spinning him off his feet; he was dead by the time he hit the sidewalk.

"McComb's dead!" Rasche shouted.

"And we're next, if we don't keep moving," Schaefer said. He stared through the mask. "They're not keeping any kind of formation, they're just milling around out there, picking targets at random—if we can lay down a fire pattern, drive 'em back . . ." He looked around for allies and spotted a cluster of Carr's men, spraying bullets in all directions.

"Lay a pattern!" he shouted. "Push them back toward the ship!"

The thugs paid no attention; Schaefer swore and charged out toward them, firing wildly to cover his own movements.

He had almost reached the group of outlaws when the shape of one of the aliens, red and gold through the mask, reared up before him.

"Oh, shit . . ."

The thing hit him with the back of its hand, sending him flying; then, when he landed, it stepped over to him, reached down, and snatched the mask away from him.

That finally got the attention of the nearby humans, and a barrage of gunfire drove the monster away before it could finish him.

"Damn!" Schaefer said as he crawled for shelter. "helmet's gone—we're blind, and they know it!"

Blue-white cannon fire took down two of Carr's recruits, and in the instant's distraction Rasche dashed forward to help Schaefer up from the pavement. Together, the two ran for shelter.

A wild shot tore through Rasche's shoulder, and he fell back, shattering what remained of a broken display window. Schaefer called his name and looked wildly about for somewhere he could take his fallen partner, somewhere safe.

He didn't see anything like safety, but he did see reinforcements coming.

At least he hoped they were reinforcements.

A squad of men in olive drab were charging up Third Avenue, M-16's firing.

And one of the men, Schaefer saw, was General Philips.

"Schaefer!" the old man called. "Goddamn you, you son of a bitch, you had to do this the hard way! The shit's really hit the fan now!"

"What's next, General?" Schaefer shouted back. "Gonna take out my boys for 'em? Still hoping to negotiate?"

"Shit," Philips said. "Maybe that's what they want down in Washington, but I was never much of a diplomat. I may not have shown it, Schaefer, but I do know what side I'm on, and it isn't some goddamn monsters'—I've got gunships, helicopters, coming this way."

"Think it'll help?" Schaefer asked. "You know how many ships they have, where they are?"

"Nope," Philips replied. "Can't track 'em that well—they make our stealth technology look like bright-red billboards with targets on 'em. But goddammit, it's *our planet!*"

The second-story wall blew out of the building above them just then; neither man had seen whether alien cannon fire or a wild shot from one of the defenders' heavier weapons was responsible, but they both bent over and sheltered their heads with their arms as debris pelted them.

Then Philips looked up and looked around.

"Can't see a goddamn sign of 'em," he said. "These damned foreigners are really starting to stick in my craw—why don't the yellow bastards *show* themselves?"

"Why should they?" Schaefer asked as he scanned the street. "It's . . . Wait a minute." Something had caught his eye, and combined with a memory. "You watch Rasche," he said.

He ran forward into the street before Philips could react, and began pawing through the wreckage of one of McComb's cruisers. He found what he wanted—a fireman's wrench. He hefted it and ran for the nearest hydrant.

He twisted the cap off the front, then turned the hydrant on full.

Water sprayed out, against the side of a burning cruiser, and then up, arcing into the street; as the water showered back, blue sparks crawled across shimmering outlines, and two alien monsters appeared.

Carr, a block away, saw what Schaefer had done; he didn't have a wrench, but he had something else—he blew the top off another hydrant, sending another spray of water spilling into the street.

That evened things up a little—both soldiers and gang bangers had targets now. Big, fast-moving, armored targets, but targets.

Rasche, lying in the store window with Philips standing by his feet, heard a rhythmic beating somewhere overhead; at first he thought it was some new attack, then that it was the blood pounding in his head.

Then the first chopper came into view over the rooftops, and Philips began shouting, "Clear the streets! Clear the streets, goddammit!"

Rasche forced himself to sit up, to watch what was happening. Everything seemed darker than it should have been—the dawn seemed almost to have faded back into night.

Rasche hoped his eyes were okay. He blinked and looked out at an expanse of twisted metal, burning wreckage, and bloody corpses. Human fighters were dodging and hiding, fading away, while the aliens stood proudly in the street, moving in sudden quick zigzags whenever they sensed a threat or a target.

One was closing in on Schaefer, cutting off each attempt at retreat the big man made, cornering him against the building on the opposite side of the street from Rasche's perch.

"Schaefer!" Rasche shouted, but his shout was lost in a sudden new, louder rumble from overhead.

He looked up, past the spaceship, past the rooftops, past the V formation of a half-dozen gunships, at the black clouds above.

Lightning flashed, and thunder rumbled again, and the first fat drops of rain spattered down. A cool wind blew in from the side streets, rustling clothing, sending litter skittering in the gutters, twisting the flames from the wrecked vehicles into spirals.

The heat wave had finally broken.

The predatory creature pursuing Schaefer stopped, and like Rasche, it looked upward.

All around, the aliens stopped.

Rasche watched them, watched them considering the weather, the choppers, the city. He wondered if they were communicating with each other somehow—they weren't speaking, but maybe they were telepathic, maybe they could read each other's scents, or heat patterns.

"Is that it?" one of them bellowed abruptly, in McComb's voice.

The one that had cornered Schaefer turned back toward the detective for a moment. Its right hand, the one with the two jagged blades, slashed out, drawing two red lines across Schaefer's chest—not to kill, but simply to mark, to let Schaefer know he was beaten.

Then the thing's other claw lashed out, but in a far subtler and more complex motion, as it picked the homing device from Schaefer's neck.

Schaefer screamed, fell to his knees, and clutched at a bleeding wound—but the blood was seeping, not spouting; the carotid had not been cut.

He knelt, his hand on his neck, and watched as the alien hunters marched back to their ship. One by one, they leaped lightly up into the open hatch, casually jumping a height no human could possibly manage unassisted.

Three of the things had been taken down in the fighting, one way or another; the survivors gathered these three up as they returned to the ship. The humans watched as the monsters withdrew, taking their dead with them.

When the last of the aliens was aboard and the hatchway closed, the humans emerged slowly from cover, moving warily out into the open.

Unearthly engines screamed, and the spaceship began to move, to push south down Third Avenue, then to rise, quickly gathering speed and altitude; its belly fin sliced a yard-wide twenty-foot path through the asphalt before coming clear.

The ship vanished from sight before it had cleared the buildings on either side, and the sound cut off abruptly, as well—the invisibility screen was back in place.

"Maybe . . . maybe we scared them off," Philips said. "They're too smart to start a fight they can't finish."

"Can't finish?" Schaefer stared at Philips in disbelief. "Shit, they could have scragged the entire city without breaking a sweat if that was what they wanted."

"So why *didn't* they?" Carr asked.

"Because that's not what they were here for," Schaefer said, looking upward to where the ship was faintly visible as a hole in the intensifying rain. "They weren't here to wreck the city, they were here to have a good time. It got out of hand, though—it wasn't *sport* anymore. It's wet, it's cold—it's just no more *fun*." He turned away. "That's what they wanted, General—no invasions, no treaties, just some good ol' boys out on a tear. And when it isn't fun anymore, you pack up and go home. You go look at your fancy radar, General—I'll bet the whole fleet's leaving." He grimaced. "And, Carr, I'd suggest you get lost," he said.

"Lunchtime today, I'm coming after you, but right now you're still clear as far as I'm concerned."

Carr grinned. "See you then, Schaefer," he said. He turned away and began swaggering west on Thirty-seventh, a machine gun on his shoulder— and Schaefer and the soldiers just watched him go.

The other surviving outlaws also began to fade away into the side streets, some taking their weapons, others dropping them here and there along the avenue.

Schaefer turned back to Philips. "General, call off your choppers—hunting season's over, and the hunters are going home." He grimaced. "See you *next* year."

35

As Rasche's stretcher was loaded into the ambulance, he raised his head, straining against the straps, and took a final look around at the scene of the battle. "Jesus, what a mess," he said.

Schaefer looked around as well and saw half-demolished buildings on either side, wreckage strewn along a dozen blocks of pavement, abandoned weapons and dead bodies lying about, not yet collected or covered. Fires were still burning in several places, despite the steady rain; the water running in the gutters was dark with blood and ash.

"Yeah, looks like they'll be rewriting the tourist guides for this neighborhood," Schaefer said. "Come on, partner, let's get you out of here."

"Partner, my ass," Rasche said. "Only until I

have a chance to resign—to hell with making pension. Soon as they let me out, I'm taking Shari and the kids and going somewhere *safe*—you know, Beirut, South Central LA, Sarajevo, *anywhere* but New York."

Schaefer smiled down at him—the warmest smile Rasche had ever seen on that stony face. "Suit yourself," Schaefer said. "You done good here."

The attendants slid Rasche's stretcher in and slammed the doors, and Schaefer stood and watched as the ambulance pulled away.

Then he turned to Philips, who had been directing the military side of the mopping up.

"Starting the cover-up?" he asked.

"Best as we can," Philips said. "After all, you think we can tell anyone what happened here? We've got no evidence—those things didn't leave any of their fancy hats behind, not so much as a pocketknife. No one's gonna believe it unless they saw it."

"Seems to me you have enough witnesses on this one. You could convince people if you tried."

Philips shook his head. "We don't *want* to convince anyone. What good would it do? We chased the bastards away."

"They'll be back," Schaefer said.

"You seem mighty damn sure of that. You seem to think you understand these critters."

Schaefer looked up at the clouds. "I think I do understand them, General. They're hunters. If a few hunters run up against the wrong prey and get themselves killed, you don't shut down the game preserve—you just issue a few warnings, make sure the next group's got the best equipment and some common sense. And the other hunters aren't scared off—you must know that. They take it as a *challenge*. We've made Earth more fun than ever, do you realize that? Sure, they lost a few, but that just adds excitement. The cities have the jungles beat all to hell for excitement. I figure they tried New York as an experiment, and believe me, from their point of view it was a rip-roaring success. So you bet on it, General, they'll be back, all right, and in a city. Maybe not here in New York, but somewhere—and the next batch may be tougher."

"And we're gonna try like hell to be ready for 'em," Philips said.

"But you're keeping it hushed up?" Schaefer asked. "You aren't going to warn anyone?"

Philips shook his head. "Nope. We issue warnings, trigger-happy farmers will start shooting their neighbors every time it gets warm. We'll leave it to the professionals to handle this." He sighed. "It'd be easier if we understood something about that technology of theirs."

"Maybe next time you can get your hands on some samples," Schaefer said. He looked around. "So how are you going to explain this?"

"Plane crash," Philips said immediately. "Fighter came down, blew up, threw a bunch of ammunition around. Terrorist sabotage suspected. Think it'll play?"

Schaefer stared at him for a moment, then back at the wreckage.

"Yeah, that'll play," he said. He shook his head. "Good luck with your lies, General."

Then he started walking away, heading uptown toward the nearest subway entrance.

"Hey," Philips called angrily, "wait a minute—where the hell do you think you're going? We've got some questions for you, Schaefer!"

"Stuff it, General," Schaefer called back.

"Goddammit, Schaefer," the old man shouted, "Manhattan's a disaster area, a dozen blocks of midtown have been leveled, and you just walk away? New York will never be the same!"

Schaefer paused and turned back. He smiled at Philips—not the warm smile he'd given Rasche, but an expression that might as well have been carved from ice.

"You say that as if it were a bad thing," he said.

Then he turned and walked away, into the canyons of the city.

About the Author

NATHAN ARCHER was born and raised in New York City, where his great ambition was to be a science fiction writer. He's been writing for his own amusement for twenty years.

That didn't pay the bills, however, so he took a government job straight out of college, working as an intelligence analyst. Since the job involved a secrecy oath, any attempt at getting published seemed like a bad idea.

When budget cuts left him unemployed in 1992, he decided it was time to give his childhood dream a shot.

Dreams can come true. PREDATOR: CONCRETE JUNGLE is his second novel, following STAR TREK: DEEP SPACE NINE: VALHALLA, and will definitely not be his last.

He's also co-editor (with Kurt Busiek) of the forthcoming anthology, THE ULTIMATE SUPER-HERO.

Archer lives in Chicago, has never married, and has no children or pets. His eyes are green, and other details are classified.

*The ultimate confrontation between the silver screen's
two most terrifying aliens . . .*

ALIENS™

vs.

PREDATOR™

ONE A RACE OF RUTHLESS and intractable killers, owing their superiority to pure genetics. The other using the trappings of high technology to render them the perfect warriors. Now, the classic conflict of heredity vs. environment, nature vs. nurture, is played out in a larger—and bloodier—arena: the universe. And in such a conflict, who can possibly win out?

Based on the spectacular hit movies from Twentieth Century Fox and the bestselling Dark Horse graphic novels, the *Aliens vs. Predator* series presents a ravaged universe in which mankind is caught in the balance.

ALIENS VS. PREDATOR: PREY _____56555-9
by Steve Perry and Stephani Perry $4.99/$6.50 in Canada

ALIENS VS. PREDATOR: HUNTER'S PLANET _____56556-7
by David Bischoff $4.99/$6.50 in Canada

**Buy all the *Aliens vs. Predator* novels on sale now wherever
Bantam Spectra Books are sold, or use this page for ordering.**

Please send me the books I have checked above. I am enclosing $_____ (add $2.50 to cover postage and handling). Send check or money order, no cash or C.O.D.'s, please.

Name _____

Address _____

City/State/Zip _____

Send order to: Bantam Books, Dept. SF 9, 2451 S. Wolf Rd., Des Plaines, IL 60018
Allow four to six weeks for delivery.
Prices and availability subject to change without notice.   SF 9 5/95
Aliens™ and Predator® © 1995 Twentieth Century Fox Film Corporation. All rights reserved.
™ indicates a trademark of the Twentieth Century Fox Film Corporation.

PREVIEW

CHARON BASE, LONG SINCE ABANDONED by its prisoner inmates, has been converted to a vast laboratory complex. Its goal: to study the aliens. A queen and her hive dwell within the carved rock tunnels, safely isolated from the human complement of the base. Or are they?

For Charon Base is under the control of Professor Kleist, a dangerous megalomaniac who is determined to breed the first tame alien and will stop at nothing to realize his dreams—even if it means killing everyone who stands in his way.

Now it is up to a few brave men and women—led by the indomitable Captain Joyce Palmer—to seize control of the base and end the professor's reign of terror. Only they do not reckon with the results of his latest experiment run amuck. . . .

Don't miss

ALIENS: ROGUE

by Sandy Schofield

Coming in December 1995 to a bookstore near you